The Tunnel

by

Ernie Lijoi, Sr.

An Eddie Pannoni Thriller

A-Argus Books
New Jersey***North Carolina

A-Argus Better Book Publishers, LLC
For information:
A-Argus Better Book Publishers, LLC
9001 Ridge Hill Street
Kernersville, North Carolina 27285
www.a-argusbooks.com
ISBN: 978-0-6158544-5-8
ISBN: 0-6158544-5-1

Book Cover designed by Dubya

Printed in the United States of America

Table of Content

Female
You have life to keep you warm
You have memories of the norm
There are actions to remember
From life's ember
You are the child of wonder
The remains that children plunder
The learning that you taught
The enjoyment that you brought
You can see the detail
You my friend are female.

Ernie Lijoi Sr.

Chapter 1

Mexico

Monday April 14, 1980

Ernie had breakfast at home and before coffee he went out to start the car. On his walk up the driveway to his car he heard the familiar sound of whistling and recognized the pitch as his old friend the mockingbird. Ernie replied and stood there in the cool morning enjoying the notes. This interaction always brought a smile to Ernie's face.

Detective Ernie Lijoi Sr. is 5'8" tall, 185 pounds, a Brooklyn-born, Italian male, with dark brown afro hair which is very curly and a full beard with mustache, brown eyes and a major scar across left eye and nose.

This scar was from a street fight as a boy in Brooklyn, New York, when he was hit with a flimsy glass milk bottle. He grew up there in the 40's and 50's, before he entered the United States Air force. Ernie was now parking his car on the street and enjoying the nice weather.

Upon arrival at the office everyone seemed happy to see Detective Ernie Lijoi and welcomed him back from his recent undercover job where his favorite saying was that the job was merely another job of chasing snow.

Detective Henry Griswold said "hi," and was busy reading a report. Henry put down the report and turned toward Ernie.

Henry: "Ernie, would you mind helping me out with something."

Ernie: "Of course not Henry."

Henry: "I'm not an undercover man, but I have this case that is pretty good and needs someone like you in your guise as Eddie Pannoni. I need someone to go and cut themselves into this guys operation for me."

Ernie: "What kind of drugs is he dealing?"

Henry: "No, no drugs. Not that I know of; guns are his game and plenty of them, I got word that he was some kind of a gun nut."

Ernie: "Henry, I'll be happy to do whatever I can for you to clear the case. When do you need me?"

Henry: "We can do it anytime, but it may take some time to set up."

Ernie: "OK, let me clear up the first half of the DEA case that I'm working on. I'll start your case as soon as I can."

Henry: "Let me know when you're ready"

Ernie: "Agreed."

Ernie telephoned Agent Slater of the Federal Drug Enforcement Agency to set up a meet. The agent told Ernie to come into the office anytime, he would be there doing his reports on their previous trip to Mexico.

Agent John Slater is a white male about 6' tall and thin, with long dirty-blond, thinning hair, brown eyes, clean shaven with no scars or distinctive marks.

At the meeting with Agent Slater it was decided to set up the second buy from Ernesto Adelanto who is the subject of the Mexican trip. Adelanto has been wanted by the United States for at least 5 years. He is responsible for hundreds of thousands of kilos of cocaine that he imports into the United States in an unknown way. Because of these drugs he created a world of illicit drugs. These drugs are being uses by the youth and future of our country and killing hundreds if not thousands of people. No one has been able to get next to him let alone close enough to get him to come into the United States except Detective Ernie Lijoi Sr. under the guise of Eddie Pannoni.

Ernie, while under the guise of Eddie Pannoni, was able to form a bond with Ernesto Adelanto on his previous trip to Mexico when he stayed at Ernesto's home with an informant.

We continue this investigation with a meeting with Agent John Slater:

Ernie: "John, something odd happened while I was at Ernesto's home. His servants and employees were mumbling as they looked at me. I couldn't make out what they were saying. It was very obvious that they were talking about me. I couldn't figure it out and it was really weird not knowing what was going on."

John: "I can guess, Ernie. I should have told you as soon as I realized it, but I really didn't know until very recently. I just found these pictures in a very old file."

Ernie: "What are you talking about John?"

John: "Here, take a look at this photo."

Ernie: "Yeah, what about it?"

John: "You don't see the resemblance, between you and the man in the photo?"

Ernie: "What resemblance."

John: "Ernie, you could easily pass for the guy in that picture, especially if no one saw you for a few years."

Ernie: "Yes, I guess I could, but he looks a lot like Ernesto Adelanto as well. Who is this guy, a relative of Ernesto or something?"

John: "You're close. This is Eduardo Adelanto, Ernesto's dead brother."

What Detective Lijoi was not aware of was that Ernesto had a brother that had been killed by a rival illicit narcotics group. This death was due to Ernesto's insistence of being correct at all times. That brother was named Eduardo and looked a lot like Detective Ernie Lijoi Sr., which unbeknown to Lijoi gave him an advantage unlike any other in the past.

Ernie: "Wow, now it makes sense."

John: "What makes sense?"

Ernie: "Now I understand why he treated me so well and protectively during that trip that I made down to Mexico with the informant to meet with him. I told him my cover name, Eddie. He began calling me Eduardo immediately. I thought it was because of his language."

John: "Yes, he was probably treating you like a brother. He had to see the resemblance."

Ernie: "Yes when he went into that bar and had those four men killed and after we were shot at by a rival group, he made sure I was not in danger. I thought that he was just being protective of his future income from me and even that would be rare for him. I guess I was wrong."

John: "Now you know and maybe you can use it."

Ernie: "I don't think I'll use it. Not unless I am pushed into a corner. It'll be good to keep in my back pocket, just in case I need it."

John: "Yes you're probably right. Do you want to make that call now?"

Ernie: "Good idea we should call Bartoli and make arrangements."

Ernie picked up the phone and dialed.

Ernie: "Hello, this is Eddie Pannoni. Is Bartoli Romero there?"

Bartoli: "Yes, Mr. Pannoni, I am Bartoli and I have been expecting your call. What can I do for you, Sir?"

Ernie: "One hundred."

Bartoli: "Yes Sir, I have that available anytime you like."

Ernie: "Where are you?"

Bartoli: "We are located in Nogales, Arizona, just across the border from Nogales, Mexico, in a lumber yard called Nogales Lumber at the intersection of Route 19 and route 82 in Arizona, USA."

Ernie: "That sounds easy enough; can my truck pull right in and load from there?"

Bartoli: "Yes Sir, we will help you load after you pay the fees involved."

Ernie: "Hold on for a moment, please"

Ernie put the phone to his chest and asked Agent John Slater when he thought would be a good time to make the pickup. Agent Slater suggested that they make it for Friday/ That would give them plenty of time.

Ernie: "Hello, Bartoli, I am sorry about that we were just trying to figure out the best time for a pickup. How about Friday afternoon?"

Bartoli: "Whatever you say, Ernesto said that you get treated the best."

Ernie: "Thank you, do I have to be there?"

Bartoli: "Yes, you must, I cannot release to just any-one."

Ernie: "How will you know if it is me, have we met?"

Bartoli: "No, but I have your picture and the picture of your partner."

Ernie: "Where did you get that?"

Bartoli: "Ernesto he trusts you, but he has a system in his home that takes pictures of all potential customers."

Ernie: "That's a great idea; but having our pictures could be dangerous for us. I must comment on that to him when I see him again."

Bartoli: "He said that you are the best and we can place a certain amount of trust in you."

Ernie: "Thank you, I will see you Friday."

Ernie hung up the phone and looked at John Slater.

John: "What's wrong, Ernie? It sounded like it all went well, but you look strange."

Ernie: "John, that prick was taking our picture while we were at his home in Mexico. This guy Bartoli Romero has the pictures at his place, where we make the pickup for identification purposes."

John: "That's not good; this could be a serious situation, we will have to be very careful after we get this guy. I'll let the bosses know about that and the rest of the team members. Just in case something comes down after this is over."

Ernie: "Yes, good idea. I'll do the same with my guys. When do you want to leave?"

John: "Let me look at this information, make travel arrangements and I'll get back to you. Anything else going on?"

Ernie: "One of my guys has a gun thing going. I'll try and help him with that."

John: "Is it large enough to bring in the (ATF) Federal Alcohol, Tobacco and Firearms Administration?"

Ernie: "I don't know enough about it yet."

John: "If you need them, you know the best guys to call, right?"

Ernie: "Yes I worked with a couple of men from the ATF in 1978, I'm sure they would be interested, but I won't bother them unless it looks like they will be needed."

John: "OK Ernie, if I can be of any help, let me know."

Ernie: "Thanks, I'm sure we'll talk in a day or two, John."

Ernie left the office and drove back to the Quincy office where he had met with Detective Henry Griswold to discuss the gun case. Henry was not there. Ernie left him a message that he would be there in the morning to discuss the weapons case and left for the day.

April 15, 1980

Ernie reported to the office early in the morning. He wanted to have time to read the reports that Henry was talking about and see what kind of a case could be made. Henry walked in about an hour later and immediately started talking about the case with Ernie.

Henry: "Ernie, this case should be fairly easy, this guy seems to be looking for customers."

Ernie: "Yes, I see his name is Ralph Piper. He hangs at the Bomb Room on Quincy Shore Drive."

Henry: "That's about all I have on him with exception of the fact that he is selling and renting guns."

Ernie: "How reliable are the people that are telling you all this stuff about him?"

Henry: "Two of them are reliable and this will be the first case for the third guy."

Ernie: "Can any of them make an introduction?"

Henry: "No, that's the problem. They are all afraid of this guy because of his gun business."

Ernie: "Have you been in that lounge?"

Henry: "Yes, it's a long bar on one side, a bunch of tables, a dance floor and a small stage. There is a small room off the back wall with four pool tables."

Ernie: "Pool tables, that sounds perfect. Does this Ralph Piper play pool?"

Henry: "Yes, as far as I know pool is his favorite game and the Bomb Room is his favorite hangout. That's one of the reasons I thought of you for this case; pool may be your way into him."

Ernie: "I don't see much of a description here, in the report."

Henry: "No that's just a preliminary I haven't finished it; he is about 5'8" tall, light, curly hair and light eyes. Nice complexion and he is 35 years old, with a scar across his right eye and nose."

Ernie: "Henry, here's what I would like to do, I would like to go to the bar, play some pool and hang out. I'll slowly get to know a few people as Eddie Pannoni. I'll be in the office very little. If the case goes that way, we'll have to meet from time to time for me to turn in my reports to you."

Henry: "You want to play it slow and see how it goes. That sounds good to me."

Ernie: "Two things, I have a case pending with the DEA. I will be working on that case as well. Your case takes second place until I am through with the DEA. In the event that your case looks bigger then we think I would like to bring in the ATF. They can take whatever areas of the case that I come up with outside of Quincy. Can you agree to that?"

Henry: "Ernie, I don't know anyone at ATF that can help us."

Ernie: "No problem I know several of the agents. I have a man that I worked with, he's very good."

Henry: "When do you want to start?"

Ernie: "As long as the captain goes along with everything we worked out, I'll try to start tomorrow night. That will give me today to clean up my work. Understand that I'll be breaking off for the DEA case each time I have to make a run with them until that case is cleaned up."

Henry: "OK, let's go and see the captain."

Ernie and Henry contacted Captain Richards via radio and asked to meet with him.

Captain: "Can we meet over coffee?"

Henry: "Yes, sir"

Captain: "Meet me at the coffee shop."

The men left the office to meet with Captain Richards and explain Ernie's plan. The captain had complete confidence in the plan and gave authorization to go ahead. They left the captain and went back to the office where Ernie caught up on most of his paperwork.

That night after supper Ernie spoke with Teresa, his wife and explained that he had to work. Ernie explained that he was doing a job for one of his co-workers and would be tied up at night from time to time.

Teresa, a beautiful Italian girl with auburn hair and dark brown eyes; easy girl to get along with. She was a family girl raised by her parents who were born and raised in Italy. She believed that family came first then she would take care of herself, then the rest of the world.

Teresa: "Ernie, I understand that you have to do your job. Don't worry about me."

Ernie: "Thanks, Teresa, this will be on and off for a while until I am able to understand how this guy works. I still have the DEA case that I will be working on. I will have to take off with Agent Slater sometime this week."

Teresa: "Just be careful, I know you have a tendency not to pay attention to danger."

Ernie: "It will be all right; I'll be leaving in a few minutes. All I'm going to do is play some pool with a few people."

Teresa: "OK, Ernie, have fun, you deserve it. I will wait up for you."

Ernie: "Thanks"

Ernie left the house and drove to the Bomb Room.

As Ernie entered the lounge, he noticed that it was filled with people standing at the bar. Others sitting at tables and hanging out in the pool room. Ernie ordered a beer and walked into the pool room where he put some quarters on the table which placed him in line for a game with the winner of the current game.

At a table, just inside of the Pool room, Ernie saw a man that fit the description of Ralph Piper, scar and all. He was speaking with two other men and Ernie could make out some of the words from the movement of their lips, but not enough to get the entire conversation. However he could read the word cocaine cross the lips of one of the other two men.

Ernie's turn to play the game came up. He wanted to attract some attention and maybe attract Piper to the table. After the break he ran the table and sank the eight ball which attracted a lot of attention. He accomplished his goal. Piper was finished with the two men that he was talking to and came over to the table. Ernie's run of the table attracted his attention.

Ralph: "You're pretty good; you want to play a couple of games?"

Ernie: "That was sheer luck, running all those balls, I haven't done that in twenty years. Rack them."

Ernie was playing pool with Ralph Piper, he got lucky and maybe he could end this case quickly.

Ralph: "You're not from around here are you buddy"

Ernie: "No, I'm not."

Piper interrupted Ernie saying, "Let me guess where you're from. New York, am I correct?"

Ernie; "Very good, you have a good ear."

Ralph: "You don't need much of an ear for that accent."

Ernie: "I guess not, my name is Eddie."

Ralph: "Eddie, nice to meet you I'm Ralph. What brings you to Quincy?"

Ernie: "I'm visiting some friends in Boston, just over the bridge. They asked me to come down here to this place and I would be called to pick something up."

Ralph: "What are you picking up or did you pick up?"

Ernie: "You seem like a nice guy Ralph, but that's my business, I'm not here to become a page in your new novel."

Ralph Piper laughed and apologized.

Ralph: "I have to be careful of whom I speak with; you may be a cop. That's why I got curious."

Ernie laughed and continued playing pool. He didn't say anything."

Ralph: "You're not curious why I don't want to talk with cops."

Ernie: "No, none of my business, I'm just here to play a little pool, maybe I'll come in again maybe I won't."

Ralph: "Eddie, you're alright. How long will you be around?"

"I don't know. I'm waiting for a call from some people and then I will take off for a few days, assuming everything goes all right I'll come back here. If not, I'll go to Brooklyn."

Ernie let Ralph Piper win the first two games by one ball and the third game Ernie won. He said good bye and left the bar. He had been playing pool with Ralph for over an hour and wanted to break off any further conversation and leave it for another night. He had planted the seed of illegal activity. Let that seed take hold and grow, that was enough for that night.

April 18, 1980

Ernie woke to the telephone ringing.
John: "Ernie, it's John Slater."
Ernie" "What's up John?"
John: "We're all set to leave at 9am from Logan Airport, two hours from now."
Ernie: "OK, I will see you there."

Ernie got ready and went to the kitchen and found a note from Teresa saying that she went shopping and would be home in a couple of hours. Ernie left his own note saying that he would be back in a couple of days. He had some coffee and left for the air port.

Ernie and John arrived in Tucson, Arizona. They were met by the local branch of the DEA and were driven to a location where they picked up a truck. Ernie and John were told that the area they are going to is hard to cover, aircraft will be used and cars will be a couple of miles away so try to hold on if there is trouble.

They got into the truck and took off for the meeting with Bartoli Romero at the Nogales Lumber Yard near the intersection where Route 19 and route 82 meet in Nogales, Arizona, USA. About an hour later they pulled up to the front gate and drove into the yard.

As soon as they entered the lumber yard appeared a man with a dark complexion, 5'6" tall about 200 pounds, with a large belly, dressed in working clothes and apparently Mexican. This man walked over to the John and Ernie's truck and asked if he could help them. Behind him were three men, all Mexican, short in stature and heavy set.

Behind the men, there was a building, Ernie could barely see through the windows of the building. Those windows were very dark with dirt. He could barely make out some men inside the building, watching everything that went on. Above the front door was a large sign with the name, Nogales Lumber Yard.

No weapons were visible on the men standing outside with Romero.

Ernie: "Sir, are you Mr. Romero?"

Bartoli: "Yes, you must be Mr. Pannoni."

Ernie: "Yes, I am and this is my partner, John."

Bartoli: "It is a pleasure to meet you both. Drive to the back of the yard, you will see two piles of uncut logs evenly separated and evenly stacked with separations between each row. I will meet you there."

The two Detectives followed the directions and observed that the yard was about a quarter of a mile long before they came to the area that was described to them. They pulled the truck over to one side and waited in the truck. They heard a voice yelling to them.

Bartoli: "Come; come let me show you where we are going."

They exited the truck; Romero came over and told them to look around.

Bartoli: "Do you see anything?"

Ernie remembered that Ernesto had said the same words to him when he was showing him his hidden entrance to his largest underground lab.

Ernie: "Ernesto said the same thing to me when he showed me the lab. Are you trying to say you have the cocaine underground?"

Bartoli: "Ernesto said you were a smart one, let me show you."

Romero walked over to the large pile of lumber and pressed a button that was almost impossible to see unless someone showed you where it was. All it looked like was a knot in the wood.

Once he pushed the button, the entire front end of the pile lifted on the end that they were standing and went up for about six (6) feet in the air leaving the back end to rest on the ground. It all stayed together. Every piece of wood had to have been bolted in place and together for them to stay that way as the entire front was raised to show a set of stairs and a large tunnel below ground.

Ernie and John were amazed, they had never seen anything like it and expressed their impressions. They didn't go down into the underground area; they were not invited to go in. They looked down into the hole and all they could see was about 500 kilos of cocaine and bails of marijuana.

Romero smiled and asked if they were ready to accept the one hundred kilo's that they ordered.

Ernie: "Yes, do you want us to load it or will you?"

Bartoli: "I must receive the payment first then my men will take care of the loading for you."

Ernie: "That's fine"

John went to the cab of the vehicle and took out a brief case and handed it to Romero who took it and placed it on the ground. He opened and checked the cash amount. Once He was satisfied, he gestured for one of his men to watch over the brief case, while Romero supervised the loading of the cocaine.

Bartoli: "You are all loaded my friend"

Ernie: "Thanks, we'll get going.

Bartoli: "Eduardo, one more thing. Ernesto told me to ask you to visit his home again since he was unable to be hospitable the last time you visited, he wants' to make it up to you."

Ernie: "Tell him Thank you very much, we will try to go down and see him."

John and Eddie left the lumber yard, dove to a prearranged area where they turned the drugs over to the local DEA officers and were driven to the Airport with the agreement that Ernie and John would forward all of their reports to the DEA in Arizona.

John and Ernie agreed to get together to discuss the future probabilities of the case and the next step in about a week.

Chapter 2

Guns a Plenty

Saturday April 19, 1980

After super, Ernie watched the boys doing their homework and was surprised that neither one of them asked any questions. The two boys were talking about baseball and hockey, Ernie enjoyed watching them talk together and thought that was the way brothers should be acting.

At 8 pm he left to go to the Bomb Room in Quincy, the lounge where he had played pool with the subject of Detective Henry Griswold's case, a Mr. Ralph Piper.

Ernie entered the Bomb Room, ordered a beer and sat at the bar for a while. Later he entered the pool room where he played pool with a man who identified himself as Pigeon, a white male dark hair and dark eyes with tattoos running up both arms. The tattoo on his right arm stood out brightly, it was a drawing of a Pigeon holding a leaf.

This man was not a very good player, but Ernie let him win one game and bought a round of beers. Ernie decided to win a few games himself. By 11pm he had four beers sitting on a table next to the pool table where he and Pigeon were playing.

Ralph Piper walked into the pool room and spoke with a couple of people then he noticed Ernie playing pool with Pigeon. He walked over to the table. He said hi to Pigeon and Ernie, who he knew as Eddie.

Ralph: "Eddie, where have you been?

Ernie: "I've been out and about, my friend."

Ralph: "Want to take me on?"

Ernie: "Why not, I'll play a few games before I leave; I've been in Texas on business"

Ralph: "Leave, where are you going?"

Ernie: "You have to be careful of those questions, my friend. You could get into trouble. Even worse, I may start thinking that you're a cop."

Ralph Laughed: "I'm far from a cop. I understand, sorry about the questions."

Ernie: "No problem, but I'll tell you this much. I leave because she is a brunette with beautiful brown eyes"

Ralph: "Now you're talking, let's play"

The two men played several games and came out even on the beers.

Ernie: "Shit I forgot to check in with the family in New York"

Ralph: "There's a pay phone right there, by the front door"

Ernie walked over to the phone and telephoned Teresa and told her that he would be home in about an hour. He asked if she wanted to go up to Maine and open the camp this week end. Teresa said no, the boys have school on Monday and it's already Saturday night. Eddie returned to the table and Piper to say goodnight.

Ralph: "Eddie, how well are you connected in New York?"

Ernie: "Pretty well, why do you ask?"

Ralph: "I'm just curious. I'm thinking about a possible project, but we can talk about that another time"

Ernie: "That's fine; I'm available for a lot of projects. Many that most people refuse to become involved with. I'm sure you understand"

Ralph: "Yes, I do, you use a weapon of some sort in this work?"

Ernie: "Again you ask a lot of questions, but yes I do."

Ralph: "What kind of weapon?"

Ernie: "Primarily hand guns, unless the situation requires long distance contact."

Ralph: "Where do you get them?"

Ernie: "Are you writing another book?"

Ralph: "No, Eddie, but I know someone that moves some things that you may be interested in. If you guys make a deal, maybe I can make a few bucks."

Ernie: "Yeah, everybody knows somebody until it comes to the nitty-gritty, then they can't find them."

Ralph: "That's not me, my friend, we must talk someday."

Ernie: "Ralph, anytime you like. I am always ready to listen, but now I have to run."

Ernie left the bar wanting to leave Piper with the few additional seeds that he planted. He wanted them to grow in Ralph Piper's mind. Ernie felt that he was creating several strong points in his favor. These points would help him close this case quicker.

Ralph thought that Eddie was a hit man and that he was connected in New York. These beliefs would work well in the future. Ernie decided not to go near the Lounge for the weekend. He thought more about the fact that it was getting close to the time to open the camp in Maine, but not this weekend.

During the ride home Ernie saw a deer on the other side of the fence running along the highway and admired it for those few seconds. This sighting brought to memory the time he went to the mountains in western Massachusetts for the purpose of hunting deer. He had been with four other men and everyone was an experienced hunter, except Ernie.

The other men were giving Ernie tips on what to do in different situations, to remember to stand downwind, to always take your time and do not jerk the trigger, things like that.

The first night they played cards until 1am and then went to sleep. Everyone was up at 4 am. They cooked breakfast and had coffee before they went out for the days hunt.

The four men left the camp, walked about a mile into the woods and at the base of a mountain each of them took a different direction. They told Ernie to go about halfway up the first hill, find a spot that is partially covered and sit. The other men would push the deer towards him. They wanted to help Ernie, get his first deer.

Ernie did exactly as he was told. He walked up the hill and found a spot where he had a seat that placed him in a position where only his head was visible to anyone or any animal.

Ernie sat there for about an hour when he heard a noise, the noise got louder it was coming towards him. A deer came through a thicket and stood right above Ernie, he looked at the deer and was amazed at its beauty, its coloring and its stance. The deer stood just above him, he could reach out and touch its leg, yet Ernie was in a position that placed him out of the sight of the deer.

Ernie raised his shotgun to shoot the deer, aimed and put the gun down. He looked at the deer again, raised his gun, aimed and put it back down. He didn't know if he could kill this innocent creature for no reason. He was not thinking about the meat. His wife purchased the meat that they needed at the supermarket. He raised his weapon for the third time and this time he made so much noise, that he attracted the deer's attention. The deer look down at Ernie, turned and ran off into the woods, disappearing faster than Ernie could register the fact that he was gone. Ernie watched the fluffy white tail disappearing into the woods.

Ernie shook his head as he told himself that it looks like this is not his sport, he should have a camera not a rifle. At the end of the day he told the men what had happened to him with the deer and they said that he had buck fever.

With the thought of that deer in mind, Ernie arrived at home went in the house which was quiet since the boys were asleep and Teresa had the television on very low so that it would not wake the children.

Ernie and Teresa spoke, he told her about the deer incident and that he was not a hunter at heart. Teresa liked the fact that he could not kill the deer. They went to bed for the night.

Sunday morning, Ernie was up early and out working in the garden. He noticed that the grass needed mowing, the first of the season. He thought about giving his son Joe the job.

He looked over the house on the exterior to see what the winter weather had done to the building. He turned on all of the exterior water facets so that they would work from outside because over the winter he had to shut them off on the inside of the house. He did not find much that had to be done with the exception of a little caulking here and there. He may have to start painting the exterior in a couple of years. All and All the house looked very good to him.

Monday April 21, 1980

Ernie went out to start the car, the temperature felt wonderful at 60, the air was crisp as he walked to the vehicle and he heard his old friend the mockingbird sing to him. He returned the tune and the symphony began. They sang to each other for a few minutes then Ernie went into the house to get his jacket and left the area. He went up to the coffee shop in Dedham square where he met with a couple of local police officers that were having coffee. After coffee he returned to his home where the phone was ringing just as he walked in.

John: "Ernie, John. You ready to go?"

Ernie: "You said to give him a week."

John: "Yes, I did, and we have to call that Romero guy and let him know we are coming down on Thursday."

Ernie: "OK, I'll come in there to use your phone; I don't want to use my house phone."

John: "Why not, it would save you a trip."

Ernie: "Yeah, but I read about this new gadget that identifies the caller and the caller's location before you answer the phone. You can bet you ass that he has that gadget. I think they call it, Caller identification. I don't want to take a chance."

John: "I read something about that, they are doing amazing things today."

Ernie: "I'll be in there in about an hour."

John: "See you then."

Ernie arrived at the DEA and ran into Mr. Alexander Dribbleski, John Slater's boss.

Ernie: "Hello, Mr. Dribbleski."

Alexander: "Hi, Ernie, call me Alex, please."

Ernie: "OK, Alex; how are things going?"

Alex: "Good, Ernie, you here to meet with John?"

Ernie: "Yes."

Alex: "He's in the back room. Follow me." Alex directed Ernie to a back office where agent John Slater was located.

Ernie: "Hi, John."

John: "Hi, Ernie. Boss, we're going to set up the meet with Ernesto and massage him a little to make sure he shows at the big buy."

Alex: "Sounds good, let me know how it all works out."

John: "Ready, Ernie?"

Ernie: "As long as this is a safe phone, let's call."

John: "There are no safer ones around. That one comes back to some person and location in California that doesn't exist at all."

Ernie picked up the phone and dialed. Bartoili answered at the other end.

Ernie: "Romero, this is Eddie Pannoni."

Bartoli: "Mr. Pannoni. What can I do for you?"

Ernie; "Would you be so kind as to let Ernesto know that we will take him up on his offer and we will be at the parking area on Thursday."

Bartoli: "I will take care of it; how was the product?"

Ernie: "Hold on a second."

Ernie covered the phone and asked John what the analysis of the cocaine was.

John: "That stuff tested almost 90% which is fantastic."

Ernie got back on the phone.

Ernie: "Sorry about that, I dropped something important."

Bartoli: "That's Ok, I don't mind waiting"

Ernie: "What was that question you asked me?"

Bartoli: "I asked how you liked the product."

Ernie: "The product was excellent, the best I have seen in a long time."

Bartoli: "I knew you would appreciate this product."

Ernie: "Give Ernesto that message for us, please."

Bartoli: "Consider it done, Bye."

They agreed to go on the trip to Mexico, Thursday and to meet Thursday morning at 8am at Logan Airport.

That night Ernie went back to The Bomb Room and shot some pool with a couple of men. At 10 pm Ralph Piper walked into the pool room area.

Ernie was playing pool with another person at that time and decided to win the game quickly which he did. Once the game was over Ernie walked out of the pool room past Ralph Piper, said "Hi,", and headed for the bar. Piper followed him and stepped up to the bar along side of Ernie.

Ralph: "Hi, Eddie; how'd you do the other night?"

Ernie: "What do you mean, the other night?"

Ralph: "You know the brunette."

Ernie: "Oh, yes, great, we had dinner and spent the rest of the evening on indoor sports."

Ralph: "Sounds good."

Ernie: "Ralph you mentioned something the other night about guns didn't you?"

Ralph: "Yea, just a passing remark, didn't really mean anything."

Ernie: "I thought so; most guys are full of shit when it comes to making contacts."

Ralph: "You think so?"

Ernie: "Just experience talking, that's all."

Ralph: "Why did you ask?"

Ernie: "My people in New York had mentioned that they were looking for a few. I saw an opportunity to make some money had you been speaking truthfully."

Ralph: "Do you have a few minutes free right now?"

Ernie: "Not really, I was going to stop by and see that girl I told you about."

Ralph: "Do me a favor, take fifteen minutes and come with me."

Ernie: "OK, what do you have? I don't have a lot of time to waste."

Ralph: "Just come with me."

Ernie: "OK, but this had better be good."

Ernie followed Piper out the door and got into his car, a red 1978 Cadillac. Piper drove. He went up Quincy Shore drive, took a left on Bayfield Rd., a right on E. Squantum St. and another left on Walker where he pulled up and parked in the driveway of 1923 Walker street, a red Cape Cod style home with a one car detached garage. This house was only a few blocks behind the Bomb Room. They exited the car and entered the single family residence.

Ralph: "Would you like a beer, Eddie?"

Ernie: "No, I had enough playing pool; I wanna go and get laid, that's what I want."

Eddie looked around and didn't see anything suspicious. No guns on the wall, no guns lying around; the first floor consisted of four rooms, a kitchen, living room, bath and a dining room area.

Ralph: "You may change your mind in a moment, follow me."

Piper went across the kitchen and opened a door in the far left corner and disappeared down a flight of stairs, Eddie followed him down into the cellar.

This cellar was broken up into three rooms. This was a very neat and clean cellar.

Ernie: "This is nice and clean down here, nothing like mine in New York."

Ralph: "Yes I like neatness."

Ernie: "Why am I here?"

"I wanted to discuss something with you that we could not discuss in the bar. I would like to show you something."

In the middle of the cellar was a small room with a TV and a few chairs, a refrigerator, a sink and a toilet, a perfect place for a single guy.

Ralph: "Eddie, how much money can you get for a .38 caliber hand gun in NY?"

Ernie: "Black market I can get about five hundred, why?"

Ralph: "I have something you should see."

Ernie: "You have a .38 that you want to sell me right. Everyone has one of those. Let's see it."

Ralph: "No I have a little more than that."

Ernie: "What are you saying?"

Ralph: "Follow me."

Piper walked over to the left side of the room and around a corner. He went up to a cabinet about 4 feet long and about 6 feet high standing along an outside wall of the cellar. The two never entered the other two rooms in the cellar. He moved the cabinet to reveal a very small door cut into the concrete wall that was about 5 feet high and about 24 inches wide. Ralph Piper entered the doorway.

Ralph: "Come on in."

Ernie walked into the room, through that same small doorway...

Ralph: "What do you think? Eventually I will make the entrance larger and more secretive."

The lights went on and Ernie looked around to see a room that was cut out of the earth with wooden and concrete walls and ceiling. Along the walls were several different racks all with hand guns, M-1's and automatic weapons standing in the racks upright. More guns were hanging on the walls. There had to be at the very least three hundred guns in that room, not to mention the boxes of ammunition. Every one of them looked ready to fire.

Ernie: "Ralph, why would you show me this, you don't really know me."

Ralph: "You're from New York so I don't have to worry about you being a cop, not with that NY accent. I'm having a hard time moving these guns because this is not a real big town, there are only 100,000 people here. So, when you spoke of the family in New York along with a few other things you mentioned, I put two and two together and I figured I would bring you in and see what we can do to move some stock and make some serious money."

Ernie: "And I thought you were a bull shitter, Ralph, sorry about that."

Ralph: "Yeah, I have a good thing going here, good, but small. I rent and sell."

Ernie: "What do you mean, rent?"

Ralph: "If someone needs a piece for a job, I have a certain group of guns that I rent specially for that type of job."

Ernie: "That's interesting, but what if the guy that rents the gun gets caught with your gun."

Ralph: "Here's how I work it. I give the gun to him, just before the job and allow two hours after the job for him to call and clear or else I report it stolen. I have yet to report one gun stolen."

Ernie: "That's a very good scam; I may use that in New York."

Ralph: "You're welcome. What do you think now? Am I still, full of shit?"

Ernie: "You are the king, my friend, the king. Where did you get all of these weapons?"

Ralph: "Normally I'd use your line about writing a book, but since you are from out of state I'll tell you that I have a guy in the Quincy Armory and a civilian in the Quincy police station. Those two people are my entire pay roll."

Ernie: "So you can acquire all you want."

Ralph: "No I have to be careful. "Every so often the police sell off confiscated guns and I buy them very cheap through this girl who works in the office and handles the paperwork. The Armory guy comes and goes so when he is in town, I pay him and get what I need. Some of the guns that he sells me come from other areas in and out of this state."

Ernie: "What about prices, Ralph."

Ralph: "I'll make a deal with you; you tell me how much money you can get in New York for each gun that you can sell. I will charge you half of your profit. We split the profit fifty –fifty after we deduct my cost."

Ernie: "That's very fair, I have to go back to Texas for a couple of days and do a thing. After that I'll go to New York where I'll talk with my people and take some weapons orders from the boss and the men. When I come back here you can fill as much of the weapons orders as you can. That will take me under a week to do. How does that sound to you?"

Ralph: "That's a deal. I'll see you at the Bomb Room in about five or six days."

Ernie: "I will make it as soon as possible."

They left the house, Piper drove Eddie back to the Bomb Room and Eddie left the area in his car.

The next day Ernie did his reports, spoke with Henry and asked Henry to hold off on raiding Piper's home. Ernie explained that was in hopes of identifying the suppliers of the guns. He wanted to eliminate the entire operation and complete the job by arresting everyone involved at one time.

They met with Captain Richards and it was agreed that they would give Ernie the chance to identify the people that are supplying Piper with the guns.

Chapter 3

Boston's Hooker's

Thursday April 24, 1980

Detective Ernie Lijoi Sr. and Agent John Slater met at Logan Airport and made last minute arrangements before boarding the plane.

John: "Ernie, I'm a bit tired, I think I will catch some shut eye"

Ernie: "Yeah, me too. I didn't sleep well last night thinking about this gun thing I'm doing"

They boarded the plane, took their seats and before Ernie knew it John went to sleep—fast, like turning out a light. It took Ernie a few more minutes to fall into a deep sleep and dream about guns, pimps, hookers and an old informant named Jean.

Memories in the dream: Spring 1976

Patrolman Ernie Lijoi was working with the Massachusetts Transportation Authority in Boston when at roll call the sergeant called his name along with Officer Joe Devoe. These two officers were assigned to work in plain clothes for that shift. This was a common practice in the department. The men would be given turns at working in plain clothes.

From time to time different men were assigned to a plain clothes detail. This opportunity gave all of the men a chance to see what being a detective was like. This also showed the uniformed men why they should be working with the detective squad. The department was young, learning from the experienced men brought in from other departments to form this Transit Authority Police Department.

The department received information about some stolen guns from the Boston Police Department via teletype. That night, Ernie received some information regarding some possibilities on a lead in the stolen gun case.

He was told that one of the ladies of the night working at a place called Charlie's Pub named Jean had some information on the case, but was very hard to speak with.

Ernie and Joe decided to go and see if they could find her. They entered Charlie's Pub, a large bar room with several tables and a circular bar. There were men sitting and drinking at the bar. There were several women walking around the bar and stopping at different men, talking for a few minutes then moving on. Sometime they would leave the bar area and enter a back room with the man that they were speaking with.

Ernie and Joe watched for a while as they enjoyed a beer. They asked around about Jean. who was pointed out by one of the patrons as the only girl, he knew, that used that name. Ernie made a mental note of Jean's appearance as being a white female, about 28 years old, 5'6" tall and taller with CFM's (Come Fuck Me) shoes as she later called them. They were the high heel shoes with the four and five inch heels. Jean was a very well-built girl and turned out to be a very smart young lady, as well.

Ernie befriended her knowing that, in her business, she comes across a lot of good information. These girls try to stay friendly with the cops. If a police officer is trusted, they will give police officers information that they find out and hear about first hand, Their goal: be to be treated right when and if they are arrested. The police will be sure to let the court know if they have been of help which at times may lighten their sentences. This is sometimes an exchange of trust.

They spoke for a while. Ernie was trying to build some trust. He knew that it would take time. At the end of the night, Ernie gave her his business card as Detective Ernie Lijoi Sr. and Joe's business card as well. They told her to contact them at anytime, even if she just wanted somebody to talk with.

Jean called Ernie many times just to talk or ask a legal question for herself or one of her friends. Ernie did his best to always get the answers to her questions if he didn't know them. One night about a month later Jean called again.

Jean: "Ernie, do you guys have any guns missing?"

Ernie: "Yea Jean, we had a break-in a while back. Why do you ask?"

Jean: "I was wondering because I heard something. It may not be true."

Ernie: "What did you hear?"

Jean—being careful—"I don't want to say right now, I want to check a few facts."

Ernie: "Jean, don't try to play cop, that's my job. I don't want you getting hurt."

Jean: "Not me; I'll get back to you."

There was nothing that he could do. Ernie didn't hear anything from Jean for about a week and was becoming concerned. Then one night he received a call from a female that he did not know. She identified herself as Angela Scardelli.

Angela: "Ernie, Is this Ernie?"

Ernie: "Yea, who's this?"

Angela: "This is Angela. I'm calling for Jean, she's hurt real bad."

Ernie: "Where is she and what happened?"

Angela: "I can take you there; her boyfriend beat the shit out of her."

Ernie: "Her boyfriend? You mean her pimp, don't you?"

Angela: "Yeah, he's both her boyfriend and her pimp."

Ernie: "OK, where are you?"

Angela: "I'll be in front of Charlie's Pub"

Ernie: "I'll be there in about a half hour, with good traffic."

Ernie spoke with his partner Joe Devoe, explaining what was going on. They left the office and about twenty minutes later they arrived at Charlie's Pub. They saw a black female, 5'5" tall, very well built, wearing CFM's, a very pretty girl with long black silky hair standing outside, in front of the bar. They pulled up.

The girl ran to the car and asked if he was Ernie. Ernie nodded his head, yes. Angela opened the back door and got in.

Ernie: "Angela, this is one of my partners Joe Devoe, you can trust him."

Angela directed them to an apartment house on Commonwealth Avenue near Massachusetts Avenue where she got out and signaled for the men to follow her.

They entered the building and were directed to a very small, two-room apartment on the second floor of that old building. The building looked very nice from the outside, but the inside needed plenty of work. Jean was laying in the bed sobbing. Ernie could see the pain in her face.

Ernie: "Jean, what happened to you?"

She lifted her head and turned toward the detectives. All they could see was red welts, blotches and bruises on her face. Then she sat up and she had long thin lines all over her arms. She stood up and those same long thin welts were all over her legs.

Ernie: "What the hell happened to you?"

Jean: "My boyfriend hit me with a coat hanger. That's what he uses all the time, but this time he hit me in the face. I hurt all over."

Ernie: "Why would he do something like this?"

Jean: "Do you remember when I called you a while back about those guns that were stolen?"

Ernie: "Yes, I remember."

Jean: "Those guns belonged to one of my boyfriend's contacts. We got in an argument over the guns and he hit me."

Ernie: "Who hit you, your boyfriend?"

Jean: "No, his friend."

Ernie: "What did you do or say for him to hit you?"

Jean: "I got pissed because he was drawing my boyfriend into his illegal activity with the guns. I told him that I was gonna call a cop friend of mine and tell about the guns, that's when he punched me in the face."

Ernie: "Then what happened?"

Jean: "Then my boyfriend hit me with the hanger for interfering in his business. Him I didn't mind, the hanger only hurts for a little while and the marks go away, but look at my face, I can't work."

Joe Devoe looked at her and said; "No sucky, no fuckie this week," and chuckled.

Jean: "This in not funny, Joe."

Joe: "I know just trying to add a little levity to the problem."

Ernie: "Jean, let's get you to the hospital, your face looks like you have some broken bones."

Ernie and Joe drove the two girls to the hospital and waited for Jean to be checked out. Jean was treated and released. The officers took a copy of the doctor's report in case they needed it and drove the girls back to the apartment.

Ernie: "Is this your home, Jean?"

Jean: "No this is my office. so to speak."

Joe said; "Oh, you raise everything here legs, pricks etc, etc," and chuckled again.

Angela: "You're a prick sometimes, Joe. Ernie, he's trying to be funny. What are we gonna do?"

Ernie: "Let's give her a day or so to heal up then we can all sit down and talk. Is that OK with you, Jean?"

Jean: "Yes, Thanks; I want to get even with that bastard. He ruined my face."

Ernie: "He didn't ruin your face. You have porcelain skin; everything shows up worse on you. We'll take care of him, don't worry. Call us in a day or two, as soon as you are feeling well enough to talk."

After they left the apartment and when they were in the car Joe started asking some questions.

Joe: "Why didn't we get all of the information right now?"

"Because these girls could be of great value to us in the future, they're treated like shit all their lives and now by their pimps. If we have some honest concern for them, which I really have, we'll make some great friends and contacts that will last for our entire career."

Joe: "I see there is a method to your madness."

The two officers went back to the office and turned in the car. They both left for the night.

Two day later Ernie received a telephone call from Jean who was feeling much better and wanted to speak with Ernie. He drove to Charlie's Pub and she got into the car thinking that they would talk in the car.

Ernie: "No, we are going back to the station house where I can tape what you say. Is that all right?"

Jean: "Yes, OK."

A few minutes later they arrived at the station and went up to the second floor where the detective office was located. Ernie gave Jean a seat and went to get Joe so that he would be witness to the conversation. Ernie got a tape recorder to record the entire statement.

Ernie: "Are you ready, Jean?"

Jean: "Yes."

Ernie, speaking into the microphone: "Present are Officers Lijoi, Officer Joseph Devoe and our witness Miss Jean Rufford. The time is 9 pm on Thursday May 6, 1976."

Ernie: "Jean, what is your full and real name?"

Jean: "I am Jean Rufford originally from New York, now from Jamaica Plain in Boston."

Ernie: "Excuse these next few questions but what is your height and weight?"

Jean: "I am 5'7" tall and I weigh 135 pounds, I have blond hair—it's real blond too,not out of a box—and blue eyes. What else?"

Ernie; "Do you have any scars, tattoos or anything like that?"

Jean: "I have two hearts on my ass. Want to see?"

Ernie: "No thanks; I'm sure you have a beautiful ass, but no thanks. Anything else you can tell me?"

Jean: "No that's me in a nut shell."

Ernie: "Jean, you mentioned that you observed several guns, can you tell us where you saw them?"

Jean: "Yes, at the home of George Dennis in Boston."

Ernie: "Do you know his phone number and where is his home located?"

Jean: "He lives in a single-family house at 427 Scouting Way in Cambridge, Massachusetts. His phone number is 555-2290."

Ernie: "In your own words will you tell us how you came to see these guns and what happened afterwards?"

Jean: "OK, I was with my boyfriend Norris Stable when he told me that we were knocking off work early that Tuesday night. Tuesday is a very slow night. Anyway, he took me to the George Dennis house and we had a party with a couple of other people that I don't know."

Joe: "When did the guns come into the discussion?"

"I'm getting to that; we were in the living room, then in the bedroom, back and forth. During a break, George said that he just did a big job and if anybody needed guns just let him know. Everybody got curious so he took everyone into his private bed room and showed us a trunk at the foot of his bed. He opened it and it was full of guns, big ones and little ones. I didn't like my boyfriend becoming involved with this man and his stolen guns so got upset. He hit me and then my boyfriend hit me with the wire hanger because I got involved with his business."

Ernie: "Jean, are you willing to testify to these facts, as you just stated in this taped conversation?"

Jean: "Yes, I am"

Ernie: "And why would you want to do that?'

Jean: "Because that son of a bitch beat the hell out of me and scared my face, I can't make as good a living because of him."

Ernie: "OK, I think we have enough for now. Joe, I want to get pictures of her arms, legs and face as evidence. Do you have any questions, Joe?"

Joe: "No, you covered it all. I'll get the camera and take the pictures; it'll just take a minute."

Ernie: "Jean, let me be clear about the facts of this case. The man's name is George Dennis and he lives at 427 Scouting Way in Cambridge, Massachusetts. The guns were at that location. Am I correct?"

Jean: "Yes, all true; no bull shit."

Ernie: "Because of your objection to your boyfriend becoming involved this guy Dennis beat you up. After that your boyfriend beat you for getting involved in his business. Is that correct?"

Jean: "Yes that's also true, but I don't mind my boyfriend hitting me. I mind being hit in the face."

Ernie: "Believe me, I understand your feelings and I am sorry for your problems. We shall do all that we legally can to help you. It is now 9:30 pm and this interview is completed."

Ernie and Joe took the pictures that they needed. They drove Jean back to the Pub and Ernie warned her not to speak to anyone about her conversation with him and Joe.

Jean: "Do you think I am crazy? I won't say a word."

Jean then left the car. Ernie and Joe drove back to the office.

Joe: "Are you going to do the affidavit, Ernie?"

Ernie: "Yes, I will. If you will confirm the address and who is living there, that will help a lot."

Joe: "When do you want to start, tonight or tomorrow?"

Ernie: "Suppose we come in tomorrow morning and start the entire thing then, if everything goes OK, we can hit the place late tomorrow night."

Joe: "Sounds good to me, I'm outta here; I'll see you tomorrow."

Ernie: "Tomorrow."

Ernie showed up in the office at 9 am with a cup of Dunkin Donuts coffee for himself and one for Joe, along with two bear claws, one for each of them.

Joe: "I'll head over to Cambridge to confirm the address and names on the residence lists, right after I finish my coffee."

Ernie: "That's good, I'll start the affidavit for the search warrant and I'll be finished by the time you get back."

Joe was finishing his coffee and bear claw and checking the phone book to see if George Dennis was listed at the home in Cambridge at 427 Scouting Way and he found Dennis was listed at the correct address with the same phone number that Jean gave them.

He left the office to go to the house and check the mail box to make sure Dennis received mail there. If he was lucky he would catch the mailman and find out from him, but he was not lucky. Joe parked the car and walked up the street to the address, up the walkway to the front door and the mail box was nailed on the right wall of the entrance just outside of the door. On the mail box was the name G. Dennis.

The entire trip took two hours and when Joe returned to the office Ernie was finished with the affidavit. They went to the Superior Court to apply for the search warrant. Once they submitted the paperwork they were told to come back in two hours because everyone was at lunch. It was almost noon, they would return at 2 pm.

Ernie and Joe returned to the court at 2 pm and were directed to the office of the Clerk of Courts where they answered a few questions and the warrant was issued.

They contacted police headquarters and let them know that they had obtained a search warrant. They made a courtesy call to the Cambridge Police and notified them that they would be doing a search warrant at 427 Scouting Way. The Cambridge police offered whatever assistance was needed and Ernie asked that a cruiser meet with them at the intersection of Harvard Street and Scouting way. It was a common courtesy to notify the local Police Department when they were doing a search warrant in that territory.

At 4pm Ernie and Joe pulled up to the Cambridge cruiser waiting for them at the corner of Harvard and Scouting Way. They explained the case history to the officers and they all went to the house together.

Ernie knocked on the door stating that it was the Transit Police.

As soon as he finished saying Transit Police the door opened.

Dennis: "What do you guys want?"

Ernie: "Are you Mr. George Dennis, Sir?"

Dennis: "Yes"

Ernie: "We have a search warrant for the premises."

Dennis: "Search warrant, what for?"

Ernie: "Guns sir, Guns."

They walked into the house. They asked Mr. Dennis to sit on the couch and not to move from there. Joe assigned one Cambridge police officer to stay with Dennis.

Ernie: "Mr. Dennis, stay right there while we search."

Ernie and Joe went into a bedroom on the first floor, but there was no trunk in front of the bed. They went up to the second floor and went into the first bed room on the right. Nothing. Then across the hall to the third and last bedroom and there it was. They opened it and saw all of the guns piled up inside of the trunk. Ernie walked down to the living room and asked Mr. Dennis if he had a gun permit?

Dennis: "No I do not have one, sir."

Ernie: "Then you are under arrest for possession of stolen property, possession of illegal weapons namely automatic weapons, possession of stolen weapons and I am sure the DA will come up with a lot more charges before he is through with you."

While finishing the search they found an ounce of cocaine and three ounces of marijuana. All of the evidence, guns and drugs were taken into custody.

After several months of litigation, postponements and attempts at new evidence, Mr. Dennis was charged with the drugs in addition to the gun charges and received five years in the State's prison.

As they walked out of the court house, Joe looked at Ernie; "Ernie, should we tell Jean that her arch enemy will be a guest of the State for the next few years?"

Ernie; "Didn't you see her in the court room, Joe?"

Joe: "No —was she there?"

Ernie: "She was sitting in the back row during the sentencing, then she left quickly. She looked at me and smiled as she went out the door."

With that dream finishing; Ernie felt the wheels of the plane hit the ground. Both he and John were awakened by the noise.

Chapter 4

The Departed Five

Detective Ernie Lijoi and Agent John Slater landed in California, rented a car and drove to the parking area where they met with the same two men that Ernie met on his previous trips to Mexico. They did not check identification this time; instead they welcomed Eddie and John to Mexico. They all got into the car that Ernesto sent and the men seemed to be going in a different direction from the past trips. During the trip Ernie took on his guise of Eddie Pannoni.

Eddie: "It seems like we are not going to Ernesto's home?"

Driver: "No sir, Ernesto gave orders that we take you to him in Loma Alvares, (Alvares Hill) a section south of here."

John: "Why"

Driver: "He is having a small get together at one of his smaller homes, as far as we know."

Ernie looked at John and John just raised his eyebrows indicating there was nothing they could do to change things now. After a couple of hours of driving, they arrived at a home while not as large as his mansion in the jungle, was at least ten rooms, surrounded by hills and had plenty of guards around.

Ernesto: "Eduardo, John, It is good to see both of you, come in and meet some of my guests. Your bags will be taken care of by my people" Ernesto walked into the house with Eddie and John following him.

Eddie: "Ernesto, this surprises me, I didn't expect such an affair."

Ernesto: "I want you men to meet some influential people in Mexico so that if you should be in need of anything these people will know that you are family. Anything can be handled easily because they will now know who you are."

Eddie: "I see your genius at work, good thinking."

Ernesto: "Thank you, Eduardo, and first let me introduce General Ortega one of my closest friends. General this is a very good customer and friend Eduardo Pannoni and this is his partner John Slater."

Eddie: "It's a pleasure to meet you, General. I have heard many good things about you from Ernesto."

General: "The pleasure is mine, Eduardo, I enjoy meeting with top-rate customers that Ernesto respects."

John: "Thank you, General, we appreciate that."

Ernesto: "Come let me introduce you to the general's top aide."

Eddie: "His aide?"

Ernesto: "Yes, the man who takes care of things for the general."

Eddie: "I see."

Ernesto: "Colonel Waurez, sir, let me introduce you to a couple of friends; Eduardo and John. They are not only friends, but good customers."

Colonel: "A pleasure, gentleman, welcome to our beautiful country."

Eddie: "Thank you, Colonel, it is always a pleasure to be here."

Colonel: "Please, enjoy yourselves tonight, if there is anything you would like, we are all Ernesto's guest, I love coming to his parties."

John: "As do I"

Eddie: "Sir, it is a real pleasure meeting you."

After the introductions there were a few other people in the room, but Ernesto said the important ones are the General and his aide. Eddie and John mingled for a while until the general came over to Eddie.

General: "Eduardo I think that beauty has her eye on you and I have my eye on her friend, shall we play?"

Eddie: "Let's go, General; I'll follow your lead."

After spending a while with the ladies, Eddie excused himself for a few minutes and walked over to John who was talking with a man not known to Eddie.

Eddie: "John, can we speak for a moment, privately?"

"Sure Eddie" John looked at the person he was speaking with: "Please excuse me for a moment, Sir."

John and Ernie walked out to the front porch area of the home.

Ernie: "John, you should have gotten a single guy for this job. I can't fuck around with these women."

John: "Neither can I; I'm married too, you know. If any one of these girls were carrying some disease, we would catch it. Do you have any suggestions?"

Ernie: "I have only one suggestion that should get us out of this easily, but we may have to sleep in the same room until we leave."

John: "That's OK with me. This guy has all king size beds, we'll have plenty of room."

Ernie: "All we have to say is that we prefer each other over any women."

John: "I didn't want to say it, but you're right; that seems like the only way out. I'm in."

Ernie: "OK, only if we have to, not before."

They each went back to the people they were speaking with.

General: "Eduardo, you are Italian, yes?"

Eddie: "Yes, General, I am Italian; my family name comes from a small town in Calabria, Italy, called Santa Andrea."

General: "Yes, I thought so. Then why are you called Eduardo, which is Spanish?"

Eddie: "My name is Edward, Ernesto calls me Eduardo, I don't mind."

General: "Now I understand. It's his brother."

Eddie: "General, I am sorry, I don't understand, what do you mean?"

General: "Ernesto had a brother who was killed a long time ago. When I saw you, I almost thought that his dead brother had come back to life, his brother's name was Eduardo He was a very nice gentleman; you remind me of him."

Eddie: "I didn't know that, he never said a word."

General: "That's fine; please, don't say that I said anything. Let him tell you in his own time."

Eddie: "Thank you for telling me, General."

General: "You are very welcome, my boy."

The two girls named, Coco and Nina were standing with them and listening to the conversation.

Coco: "You men are just going on and on, we're getting bored."

General: "You girls come with us and we will take care of that boredom."

The general took both girls with him up the stairs and Eddie was relieved.

Eddie: "You go ahead, General. I still have to meet a few people, I don't want to show any disrespect to Ernesto"

Eddie joined John, they went over to Ernesto; they told him that they had been awake since 5 am and were quite tired. Ernesto offered to show them their rooms so they could rest.

Ernesto: "We have a big day tomorrow, men."

Eddie: "What do you have planned for the day, Ernesto?"

Ernesto: "I want you to see my jewel; it is about two hours from here, but a pleasant ride most of the way."

Eddie: "Thank you, that sounds like it will be enjoyable. I assume that we'll leave after breakfast?"

Ernesto: "I shall see you then."

The two men went to their bed room. Ernie was amazed at how quiet the room was, even with a party going on in the house. The quiet gave credit to the concrete that the building was made of. He got into bed and slept like a log.

Before he knew it he could feel the morning sun drenching his body as it came in through the window, slowly waking him from a deep sleep.

After breakfast they all sat in Ernesto's Ford Bronco where Ernesto introduced the driver as Ramón.

John: "Ernesto, this vehicle is much more comfortable then the truck, thanks for using this one."

Ernesto: "Yes, I like this vehicle much better."

There was not much conversation during the ride. Ernesto had his eyes wide open, looking around constantly like a shotgun guard on an old western coach.

Eddie: "Ernesto, it's obvious that you're looking for something. What are you looking for? Maybe we can help."

Ernesto: "No, you do not know the signs. We have a new group; they are always coming up looking to take on the big man in the area. Because of them, I look for signs like the jungle turned down, a new walkway or someone in a tree along the road. Thank you anyway."

Eddie: "I thought we could help. By the way, after we see your jewel and once we are back at your home, we would like to discuss our upcoming order; no hurry."

Ernesto: "Yes, when we get home or after breakfast in the morning, we will discuss. That is not a problem."

Eddie: "Thanks."

As Eddie spoke the word, thanks, a shot came through the front window of the truck hitting the front seat and just missing Ernesto. The shot missed him because he was half turned speaking with Eddie and John. The car swerved off the road, went into the jungle and stopped. They heard a couple of more shots go off then it went quiet.

John: "Who the hell did that?"

Ernesto: "This is what I am talking about; we have a few people to speak with before this ends. I will take care of this immediately."

Ernesto spoke in Spanish to the driver who took off back the way they came and stopped at a small building that apparently sold food. Neither John nor Eddie had noticed the building as they passed it the first time. Ernesto got out of the vehicle, went directly to the pay phone and made a call.

Ernesto spoke in Spanish, listened for a moment to the people at the other end of the line, his face changed to that hateful look. Eddie has observed this look in the past, when he was visiting Ernesto. Ernesto spoke some more Spanish then hung up the phone.

Ernesto: "Eduardo, we must make a short stop in route to our destination."

Ernesto made another call and spoke with someone for a short while, then got back in the car and spoke with the driver. They left that area and went back towards the area where the shots were fired.

The driver turned off onto a very thin jungle road that was very bumpy. They drove for about twenty five minutes to a location where the road opened to a small town. This looked, to Eddie, like an old western town you would see in one of the cowboy movies on TV in the United States.

They pulled into a small alley next to a building that had 'Policia' on the front of the building. Ernesto got out and went into the Police building stayed for a couple of moments and came back to the vehicle. Shortly thereafter three police officers came out of the building got into a car and drove off.

After the police left the area, the driver began driving again and drove off in a different direction. Ernesto was directing the driver in Spanish. Eddie and John heard the word "parade." Eddie thought that this was a Spanish word for stop, which is what the driver did. They had no idea what was about to happen.

Ernesto got out of the vehicle and waved to a blue car. Four men got out of the blue car and walked across the street to what looked like a small cantina, they were all carrying guns and one had a shotgun.

Eddie, John, Ernesto and the driver all heard several shots going off, then both barrels of the shot gun were heard. Four men walked out of the cantina, calmly, one of them making a hand gesture to Ernesto that indicated that everything was OK. They got into their blue car and drove off.

Ernesto: "Come, Eduardo, John; see my excellent work."

They walked into the cantina and saw that there were five bodies on the floor, all looked dead and all had been shot.

Ernesto: "This is what happens when someone shoots at me."

Eddie: "Ernesto, remind me never to shoot at you," and they all laughed.

John was curious, "Are you sure that all of these people were involved?"

Ernesto: "Yes, this one (Ernesto moved the body with his foot) told me to my face that he was taking over my operations."

John: "What did you do at that time?"

Ernesto: "I just laughed at him. I knew that he did not have a chance."

Eddie: "It's obvious that they did not have a chance. Too bad they didn't realize it sooner."

Ernesto: "I do not like doing this to people, but it is necessary for my business. If I did not take care of things like this, in this way, word would never get out and I would be dead like my brother."

Eddie let the entire comment about his brother slide.

They left the bar and went back to the vehicle. Ernesto spoke to the driver in Spanish. The driver drove out of town and back onto the small road that was very bumpy. They finally got back onto the original road that they had been on earlier and started back towards the location of the original shooting incident and drove right through, no trouble this time.

A while later they arrived at a clearing in the jungle. Ernesto exited the vehicle and the others followed, he walked over to a very large tree, behind the tree he cleared a small hole in the ground, placed his hand in it and two doors opened, like the old city cellar doors on a large city street, where deliveries were made.

Inside were a set of stairs going down about 10 feet to an opened area. Underground, they saw four 15 foot, homemade tables stretched out in two's and on the tables were piles and piles of marijuana cuttings, straight from the trees.

Eddie: "Ernesto, I didn't see any marijuana trees."

Ernesto: "No, one day I will show you my farm, It is a long way from here, in the mountains."

John said, "This is fantastic."

Ernesto: "Thank you, John, but come, let me show you the rest of the place."

Ernesto guided the two detectives through four other rooms, all underground and all like the first one. Then they were handed some masks for their faces. They put the masks on and entered a fifth room that was closed off by hanging plastic. This room had cocaine in it. The cocaine dust was hanging in the air. Everyone working in the room was wearing a mask. The cocaine was being dried after being cooked down. After cooking and drying the cocaine it is pressed into tight kilos for Ernesto's customers.

John: "It surprises me that you have cocaine here, Ernesto, when you have it in that other location that Eddie spoke of."

Ernesto: "Yes, John, this room is just a backup in the event that something should happen at the main location."

John: "I can see that you are a thinker and a smart man, Ernesto."

Ernesto: "Thank you, John; it is not often that I meet nice people like you two."

After the tour they left the area and drove to Ernesto's home, when they arrived it was about 10 pm and they all went to bed.

Chapter 5

Phase Three

Sunday April 27, 1980

They woke up, looked out the window and saw that familiar mist hanging in the air, which seemed to be soothing as well as beautiful as it hung just above the jungle tree tops. They got dressed and went down to breakfast.

At breakfast John began discussing the lab and how well it was constructed which bolstered Ernesto's ego and kept him in a good mood. After breakfast they had coffee in the living room and spoke of their upcoming order.

Ernesto: "Eduardo, you wanted to speak about your order, I hope everything was to your satisfaction."

Eddie: "Ernesto, it could not have been better. Because of your product, we have increased our customer base by almost ten percent, which is wonderful. Because of the high quality of your product we have made a decision."

Ernesto: "This makes me very happy, what kind of a decision did you make?"

Eddie: "We would like to give you all of our business."

Ernesto: "Eduardo, what are we speaking about?"

Eddie: "We will need one thousand keys every three or four months and a better price then ten thousand dollars per kilo."

Ernesto: "At that quantity and because it is you, I will give you a small break and come down to nine thousand per kilo, but please, do not push, I can go no lower. I do not need your order as much as I enjoy your company. That would make your bill nine million American dollars."

Eddie: "Yes, we understand that and that is the problem."

Ernesto: "I cannot lower the price I am sorry."

Eddie: "No the price is fine; we do not wish to hand over nine million dollars in United States currency to a subordinate."

Ernesto: "What is this subordinate?"

Eddie: "A worker, an employee that can walk off with it and never be seen again."

Ernesto: "Eduardo, this is not a problem, my men can be trusted."

Eddie: "I am sorry, but with all respect, we cannot go along with that."

Ernesto: "Then what do you want?"

Edie: "We want to put the money in your hands only and on the day we pick up the product."

Ernesto: "That is not a problem. For you two men, I will be there, as long as you give me enough notice. I will be sure to be there."

Eddie: "What is enough notice?"

Ernesto: "Two days should be enough."

Eddie: If I tell Bartoli that I will pick up on a certain date, will he relay that to you so that you can be there?"

Ernesto: "That order will be given and this will not be a problem."

Eddie: "Thank you, Ernesto. You are as understanding as you are hospitable."

After the meeting, Ernesto walked them out to the car and got into the car with them.

John: "Ernesto, are you coming with us?"

Ernesto: "Yes, part of the way, you men have a lot of time before your flight, I will show you a little enjoyment before you leave."

They drove off and about half way to the airport they drove onto a dirt road. That road led to a large barn where they parked alongside several other cars.

When they entered the building there were about 50 men all standing around a small walled ring in the center of the barn This was obviously a cock fighting ring which the locals referred to as a Galina or Gallera. Ernie was unable to make out exactly which word they were using and it wasn't important enough to inquire about.

Ernie and John were later told that the Galina or Gallera is the facility for the championship cock fighting bouts for the entire area. Throughout the area there are small rinks where the minor bouts take place all year long in an effort to make it to the Galina for the championship, which is held on a regular basis.

Ernesto: "Do not bet on any of the fights until I tell you."

Eddie: "OK, Ernesto"

The first two cock fights were very strange to a person who was raised in Brooklyn, New York where this type of animal fighting is never observed. This was a way of life for these men, they took this as a sport and very seriously. The same way Americans look at football or baseball.

As the birds were brought out, they were weighed, then shaved under the wings and paraded around the ring to the people waiting to pick their favorite to bet on in the third fight. The referee would attach a blue band to one bird's leg and a white band to the other bird's leg for the purpose of distinguishing the difference in the birds after the blood started flowing. In addition the referee added long, razor sharp talons to the legs of both birds which added to the viciousness.

The spectators had been betting on all of the fights, but this one seemed to create a much larger fuss like a championship bout.

Ernesto: "This is the one to bet on, Eduardo, you see the large red bird."

Eddie: "Yes, I see him."

Ernesto: "Place your bet on him, he is a champion, has never been beaten and will win today."

Eddie: "Ernesto, how much should I bet?"

Ernesto: "In American bet fifty dollars, that is a lot of money to these peasants."

Ernie and John placed a bet of fifty dollars each on the red bird. This bird was fighting the black bird that looked just as strong. After fighting for about thirty minutes the red bird was victorious. The man taking the bets came over to Ernesto, John and Eddie and paid them their winnings.

After the fight Ernesto indicated that Eddie and John should leave so that they would catch their flight.

Eddie: "What about you Ernesto, how will you get back?"

Ernesto: "That is very good that you show concern for me, Eduardo, but I have people here that work for me and they will make sure I get home."

"OK as long as you are all right I will not worry.:

The two detectives left the area and were driven back to their car then left for the California airport. On the ride back they had a discussion.

Ernie: "John, we discussed the intelligence on Ernesto's brother?"

John: "Yes, his name was Eduardo and he looked a lot like you. All of the information is in the file, including a picture of Eduardo which you looked at, Ernie."

Ernie: "Yes, I remember, how could I forget that?"

John: "Ernie, in the beginning it never even dawned on me that it would come up, how did his brother's name come up?"

Ernie: "That general told me about him and said that I looked so much like Ernesto's brother that he thought I had come back from the dead."

John: "Yeah, you do look like his brother. Maybe that's why he's so nice to you. He seems to be protective of you, he makes exceptions for almost everything you say and do and he's nicer to you than anyone. With others he gets upset, never with you."

Ernie: "As much of a murderer as he is; I'm going to feel a little bad about this one for a while."

John: "Feel as bad as you like, Ernie, but if he decided to go after anyone it will probably be you. We have to be very careful after this is over."

Ernie: "Yea, now you know why I use Eddie Pannoni."

They boarded the plane and were back in Logan International Airport in Boston, that evening. They telephoned for a ride and called their wives, they were home, from the airport in two hours.

They agreed to meet on the next Friday to go over the reports and start the closing of the Ernesto Adelanto case.

Friday May 2, 1980

Ernie had his morning breakfast. Spring was in the air, the birds were singing, It seemed like all of the birds were gaining weight or becoming pregnant, dogs were losing their winter coats, the squirrels tails were getting very thin and the horse's at the stable, that Ernie passed from time to time when he traveled through the Blue Hills on the way to his office, were losing all of their winter hair.

Ernie walked into the office and sat at a desk. It almost seemed strange to him with all of the traveling in the Mexican case, but the feeling of home returned quickly.

Henry, one of his partners, walked over to him and handed Ernie the phone, smiling and saying that it doesn't take these people long to know you're here. Ernie took the phone and smiled.

Cobra: "Hi Eddie, this is Cobra."

Ernie: "Cobra, nice to hear from you, how are you making out?"

Cobra: "OK, I guess. Can I meet with you?"

Ernie: "When and where do you want to meet?"

Cobra: "I'm at the coffee house, on Franklyn St., can you come down?"

Ernie: "Sure, I'll be there in about twenty minutes."

Ernie hung up the phone and Henry looked at Ernie, "Another trip?"

Ernie: "Just to the coffee house, want to come?"

Henry: "Will I be in the way?"

Ernie: "Not at all. Don't worry Cobra don't bite, I just have to make one call first."

Ernie picked up the phone and telephoned Agent John Slater of the DEA.

Ernie: "John, Ernie here"

John: "Hi, Ernie, I was just going to call you."

Ernie: "What's up?"

John: "Ernie we want to put this meeting off until Wednesday afternoon at two. Is that OK with you?"

Ernie: "I don't mind, but what is the hold up?"

John: "I have an agent coming in from out west. He's familiar with that area. Maybe he can be of some help to us, you never know."

Ernie: "OK, then I will see you Wednesday at 2 pm."

Ernie and Henry left the office together and went to the coffee house where they met with a white male, 5'9" tall, with dark hair and dark eyes whose real name was Francis Tapper.

This man had a stiletto knife tattooed on his right arm with a cobra snake sliding through it which is the reason he was called Cobra. His face was young looking even though he was 40 year of age, very clear and soft. His personality was explosive; he could strike out at any second. Especially when he didn't like what was going on around him. These traits tied him to the name Cobra.

Ernie has known Cobra for a while. At one time Cobra was involved in drugs and Ernie was working deep cover. Because of that investigation Cobra did a short stint in the county jail. Ernie wasn't totally sure of Cobra and wanted to know what Cobra may want from him. He invited Henry along at this preliminary meeting as a witness to any conversation. Over a year had passed since Ernie had heard anything from Cobra.

At Ernie's last meeting with Francis Tapper, AKA, Cobra, Ernie was locking him up on narcotics charges and Cobra was not very happy about that meeting. Ernie wanted to keep one hand high for a while with Cobra.

Ernie and Henry arrived at the meeting. Ernie introduced Detective Henry Griswold as one of his partners and asked what it was that Cobra needed?

Cobra: "I have something of interest, Eddie. I believe that you can use it."

Ernie: "First of all, call me Ernie, my real name is Detective Ernie Lijoi Sr. Second: Why help me out, after I arrested you?"

Cobra: "You'll understand. First let me say, I'm happy that I'm off drugs and out of that business. Now I can concentrate on my family. You did that for me and I appreciate it. Not at first, but after some time I do appreciate what you did. Let me ask you something first, I have never done anything like this before, how does it help me out?"

Ernie: "Cobra, you have a family right and you're clean?"

Cobra: "Yes, why"

Ernie: "Do you want to stay that way? Do you want your kid to stay clean?"

Cobra: "Of Course I do, they are my life now, no more drugs."

Ernie: "Then that's why you will help me out."

Cobra: "Yes, but Eddie—I mean Ernie—I am in bad shape and could use some financial help until I get on my feet."

Ernie: "OK, now we're being honest. You want to sell your old contacts. Am I right?"

Cobra: "That's part of it. Can you do anything in Florida?"

Ernie: "I can make arrangements to do anything anywhere; talk to me."

Cobra: "I have a situation where a guy is so well connected to this joint in Miami, Florida that he goes down there and makes arrangements to have thousands of pounds of marijuana and hundreds of kilos of cocaine shipped here and he distributes it from his barn here in Quincy."

Ernie: "Cobra, he ships the drugs by truck?"

Cobra: "Sometimes by tractor trailer and sometimes he takes as much as a thousand pounds on his 35-foot boat and has the pickups just off shore. He does different things at different times; he's very smart."

Ernie: "Yes he sounds like a genius. What do you need and what can you do for us?"

Cobra: "I need about ($10,000) ten thousand to carry me and my family, but I can cut you into this guy easily. Then it's up to you."

Ernie: "That's a lot of money for a simple introduction."

Cobra: "This guy is the head of a small mafia family and they think nothing of murder. I'm putting my life on the line here."

Ernie: "I'll be honest with you, if I go back to my boss and the DA, with a request like that, my bosses will throw me out of the office."

Cobra: "Well then, see what they will do, I'm reasonable, I'll work with you. When you were Eddie we always got along, right?"

Ernie: "Right, we did get along, but I have to think about your safety first so let me speak with some people and set something up. As far as the money goes, you're more interested in helping out your family right?"

Cobra: "Yes, I need to get them started on the right road, find a job and stay with it and with them."

Ernie: "Instead of approaching me with the sale of an old supplier of friend, why not just ask me to help you get a job. That would solve your problems?"

Cobra: "Ernie, you're right, that would be great, if you could get me maybe a grand or two and a job. That would be wonderful."

Ernie: "We'll talk, I'll be away for a while; I'll call you within two weeks."

Cobra: "Sounds good to me, you have my number, right?"

Ernie: "The same number as before?"

Cobra: "Yes, just call me there, you know my wife Annie."

Ernie: "Yes, I know her; I'll call you around the end of next week."

Cobra: "Thanks Eddie. I'll take any help I can get."

Cobra left the coffee shop, Ernie and Henry sat there for a while talking about Cobra.

As they walked to the car Ernie told Henry that he would speak with the DA on Monday and see what he thinks of the Job and a thousand dollars.

Henry: "We can get him a decent job, but that cash may be a problem. What about the Fed's, do you think they may want in?"

Ernie: "It's possible, but I'll speak with the District Attorney first, then see how it goes from there."

The two men drove back to the office and Ernie worked on his reports for his department and for the Fed's.

Monday May 5, 1980

Ernie left the house and didn't have to warm up the car; the weather was getting warmer, the days longer and the sun stronger. He whistled to the mockingbird, got in the car and drove off.

The first stop of the day would be the District Attorney's office to see John Hageman. Ernie knew what he would say about the money that Cobra wanted, but he gave it a shot anyway and he was not disappointed.

John Hageman: "Ernie you know better than that; we can't afford all these guys. We have to find another way."

Ernie: "John, what are you willing to pay him assuming that the case closes the way he predicts?"

John: "We can afford a couple of grand, but that's about it."

Ernie: "If he will not accept our deal do you have any objections to me taking it to the Feds or the DEA?"

John: "No objections whatsoever; go for it?"

Ernie: "Thanks John."

After his meeting Ernie started off to go to the Quincy office and while on route 128 heading towards Quincy, he noticed a 1975 red Cadillac. He recognized this car as being one of the cars that a member of the Suriano Family uses, but he could not see who was driving.

The Suriano Family started out with two or three brothers back in the very early 1900's who made a good living in the construction industry. Their children also made a great living in construction, but they became extremely powerful in the town of Dedham and the third generation became very much involved with illicit narcotics and gaming.

Ernie followed the Cadillac into Quincy where the driver drove around for a while then drove back towards Dedham. Ernie thought that the driver saw him following and that's why the Cadillac driver left Quincy. He made a note of the incident and then a report that was given to the cruisers. If that car came into Quincy again Ernie would know who the driver was and the areas that he was in.

At the office Ernie telephoned Cobra and asked to meet with him at the coffee shop at 1pm. Cobra agreed.

Ernie ordered a cheese burger and fries for lunch and sat in the coffee shop. A little after 1pm Cobra walked into the shop and over to Ernie.

Cobra: "What did they say?"

Ernie: "The DA didn't like the situation as I laid it out. They can't afford the money part. They're starting their audit for the season and as you know money is tight everywhere."

Cobra: "You mean they want me to do this for nothing?"

Ernie: "I can do the job thing for you almost immediately, which will help out. As far as the money goes; I'll get you a grand only if we get more than that from the case. You'll get it after the money is turned over to the DA's office by the court."

Cobra: "I'll take it. When can you get me the job?"

Ernie: " You go and see this man." Ernie handed Cobra a piece of paper with a name and address on it. "It's a construction job, driving a truck. This job will help you to get on your feet and you'll have the income from the job. You understand that you do not get paid until a few days after the case closes and it all goes as planned."

Cobra: "OK, I guess that's only fair, I was hoping to get paid now."

Ernie: "Sorry, but the case closes first."

Cobra: "How long do you think it will take?"

Ernie: "I don't know anything about it yet. Once I have the information and form a plan then I can estimate the time factors."

Cobra: "OK what do you need to know?"

Ernie: "Right now, how good this cheeseburger tastes."

Cobra: "When do you want to start this case?"

Ernie; "We can meet tomorrow tonight. I want you to write down as much information as you can remember about this guy; his home, his car and anything else you think of no matter how trivial."

Cobra: "Should I telephone you?"

Ernie: "No, I'll call you about the same time tomorrow. After that I have to go away for a few days, a family matter, and when I get back we can start on this case."

Cobra: "OK, I hope everything is OK with your family."

Ernie: "Not a major problem, I'll see you tomorrow; you want a burger?"

Cobra: "No thanks, I have to meet my wife for lunch now. I'll talk with you tomorrow."

Cobra left the coffee shop; Ernie finished his lunch and then started back to the office. While driving to the office along Franklyn St. he came to the corner of Bradford St. where he noticed three teenagers all huddled in a door way and all three of them had paper bags. This seemed odd; Ernie pulled his car up and called for a cruiser to meet him.

It took about five minutes and the cruiser came up the street right past the three teenagers. Ernie was watching their reaction to the cruiser through his car mirrors. They could not take their eyes off of that cruiser until it got well past them.

Ernie spoke with the driver of the cruiser, Patrolman O'Rielly, and asked him to hang around while Ernie went over to check out the boys. He left the cruiser and began walking towards the boys. They were still watching the cruiser and saw Ernie talking to the driver.

The boys didn't know what to do. One of them began to run then a second and Ernie grabbed the third just as he tried to get away.

Ernie; "Where are you going, young man?"

Boy: "Who are you?"

Ernie: "I am a police officer, Detective Ernie Lijoi Sr. I'm just curious; why are all three of you carrying a bag the same size and why you're so interested in the cruiser?"

The boy handed Ernie the bag.

Ernie: "I guess you don't mind if I take a look?"

Ernie opened the bag and in the bottom was a small amount of loose marijuana.

Ernie: "What did you guys do split a half ounce."

Boy: "Yes, Sir, we weren't hurting anyone."

Ernie: "No? That's questionable, young man."

Boy: "Who are we hurting?"

Ernie: "Young man, by law you are not allowed to hurt yourself. With this stuff you are hurting yourself, your parents, you sisters and brothers and more, in one way or another. I don't expect you to fully understand, but in time you will. Right now you should worry about a future drug record. Would you hire someone that had a drug record?"

Boy: "No Sir, I wouldn't. Will I get a drug record now?"

Ernie; "You're being taken into custody; I'll say that much, you and your friends."

The cruiser went after the other two boys and picked up both of them. They each had a small quantity of marijuana in their possession in each of their bags.

Ernie had them all transported to the station where he called in the juvenile division to take care of the boys, look into their school and home life. He recommended that a good scare be put into them and that they not be arrested this time, but a file should be set up for any future problems.

The juvenile officer took the evidence smiled at Ernie and said that they would take care of it. The detectives then took the boys to their offices. That was the last Ernie ever heard of it with one exception. One day, one of the boy's fathers contacted Detective Lijoi and thanked him for catching his son and for not prosecuting him. Ernie told the father that he didn't like prosecuting kids; he would rather scare the shit out of them and hope that they smarten up. "We'll see in your son's case, Sir."

That ended the day shift. Ernie had a lot of reports to make out. The next day he decided to go directly to the office in the morning, he had to get the office work completed or at least caught up.

Wednesday May 7, 1980

At 2pm Ernie walked into the federal building and went to the offices of the DEA to attend the meeting with Agent John Slater and other agents in his office.

Ernie was escorted into the meeting room. He looked around and saw faces that he knew as well as faces he didn't know. On the table, were a lot of files and dozens of pictures of Ernesto's home, the lumber yard, some of the labs and more, all taken during surveillance from a high altitude airplane.

Agent John Slater: "There you are. We've been waiting for you."

Ernie: "Sorry John, I'm a little late."

John: "No problem let me introduce you to Agent Jesus Martinez from Arizona. He is familiar with this operation; he may be of some help to us."

Ernie: "It's a pleasure to meet you, Jesus. Wow that sounds strange to me, very religious."

Jesus replied biblically: "That is alright, my child."

The whole room laughed.

Ernie: "So where are we, John?"

John: "We are trying to figure a strategy to close this end of the investigation. I was just going to ask if anyone had any ideas."

One agent stood up and said that he thought they should go in guns blazing in view of all of the cover.

Jesus stood and stated: "That won't work. All they have to do is run down that storage hole. We'll never get them out of there. I'll bet they have a few areas of cover that we're not able to see from the plane."

Another agent offered an idea that John and Ernie go there, view the drugs and say the money has to be brought in by someone holding it for them and then they close in.

Ernie was listening to all of the comments:

Ernie: "I have an idea to throw out. What if John and I go in by car, confirm that Ernesto, the man we are after is there, confirm that the drugs are there and once everything is confirmed one of us leaves to get the money? We claim that the money is in a truck, parked close by and the truck is for transporting the drugs. That's a very common, logical and cautious way of doing business as you all know. One of us leaves to get the truck, the other stays with Bartoli and Ernesto. The one that goes after the truck brings it back with all of our men in the truck. The truck will also give all of us some good cover to use, if needed, and I think we may need it."

Jesus: "That sounds very good, Ernie. It gives us cover which is not easy to find out there. Does anyone have any other ideas?"

There was no answer to Jesus' question.

John: "OK; as far as I'm concerned, I like Ernie's scenario the best. It gives us an out if Ernesto is not there. We'll go with that plan. Are there any objections?"

There was no answer to John's question.

John: "Next step is that we place the order and set up the pickup date and time. Ernie, what days are good for you?"

Ernie: "John, there are no good days for something as dangerous as this, but the first of the week is best if no one objects."

John: "Jesus, is that OK with you? Will your men be available at that time?"

Jesus: "That's fine for us; whatever works for you guys."

Ernie: "John, I thought that your men were going out there with us?"

John: "No, Ernie, we speak that way for mental effect it makes the upcoming raid seem realistic in our minds as we discuss it. We'll use the Arizona people for this. We'll need a picture of you and me since we are going in. We'll make one for every agent that goes on the raid. They will know what we look like in the event of trouble or a shootout. Before you leave we will take those pictures."

Ernie: "John, when do you want to call and order?"

John: "Do you think Friday will be OK?"

Ernie: "Yes, that should be fine; Ernesto said that he needed two days and that he has stock piles of cocaine so I would imagine he will be ready."

John: "OK, let's get together on Friday at noon. We'll make the call and set it all up."

Ernie: "We are going to fly into Arizona this time?"

John: "Yes, the airport is not far from the DEA offices and close to the Nogales Lumber yard."

Ernie: "Sounds good; see you on Friday to set up the deal."

Ernie left the federal building and went home to Dedham. He walked in the house and kissed Teresa hello with a small peck on her check. He went in to speak with the boys before he went out into the garden to water and feed his plants.

At one end of the garden Ernie had a 55 barrel drum filled with water. This was Ernie's five o'clock tea which he learned about growing up in Brooklyn from his grandfather who had a beautiful garden right in the middle of the city. The garden was in the back yard behind his three-family home.

In the bottom of the barrel Ernie would place a five pound bag of cow manure every two or three years then fill the barrel with water then allow the rain to fill the barrel as he used the water.

At five o'clock two or three times a week he would use that water to water the garden. He had to make sure that he did not get any of that water on the plants themselves. The acid in that water mixture, would burn the plants. The mixture went into the ground around the base of the plants. Once he was finished, aerating or turning up the soil around the tomatoes and watering everything it was time for supper.

At the table Teresa seemed a little depressed, she was being extra quiet and Ernie could not understand why.

Ernie: "What's wrong, Teresa?"

Teresa: "It's nothing; I am just stupid that's all."

Ernie: "Not you, you're the smartest girl I know. What happened?"

Teresa: "I was at the market in the square; I loaded the bags in the car, got into the car and started to drive off from the parking spot."

Ernie; "Then what happened?"

Teresa: "Don't laugh at me."

Ernie: "I will not laugh, I promise."

Teresa: "As I pulled out of the parking spot I hit a cab that was parked in front of me. I sort of scraped his rear bumper and scratched my car."

Ernie: "Was anyone hurt?"

Teresa: "No nothing like that, just a little damage to my car, the cab didn't get anything."

Ernie: "OK so when do you want to start."

Teresa: "Start what"

Ernie: "Your parking lessons," as he began laughing.

Teresa: "I said, don't laugh."

Ernie: "OK, no problem. As long as no one got hurt, that's the important thing. The car can be repaired."

After dinner Ernie and the boys found little ways to tease Teresa about her accident. She took it in good humor. Ernie went to bed early, he said he was tired.

Chapter 6

COBRA

Friday May 9, 1980

At 7 am Ernie got out of bed. He went down to the kitchen for coffee, the boys were just finishing breakfast and Teresa was getting coffee for him. The boys left for school.

Ernie: "Teresa, I'm going away on Monday, to Arizona; hopefully this will be the last trip there."

Teresa: "How long will you be gone?"

Ernie; "As long as everything goes right I should be back by Wednesday the latest."

Teresa: "Then we should spend the weekend together with the boys."

Ernie: "OK, you think about what we should do, I don't want to go to Maine. I want spend some time in the garden this weekend. It's all turned, the tea is ready and I'm ready for planting."

Teresa: "OK, I'll figure something out that is simple and won't take us far from home."

Ernie: "Good, I have to run, I'll see you tonight."

Ernie left the house. He walked out the door and heard the whistling of two mocking birds. They seemed to be whistling to each other. Ernie tried to chime in, but neither of them paid any attention to his song. They kept singing to each other. It must have been true love.

Ernie drove off to the office. He drove past a park area in Dedham, where he observed two men playing chess. This brought to mind his sons and how he taught them to play.

SEVERAL YEARS EARLIER:

When Ernie's boys were three years old he would teach them to play with a chess set and as the time passed they learned how to play the game so well that he had them join a chess club in the town.

Each Wednesday night he would take them up to the Endicott Estate in Dedham, which was a mansion left to the town of Dedham by the Endicott Family when they passed on.

The boys would play chess against other children. At the end of the season the parents would get together and throw a party for the children. They would award every child that played a special award for playing the game. Everyone had a lot of fun and the boys became so good at the game that Ernie was only able to win a game once in a while.

At the office:

Ernie arrived at the office, all of the men wh\ere there and were talking about the Cobra case.

Detective Jerry Gibson: "Here he is now. Ernie, what do you think about this guy Cobra?"

Ernie: "I always got along with him, but he was a junkie. He says he has cleaned up his act. His motivation is perfect for us and for him. I'll listen to what he has to say and play it carefully for a while until I can confirm him and his information."

Detective Jack Wade: "How does the case sound to you?"

Ernie: "I didn't want to let on to Cobra and I didn't say anything to Henry, but I think I know who it is that Cobra is talking about. When I was in deep cover I heard a lot of rumblings about a guy connected to Boston and Rhode Island Mafia. He is supposed to be a vicious bastard and very careful."

Jack: "You never met him?"

Ernie: "No I don't think so, but you never know, we will definitely find out in time."

Jerry: "How do you want to work it?"

Ernie: "I have a meeting at noon with the DEA. On Monday I'll be going on a little trip to hopefully close out the DEA case. Once I finish that case and get back home, I'll meet with Cobra and look at this thing more closely."

Jack: "We have a lot of things pending, but that Cobra case sounds better then all of them. You know we are here if you need us for anything. Just let us know."

Ernie: "Thanks guys I appreciate that."

Ernie contacted Cobra and told him that he had to go away and would call him as soon as he returned from his trip. At 11am Ernie left the office for the Federal building and arrived at the offices of the Federal Drug Enforcement Administration in Boston at the correct time, noon.

Ernie: "Hi John, are you ready to telephone and confirm the order for the blow?"

John: "Yes, by the way, here is a copy of the pictures we took the other day. Jesus has the rest."

Ernie dialed the phone number for the lumber yard located in Arizona.

Ernie: "Hello, is Bartoli there?"

Bartoli: "Bartoli Romero here. Who is speaking, please?"

Ernie: "This is Eduardo Pannoni."

Bartoli: "Yes, Mr. Pannoni we are all ready for you, whenever you are ready."

Ernie: "One thousand, correct?"

Batoli: "Yes that is correct, Sir; when do you want them?"

Ernie: "We will be there sometime Monday during the day. Is that all right?"

Bartoli: "Ernesto and I will be waiting for you."

Ernie: "See you then."

Ernie hung up the phone and spoke to Agent John Slater: "John, we're all set for sometime Monday. He told me that he and Ernesto will be there."

John: "Great, I'll see you at the airport at 7am Monday morning; how about some lunch?"

Ernie: "Sorry, John. I have too much to do. I'll see you Monday morning."

Ernie left the Federal building and went back to his office in Quincy. Later he went to the main station and spoke with Captain Richards, informing him of the Mexican case and where it stands.

Captain: "OK, Ernie, just be very careful and call me as soon as it's over and I'll call your wife for you."

Ernie: "I will, Captain. Now I am going to head home and get some things done, see you when I get back."

Ernie left the station and drove towards home, along the highway to the Dedham exit. He drove with the driver's window opened for the first time since winter and enjoyed the warmth of the air surrounding him.

As soon as Ernie arrived at his home he changed clothes and went out to the garden. He unrolled a twenty five foot long roll of black plastic that was sixteen feet wide when it was opened up. Ernie spread it over the garden area holding the ends down with lengths of wood and rocks.

The next step was to figure out where to cut the holes for the plants and then plant the tomatoes, squash, peppers and eggplant and more. He would plant the next day.

He took a small area and placed 1X3 lengths of wood forming a box and dug two inches into the ground, about a foot long in two separate locations. This would be his lettuce patch. Ernie found that planting lettuce this way in a couple of places was the best way because he or Teresa would cut the baby stalks down in to the ground for salad in one patch, and within a day or two they grew back. This procedure lasted all summer and fall each year. They went back and forth between patches taking what they needed for that day and leaving the second patch for the next day.

Saturday morning Ernie left the house before anyone got up and went to the Endicott Estate. To an area in the back of the property where there was a hot house (House made of glass) that was originally used by the property owners. Some of the older men from the town would grow the plants from seed and then sell them to the public very cheap and Ernie bought his plans there.

Ernie: "Hi, Bill."

Bill was one of the town elders that enjoyed working with the plants.

Bill: "Wow, Ernie you're buying a lot of tomatoes in this year."

Ernie: "My mother-in-law wants to put up jars. I promised her I would plant at least 50 plants."

Bill: "Yes, I can understand that. She always put up jars when your father-in-law was alive. He used to plant a hundred or more tomato plants for her to jar along with his corn. I remember as a boy we would go in and steal some corn from him, late at night. He never said a word, he was OK."

Ernie went home with his plants. He began planting the baby plants. This was the start of his garden for that year, as he had always done.

Teresa looked out of the window at Ernie working in the garden. She told her boys that Dad was in the garden for the day.

Teresa: "Boys, tomorrow we'll be going out for lunch and after that we'll go and play some miniature golf. Later, after we play golf tomorrow afternoon, we will go to see a nice movie. Take a look at the movie schedule in the news paper and let me know which movie you would like to see."

The boys got the paper went through it and decided that they wanted to see Mad Max.

Joey: "Mom we want to see Mad Max."

Teresa: "Sorry, I don't think that's a good movie for you guys. Pick another one.

Joey: "How about Star Wars Ep. V: The Empire Strikes Back, Mom, is that OK?"

Teresa: "Yes, that one is fine, we'll see that movie."

Ernie spent the entire day getting all of the plants in the ground then went into the house.

Ernie: "I could eat a horse."

Teresa: "Not until you wash up and change those dirty clothes."

Ernie: "OK, Teresa, will you make me something?"

Teresa: "Just wash up, I'm cooking now."

At supper Teresa told Ernie that they were all going out for lunch and then to play golf and after that to a movie. The boys picked the new Star Wars movie. Ernie looked up and said:

Ernie: "I wanted to see that new movie about *Superman*. That's with Christopher Reeve, Gene Hackman and Marlon Brando, but the Star Wars is a better idea; thanks, guys."

The next day, they spent the entire day together; enjoying all of the things that they spoke about. Monday Ernie would be back at work as Eddie Pannoni.

Monday May 12, 1980

Ernie and John met at Logan international airport, boarded the plane and took off for Arizona. When they arrived in Tucson, Arizona, the DEA agents from the local area was there to meet them, take care of their bags and transport them to the offices in Tucson.

They met with several of the Arizona DEA Agents. The rest of the agents were already staked out near the lumber yard, building information for the team that will be going in; and still others were at an undisclosed airport boarding two helicopters that are owned by the DEA.

John and Ernie took a car that had been picked out for them in advance. This car had ears; the front of the car was rigged with extra sensitive microphones and cameras, built into the grill. The back of the car had microphones and cameras built into the bumper. Every conversation could be heard and recorded at the command center. This car also had front and rear cameras that transmitted the pictures to the command center for later use in court. This was a very special car far ahead of its time in the field of police work.

Ernie was very impressed. Agent Jesus Martinez explained the vehicle and all of its specialties then said that it would be best if the car was parked with the rear towards the storage area at the lumber yard then no one would be suspicious of it.

Ernie: "Wait a minute, do you mean to tell me that this car has cameras in every direction, with microphones to hear?"

Jesus: "Exactly, and it is bullet proof, so the best place to be in a shootout is inside this car."

Ernie: "That's amazing; pretty soon they won't need us anymore."

Jesus: "Ernie, I know I can trust you, but this car is top secret; no talking about it when you get back to Massachusetts."

Ernie: "No problem, I may tell my wife some day, but other than that, I Know nothing."

John and Ernie took off and drove to the lumber yard.

When they entered the gate and stopped the car. Bartoli Romero, Ernesto's employee, walked over to the car with a big smile on his face.

Bartoli: "It is wonderful to see you again, Mr. Pannoni; I think this will be a long friendship."

Eddie: "Yes, Bartoil, my plan is for us to be associated with you and Ernesto for a very long time."

Bartoli: "That is wonderful. If you will, please, follow me I will show you the stock."

John and Ernie followed Bartoli to the storage area in the rear of the property. John parked and turned the car around so that the rear of the vehicle was facing the storage area. They both got out of the car and walked down a long set of stairs into the underground tunnel. When they reached the bottom they saw a very large room built like an underground mine with large wood posts across the ceilings and wood walls.

In front of them were two golf carts, which Ernie could not figure out; they didn't seem to fit. They walked a few feet and turned a very wide corner and then the golf carts made sense.

John and Ernie were at the beginning of a long tunnel that had to be several miles long, this tunnel stretched out in front of them in a southerly direction. The work that had to be involved in building this tunnel brought to his mind the Egyptians and the pyramids and the tunnels under them.

Eddie: "Wow, Bartoli, this is some tunnel. You did this your selves and no one has discovered it?"

Bartoli: "Yes, it took us two years to dig this out and set it all up, the dirt that we took out of here is all over the area desert."

Eddie: "Fantastic job; you were showing us the order that we requested?"

Bartoli: "Yes, here in this room." Bartoli directed John and Ernie into a room that had at least ten thousand keys of cocaine stock piled, waiting for pickups by customers. Ernie figured that they were looking at a billion dollars or more in street value.

John: "OK, we will accept the fact that our shipment is here, where is Ernesto?"

Bartoli: "Get into the carts and we will drive over to him."

Eddie: "Drive over to him? What do you mean?"

Bartoli: "The other end of this tunnel ends at Nogales, Mexico in another lumber yard there. He is waiting there for us."

John: "How do I get nine million dollars over there?"

Bartoli: "We take it with us?"

Eddie: "No, we have rules, just like Ernesto has rules; the first rule is that our money never leaves the United States. Not until it is turned over to the seller, then he does what he wants."

Bartoli: "I am very sorry, but Ernesto does not come into the United States. He and the United States do not agree on a lot of points."

Eddie: "OK, I understand. It appears that we will not be able to make this purchase. Thank you very much for all of your courtesy. We will be leaving now."

Bartoli: "Wait, Wait, Wait a minute, let me telephone Ernesto before you leave."

John, Ernie and Bartoli returned to the surface where Bartoli entered a small building on the grounds with a thousand wires running into it and out of it. Bartoli spoke on the phone and came out of the building.

Bartoli: "Eduardo, I just spoke with Ernesto, he would like to speak with you."

Eddie walked over to the little 3X4 building and when he entered he saw a maze of wires inside with one phone on a shelf that was just high enough to use as a writing area.

Eddie: "Hello, Ernesto?"

Ernesto: "Yes, Eduardo, why do you want me to come to you? I will be happy to take the money at this end of the tunnel?"

Eddie: "I am very sorry Ernesto, it is actually embarrassing that I must insist on this, at least the first time that we do this large of a load."

Ernesto: "But, why should we have to do it this way?"

Eddie: "Ernesto, you have certain rules and precautions that you follow to the letter or you would not be so successful and so do I. We like and respect you, but we cannot change our rules or make exceptions for anyone. In time we will make an exception for you and you will be the first exception in a very long time."

Ernesto: "Eduardo, I like you, why don't you leave that life in the US and come to work with me. You can make ten times the money as my partner, I will start you with twenty percent and in time you will be up to forty percent, between us we can rule the coca world. You have balls, you're smart and I like you. I sometimes think of you as a brother."

Eddie: "Thank you, Ernesto, maybe we can speak of that another time. If we cannot do a simple thing like this together, how could I consider a partnership?"

Ernesto: "I break my rule and come to you; I will be there in five minutes."

Eddie: "Good and thank you for understanding."

Ernie went outside and told Bartoli that Ernesto was coming over and that John would go and get the money and the truck to transport the cocaine.

Bartoli: "He is coming here? That is very strange; he must really like you, Eduardo. He never comes here."

John got into the car and went to meet the Arizona DEA which took about fifteen minutes. Shortly after John left the area, Ernesto showed up and asked where John had gone.

Eddie: "Ernesto, thank you for coming to meet us in person. He went to get your money and our truck for transporting the product."

Ernesto: "Eduardo you should take my offer seriously. I mean to have you join me; I do look at you as I would look at my own brother."

Eddie: "I will, Ernesto, let's talk about it tomorrow."

Ernesto: "Good, call me at this number in Mexico," Ernesto handed Eddie a slip of paper with a phone number on it. "This is a private number, do not give it out."

Eddie: "Ernesto, I would not do that; here comes John with the truck."

John stopped in front of Ernesto and Eddie then waived hello to Ernesto from the truck as he slowly turned the truck around backed it up to Eddie and Ernesto, placing the truck between Ernesto and the building where his men were standing guard. John stopped the truck, got out of the truck saying: "Nice to see you, Ernesto."

Ernie (Eddie) walked up to the back door of the truck as John walked from the front to the back. John unlocked the truck and turned as if to speak with Ernesto then all hell broke loose.

The rear doors to the truck opened and 20 men flew out of the truck, all holding guns. The first people that they grabbed were Ernesto and Bartoli. The agents cuffed them and placed them behind the truck, which was located between them and the men in the lumber yard office which was about eighty feet away. It only took a few seconds to place them in a safe position and cuff them. Then shots rang out.

The shots were coming from the office building and the DEA agents were returning gunfire sporadically. A man in the office building was shot and fell through the window, his body was hanging in the window, half in and half out. Another man came to the window and used the dead man that was hanging from the window as cover.

An agent took a bullet in his left leg and all he said was: "Son of a bitch, not again."

Ernie was firing and hit one man on the first floor who fell backwards into the building and another man came over and took his place.

John was covering the two prisoners and Ernesto was screaming at the top of his lungs, yelling to his men in the building:

Ernesto yelling: "Kill them, Kill them all."

Ernie Turned to Ernesto, took out a pocket knife, cut and ripped Ernesto's shirt with the knife. He used a piece of Ernesto's shirt as a gag for Ernesto and Bartoli.

After a few minutes all of the firing stopped and the men in the building yelled out in Spanish, one of the agents answered.

Agent Jesus: "They say that they have one dead and one seriously injured. They want to come out."

The agent told them in Spanish to throw out their guns, put their hands on their heads and walk out backwards. A couple of minutes later the door opened and they complied with the orders. Everyone was taken into custody, cuffed and placed in the back of the truck.

After the prisoners were secure John took half of the agents down to see the infamous tunnel. They looked around before returning to the truck. They saw the drug room and the stock and while looking around found a third room that John and Ernie had not seen. This room was the armory room which had at least two hundred weapons and several thousand rounds of ammunition, enough weapons and ammunition for a small army.

John: "Ernie, go down and take a look at the armory room, we missed that one."

Ernie took the second group down while the first group watched the prisoners and was amazed when he saw the weapons room. He returned to the surface.

Ernie: "John, should we call the (ATF) Alcohol Tobacco and Firearms Division?"

John: "I did, while you guys were looking around."

Ernie: "What do you want to do next?"

John: "I think we should take these prisoners in. Once they are booked, we should interview Ernesto and Bartoli."

Ernie: "Sounds good to me."

Chapter 7

The Interviews

That night Ernie telephoned his wife Teresa and told her that he was OK, the case is closed. He explained that they were going to interview some prisoners and would be home in two days at the latest. After he finished talking with Teresa he called his boss, Captain Richards and gave him the same information.

Captain: "Take your time, Ernie, and take a day to rest up; I understand you have a good-looking case pending"

Ernie: "That's true. A guy that I arrested during an old investigation contacted me on what looks like a very good case. I couldn't do anything until the Ernesto case was over. Now that it's completed, I'll go back to that case."

Captain: "No rush, take your time."

The next day Ernie met with John and Jesus for breakfast.

Ernie: "John, I have a case pending that may lead to Florida, down the line. You interested?"

John: "Ernie, anything I can do, I will be happy to do. Just let me know when you need me; what are the particulars?"

Ernie: "I don't really have the whole story yet; I'll let you know if I need any help,in a week or two."

John: "OK, just call. I'll do all I can to help."

Jesus: "Shall we go and interview these guys?"

They left the restaurant and headed over to the federal offices.

Bartoli Romero and Ernesto Adelanto were placed in different rooms for the interviews. Ernie was asked to take the lead and John was asked to assist in conducting the entire interview on both subjects.

Ernie and John walked into a small room painted gray with a table, three chairs and a microphone that was connected, electronically, to a recording device and speakers in another room.

Ernie: "Good morning, Mr. Romero."

Bartoli: "You son of a bitch, you were trusted and treated like a close friend."

Ernie: "Yes that's true. As long as I paid for the drugs I was a friend. I'm not going to apologize for what I do, Romero. I just want you to know that you're being charged with, illegal possession of a gun, attempted murder, resisting arrest and several other narcotic-related charges that will be placed on you at a later date by the Attorney General. He'll place those additional charges in time for your trial."

Bartoli: "What do you want from me?"

John: "We want you to testify against Ernesto. We don't need you, but the more we have the better."

Bartoli: "What can you do for me?"

John answered; "We can advise the Attorney General's office of your help; from that point it's up to the courts who are very lenient with those that help us out. Remember, our main goal is Ernesto. You are just an extra gift and we can do without you if need be."

Bartoli: "Eduardo, Ernesto told me that he thought of you like his brother and you do this. Why?"

"Bartoli, I am a police officer, this is my job. The people of my country pay us to find, arrest and put out of business suppliers like you and Ernesto. The people of this country are sick and tired of watching their children and relatives die from your poison. You know that, why do you ask me a question like that?"

Bartoli: "We did not hurt anyone, we only sell the coca."

Ernie: "You sell the drugs to people that sell the drugs to others and down the line. Eventually that line gets down to the little people and the weak people who cannot control themselves. They cannot control the effects of the drugs, which sneaks up on them like a thief in the night, stealing their logic and sense of common decency; not counting the thousands that have died because of allergies to the drug. You're playing stupid. Don't do that. You are not a stupid man, you know what you have been doing."

Bartoli: "I must think about your offer. Ernesto is not a man to be in opposition to, he has been a good friend for many years."

Ernie: "OK, you think about it and ask for Agent Jesus Martinez if you want to discuss it any further. Remember yesterday when I said my plan was for us to be associated for a long time? I believe that to be true."

Bartoli: "Let me think about this for a while. Why can't I ask for you?"

Ernie: "I have to leave this area to work another case."

Bartoli: "Where do you go?"

Ernie laughed at Bartoli as he asked that last question, and left the room. Outside of the room John and Ernie talked about Bartoli who they believed would come around to their way of thinking in time.

Ernie: "Yes John, I hope it's soon, because once the process starts it may be too late. The DA may decide that he doesn't want or need him as a witness, we have plenty. The best thing about him is that he knows the other players, the ones that can take Ernesto's place while he's away."

John: "That's true. Do you want to interview Ernesto now or wait till this afternoon?"

Ernie: "Jesus, I think we should have them take Ernesto back to the cell for a while. Make sure he knows we spoke with Bartoli and wait a couple of hours, get his mind working."

Jesus: "Sounds good, I'll take care of it and meet you out front. Let's take a look around Tucson. I'll be out front in just a few minutes." A few minutes later, John came out with Agent Jesus Martinez who offered to take them to lunch and show them around a little."

They went to a place called the Revolutionary Grounds for coffee then to the Rod's KC Barbeque to try the real barbeque experience. While you're waiting at the counter, you can watch your meal being prepared right in front of you with mouth-watering sauces made from scratch, then over to see the Coronado National Forest which covers 1,780,000 acres of southeastern Arizona and southwestern New Mexico. Elevations range from 3000 feet to 10,720 feet in twelve widely scattered mountain ranges or "sky islands" that rise dramatically from the desert floor.

Ernie: "Wow what a day! Thanks Jesus, I can't wait to tell my wife, I'll probably never see this stuff again."

Jesus: "My pleasure, you guys deserve it, you did a great job."

They arrived back at the office; it was time to interview Ernesto. John and Ernie got three cups of coffee and went in to speak with Ernesto. They entered the same room; everything was the same, except that Ernesto was sitting handcuffed to the chair this time, the same way that Bartoli was in the earlier interview.

Ernie: "Good afternoon, Ernesto."

Ernesto nodded his head and looked away from the two detectives.

Ernie: "If you prefer not speaking with us, we understand, but it may be to your advantage to talk to us, this may be your last opportunity."

Ernesto: "Why, why did you break my heart like that?"

Ernie: "What do you mean break your heart?"

Ernesto: "I liked you, I treated you like a brother and I wanted you to become a part of my organization and you do this to me."

Ernie: "Ernesto, I do not apologize for doing my job, we both know that I'm not wrong in this case."

Ernesto: "I am not speaking of my operations; I treated you like a brother."

"It is true you treated me well, but I was a very large buyer for you. If I had not been a police officer you would have gained much from me. If I were not a large buyer of your product, you would not have wanted to speak with me."

Ernesto: "Then we have nothing to discuss"

Ernie; "So you're not worried about your operations in the US and in Mexico?"

Ernesto: "This does not bother me. My business will go on forever no matter where I am and I will control it from wherever I am. It's you that disappoints me."

Ernie: "Then you should know that as we speak your tunnels are being emptied of people, drugs and being destroyed so that they are of no use. Your gangster friends are being arrested in Mexico where they will spend many years in jail. If anyone ever remembers them at all and that includes the General and the Coronel."

Ernesto looked up at Ernie as he spoke of the things that are going on in Mexico and his face became hard and looked as though he wanted to kill.

Ernesto: "Eduardo, you men could be very wealthy, I can make sure of it, can we not agree on that?"

Ernie: "Yes, we can agree that you could have made us both wealthy at one time. I would rather have a clear conscience."

Ernesto: "What do you mean; 'at one time'?"

Ernie: "Did we forget to tell you, I am sorry, The Mexican Government was very happy to hear about your many financial arrangements throughout Mexico and is attaching as much of your money as they can. Of course they cannot touch the accounts in the Cayman Islands, but the US Attorney General will tie that up during your trial as potential evidence for records and all that. and you will have a long wait to get your hand on any of that money, if you ever do at all."

Ernesto: "You have destroyed me, Eduardo I will destroy you in my own time. You will pay for this deception."

Ernie: "I guess we are done here."

John: "Ernie, wait a minute, I want a word with Ernesto."

John: "Ernesto, I can understand how you feel, but you may be able to help yourself here."

Ernesto: "John, what do you want from me? You already have everything."

John: "Ernesto we want you to place us in a position to contact the other suppliers in Mexico."

Ernesto: "I see, you want me to introduce your people to my competition."

John: "Exactly"

Ernesto: "And this will keep me out of jail and free up my money?"

John: "We will do our best for you as far as the Cayman Island money goes, everything else is in the hands of the Mexican Government and we have no control over that."

Ernesto: "Let me think about it, but I do not give it much hope."

John; "OK, you can ask for me or Agent Jesus Martinez, when and if you are ready to discuss it further."

That ended the interview and Ernesto was taken back to his cell.

Ernie: "John, I guess you liked that Cayman Island bluff. What do you say we get out of here and head home?"

John: "That was brilliant strategy, Ernie. That's why I followed it up with my comments. I hope it works. If we leave now, we will not get home until the middle of the night."

Ernie: "That's ok with me, how about you."

The two men went to their hotel rooms packed and were driven to the airport where they boarded their plane and took off for home.

Ernie and John were both satisfied that the courts will now handle the case. They gave Ernesto and Bartoli an opportunity to work with the DEA on future cases thereby easing the time spent in a United States Prison. The prisoners refused for now, but they would come around in time, especially Ernesto, who has millions of dollars at stake, even though it was a bluff. The DA will apply to hold the funds and may get some results, but in the end Ernesto's money will remain Ernesto's money. No matter what the courts or the district attorney do or say. One day the international law on this subject may change for the better.

That was the way it seemed to Ernie. The case was over and done with for now. Ernesto would be safely put away where he couldn't destroy any more lives. If he cooperates he will get less time. That's what Ernie and John thought.

During the flight they both fell off to sleep and Ernie must have had prisoners on his mind because he dreamt of two prisoners that were being taken back to the county jail from the court house one day when the guard that was supposed to be taking care of them turned his back for a second and the two men ran off.

The guard sounded the alarm via radio and started after the prisoners. He was following them as they ran up the street from the court house cuffed to each other and they were running as fast as they could.

They came upon a pole on a corner that instructed drivers to be cautious. One of the prisoners went to the right of the pole, the other to the left of the pole they were both ricocheted backwards. The cruiser pulled up and took them into custody as they lay on the ground dazed and not knowing what had happened. Seeing this happen was like seeing an old Charlie Chaplain silent comedy.

After they landed in Boston, Ernie took the next few days off and returned to work on the following Monday.

Monday May 19, 1980

Ernie arrived at the office and spoke with Henry and told him that he was going down to see Ralph Piper the gun dealer that night. He began telling Henry about Mexico and just then the rest of the men walked into the office including the captain. Everyone was glad to see Ernie back and they were asking questions about the case that he worked on.

Ernie told them all about the tunnel, the drugs, the murders and the arrest. They were all amazed and began asking all kinds of questions. The last point made was by Captain Richards who said that he was looking forward to completion of the cases they were working on.

Ernie: "Henry, do you want to continue with me on this Cobra case? We can do that during the day, you can do some of the leg work while I will close out the Ralph Piper case for you at night?"

Henry: "Sure, I was looking forward to it, both cases look interesting."

Ernie: "Then I'll telephone Cobra and set up a meeting." Ernie picked up the telephone and dialed.

Ernie: "Hi, Cobra, it's Ernie."

Cobra: "Yes Eddie, I mean Ernie; you're back, is everything all right with your family?"

Ernie: "Yeah, it's all good; do you want to get together and start this project?"

Cobra: "Yes, just let me know where and when."

Ernie: "This afternoon, in Boston. So that no one recognizes who we are, let's meet at Faneuil Hall in front of the Comedy Connection. We'll meet at 2pm. We can talk there or go somewhere from there to talk."

Cobra: "OK, I'll see you then."

Ernie and Henry had lunch at noon then went into Boston to meet with Francis Tapper, also known as Cobra. The two detectives were standing in front of the Comedy Connection when Cobra came walking up the street.

Ernie: "Cobra."

Cobra: "Hi, guys, can we get some coffee?"

Ernie pointed across the street: "Yeah, let's go over to that small shop, Al's State Street Café. We can have coffee in one of the back booths."

The waitress came over, took their order and brought coffee for the three of them

Ernie: "Cobra, first of all I want you to get to know Detective Henry Griswold, one of my partners. He may call you from time to time for clarification on different points."

Cobra: "OK, that's fine with me."

Ernie: "Did you make that list of information that I asked you to make for us?"

Cobra: "Yes, I have what little I know about him and his business."

Ernie: "OK, Henry will follow up on that information."

Ernie: "Cobra, will you tell us what you can about this dealer, please?"

Cobra: "OK, he goes by the name of Pigeon. They call him that because he travels from one place to another like nothing. He has a bird tattoo on his arm, he's here one day then gone the next. He's very secretive unless he knows you and he trusts you."

Ernie: "What do you mean by; 'Unless he knows you?'?"

Cobra: "He has to know you or you have to come to him through someone he trusts."

Ernie: "Pigeon, what's his real name?"

Cobra: "I don't really know, but he drives a red Cadillac, I think it is a 1978."

Ernie: "That is interesting. Can you describe this Pigeon?"

Cobra: "He is a white male, dark hair and dark eyes with tattoos running up both arms and one tattoo stands out of a pigeon holding a leaf, and he must weigh about 200 pounds."

Ernie looked at Henry. They both had the same thought. Piper the gun dealer drove a 1978 red Cadillac. Ernie played pool with a guy that seemed to be a friend of Piper's named Pigeon, at the Bomb Room a while back. He was thinking and wondering if these two men could be working together?

Ernie not wanting to let on that he knows who Pigeon is: "How tall would you say he is?"

Cobra: "He must be about 5"9" tall."

Ernie: "Do you know the name of his boat?"

Cobra: "Sorry, I never saw the boat."

Ernie: "OK, is there anything else that you can tell us now?"

Cobra: "No not really."

Ernie: "Can you make an introduction to him?"

Cobra: "Yes, I'm sure that I can without a problem. After all I did time and kept my mouth shut about his operation. He should trust me and through association, he'll trust you."

Ernie: "We will try not to use you directly unless absolutely necessary; I'd like to keep you as far away from the actual case as possible. Let me analyze this info and see what kind of a plan that we can come up with. We will be in touch with you, soon."

Cobra: "Just let me know when you're ready. I'll tell my wife that you will be calling, Henry, but I will not tell her you're a cop."

Henry: "That's fine. I won't indicate otherwise."

Cobra: "Thanks, guys, call when you're ready."

Henry: "Bye, Cobra."

Cobra left the building.

Ernie and Henry sat there finishing the coffee and discussing the case.

Ernie: "Henry, do you remember the reports on Piper, the gun dealer?"

Henry: "Yes, I saw you look at me when he said that."

Ernie: "These two guys are somehow related, by association or something."

Henry: "How do you want to work it, Ernie?"

Ernie: "Let's get a listing on Piper's car. Maybe we'll get lucky and it belongs to this guy Pigeon."

Henry: "That's a good place to start."

Ernie: "I'll work that bar and get to know them both much better."

Henry: "Sounds like a starting plan to me. This looks like it may become a much larger case than we thought."

The men left the coffee shop and drove back to Quincy where they called it a day. Before they split up, it was agreed that Ernie would go to the Bomb Room that night for a short stay and a few games of pool.

Henry would cover from outside until the red Cadillac showed up, take the vehicle plate number and leave the area of the Bomb Room.

That night at 10pm Ernie entered the Bomb Room. As he walked in he could see Pigeon at the pool table playing alone. He purchased a beer and approached Pigeon.

Ernie: "Hi, Pigeon, how are you doing?"

Pigeon: "Pretty good actually, I could never really get the hang to shooting this game very well."

Ernie: "It's like anything else, takes years of practice if you have the interest in spending the time."

Pigeon: "How are you doing, Eddie?"

Ernie: "OK, looking for Piper; have you seen him?"

Pigeon: "Yeah, I just left him; did you get your order?"

Ernie: "What are you talking about?"

Pigeon: "Piper and I have no secrets, he told me about you."

Ernie: "That's nice; he didn't tell me about you."

Pigeon: "He will, here he comes now. He's just walking in."

Ernie: "Oh, good I want to speak with him about a little deal."

Pigeon: "I'll give you guys the table, when he gets over here."

Piper went to the bar, ordered a drink. He stopped to speak with a couple of people and when he was finished with them he walked over to the pool table where Eddie Pannoni and Pigeon were playing.

Piper: "Hi, Pigeon. Eddie, I've been waiting for you to show."

Ernie: "Yeah, we must talk; wanna play a game or two?"

Piper: "Sure, let's not talk here, too many ears, you know what I mean?"

Ernie: "Let's play pool."

Eddie and Piper played three games of pool then Piper suggested that they go over to his home to talk. Eddie agreed.

Piper: "Pigeon, are you coming home?"

Pigeon: "No, not now I'll be there in a while."

In the car Eddie decided to speak to Piper and ask some questions.

Ernie: "Ralph who is this guy Pigeon, he seems to know my business and that's not right?"

Pigeon: "He's my partner, a smart man. We live together and do most things together, You can trust him, Eddie."

Ernie: "OK, I'll take your word for that and I will hold you responsible."

Piper: "Believe me, it's not a problem."

They arrived at Ralph Piper's home, parked the car and entered the house.

Piper: "Eddie, what do your people need in New York?"

Ernie: "Look, Ralph I didn't speak with anyone there about this because I never made it to New York. I have to go down this week."

Piper: "If it's not being too personal, why didn't you go?"

Ernie: "I was supposed to do a pickup out west and I got fucked. The guy I'm buying from was busted and he's out of business for a while. I'll have to look for someone in this part of the country."

Piper: "What are we talking about?"

Ernie: "Blow, I don't know if you use it. I don't, but my people do. I don't believe in putting the profits up my nose."

Ralph Piper stood in front of Eddie laughing.

Ernie: "What are you laughing at?"

Piper: "What do you need a couple of ounces?"

Eddie laughed: "No, I do something a lot more than that; I can buy ounces anywhere."

Piper: "Wait a minute; you move keys?"

Ernie: "My friend you already know more than I like people to know about me, but yes I do multiple keys."

Piper: "I think we should have a meeting with my partner."

Ernie: "What good will he do me? I need a supplier not a dealer."

Piper: "Believe me he may be able to help you out, depending on how he takes you and I get the impression that he took a liking to you."

Ernie: "I'm game to talk to anybody at this point or else I'm out of business for a while."

Piper: "Let's go back to the lounge and let me speak to him first."

They left Ralph Piper's home and drove to the Bomb Room.

Ernie: "Ralph, why do they call that place the Bomb Room?"

Piper: "I'm not really sure, but I heard the owner talking one day about something to do with World War Two."

Ernie: "That's interesting; maybe he got bombed during the war overseas?"

Piper: "Anything is possible."

They arrived at the Bomb Room and Ralph Piper asked Eddie to stay in the car while he went in to get Pigeon. A few moments later Piper came out of the lounge with Pigeon, they spoke for a couple of moments, then Piper went back into the lounge and Pigeon walked over to the car and got in.

Pigeon: "Eddie, Ralph tells me you have a problem?"

Ernie: "Yes, I don't know what you can do for me, but I'm willing to talk to you because Ralph said you were OK."

Pigeon: "The same here, he told me you were a straight shooter. I like the fact that you took offence to me knowing about the gun deal while we were playing pool, it shows that you are cautious and that's important in this business."

Ernie: "A rule I try to live by."

Pigeon: "Yeah, me too. What do you need?"

Ernie: "I'm not sure that I know what you're asking?"

Pigeon: "How much blow do you need?"

Ernie looked at Pigeon and smiled: "I'd have to figure it out, but I'm not talking a small deal here, we deal in 40-50 keys at a time."

Pigeon: "I thought you needed allot of coke, that's easy."

Ernie: "I can use 100 every other month in reality. I was trying to slim it down for you to give you an idea of the type of business my family does."

Pigeon: "Don't slim down your needs. There's no amount that is too much for me."

Ernie: "You're kidding; in this little burg? you're dealing that much product?"

Pigeon smiled and looked at Eddie then told Eddie that he has one of the best connections coming out of the Caribbean and can do any amount needed for the right price.

Ernie: "If that is true and I don't doubt you. When can I get a taste?"

Pigeon: "Will you be around tomorrow night?"

Ernie: "Yes and then I have to leave for New York and get some business taken care of."

Pigeon: "I'll see you tomorrow night around 9 pm."

Ernie: "See you then."

Ernie left the red Cadillac, got into his car and drove off.

Chapter 8

QUINCY

Tuesday May 20, 1979

Ernie reported to work late that morning and went to the coffee shop to see if Henry was around. He was eating breakfast and Ernie joined him.

Ernie: "Henry, did you get the plate number?"

Henry: "All set, the red Cadillac lists to 1923 Walker Street here in Quincy, the house you were in. But it does not list Ralph Piper, the owner of the red Cadillac is Arthur Pigeoni."

Ernie: "Does he have a record?"

Ernie: "This guy has been into everything' robbery, drugs, guns and attempted murder which he beat by getting a girl friend to lie for him"

Ernie: "That's good information; I am into him as of tonight, he wants to give me a taste. He agreed to sell me the blow I want and his partner is waiting for my gun order."

Henry: "They're partners? Sounds good; do you need any cover?"

Ernie: "Yes, they are partners, they both live in that house, makes it easier for the warrants, as of now. No, I don't need any cover yet, I'll go there tonight. It will probably, take a few days to put things in perspective and decide what we want to do."

Henry: "I'll run by tonight and take all the plates I can for evidentiary purposes, we will be able to confirm that your car and his car were there if need be."

Ernie: "That's fine, thanks."

Henry: "Ernie, I'm sorry that you got caught in the middle of this, I expected a wham bam thank you ma'am. Not an extended investigation."

Ernie: "Henry, this is what we're paid to do. Don't worry, the more assholes we get the better. It's the end that counts not how long it takes or how hard it is. The important thing is that we get the drugs off of the street. God only knows how many lives we save with each arrest so don't apologize for that."

Henry: "Thanks, Ernie."

Ernie: "I'll be there tonight about 9 pm, please let the Captain know what's going on."

Henry: "I will take care of it."

Ernie left the coffee shop and went to his home, where he prepared to become Eddie Pannoni for the night work.

That night at 9 pm Eddie walked into the Bomb Room. By this time he had become familiar with several people. He was speaking with a man about a pool game when Ralph Piper walked in with Arthur Pigeoni, AKA Pigeon.

Pigeon gestured to Ernie to come outside and Ernie shook his head to the affirmative, finished his conversation about the pool game and then walked outside.

Pigeon walked out of the lounge and asked Ernie to walk over to his car. He opened the trunk and lifted the carpet. He then went into the spare wheel section, lifted the spare and underneath he had a piece of rubber that looked like the bottom of the trunk, he lifted the rubber and underneath were eight kilos of cocaine and one small ½ ounce package which he took out and handed Eddie/ Ernie.

Pigeon: "Eddie this is for you—call it a gift. I hope to make some serious money with you."

Ernie: "What kind of quality is this?"

Pigeon: "It is the best, uncut and untouched; I don't cut my product."

Ernie knew that Pigeon was lying. Every dealer cuts a small portion to increase profits, especially someone as large as Pigeon. He would find out the truth, once the lab test was completed.

Ernie: "I'll check this out when I get to New York. Hopefully, we'll do something when I get back."

Pigeon: "You'll find that this is top shelf. Whenever you're ready, I'll be ready."

Ernie: "Now I have to speak with Ralph about my deal with him. This is going to work out great for me, like all-in-one shopping. You guys are my supermarket, what a break for me, no more traveling all over the country to get supplied."

They both laughed and walked into the lounge together. Ernie walked over to the pool table where Ralph Piper was playing with another man.

Ernie: "Hi, Ralph. We have to talk about those cars we discussed."

Piper: "Yes, we do, Eddie; I'll be finished in a moment."

After the game Ernie and Piper went outside to talk.

Piper: "Eddie I'm not worried about it, I'm sure you will eventually give me an order."

Ernie: "Good, I didn't want you to think I was stringing you along. When I get back from New York I'll have some decent orders for you."

Piper: "You know where the house is, just stop by anytime during the day. At night we are here at the lounge."

Ernie; "I will, thanks, Piper."

Piper: "Oh, by the way, do you have to leave tomorrow; can you put it off until Friday?"

Ernie: "I can, I just have to make a couple of calls, that's all. Why do you ask?"

Piper: "Arthur believes that we are going to be good friends and I agree. Why don't you put your trip off one day? We're having a special party tomorrow night for close friends only, at our house and some special people will be there that you should meet."

Ernie: "What time?"

Piper: "Anytime after 8 pm."

Ernie: "OK, I'll be there. I can drive to New York later, if I'm in good enough shape."

Piper: "Great. You'll like these people, but you don't steal any of our customers or suppliers."

Ernie: "I wouldn't do that to you guys, especially after you've been so nice to me."

Ernie left Ralph Piper, got into his car and left the area. While in route home he thought about the possibilities of this upcoming party. He hoped that he would meet the girl that fixed the paperwork for Piper and worked at the police station. He may even meet the serviceman that is selling guns and God knows what else. It sounded like a great opportunity for Eddie Pannoni. Ernie arrived at home and about five minutes later the telephone rang.

Henry: "Ernie, it's Henry."

Ernie: "Yes, Henry, what's up?"

Henry: "I just thought that you would like to know that I took pictures of you and each of those guys as you were talking with each of them in front of their cars and I got the plates in the pictures. These photo's will support your reports."

Ernie; "Thanks for letting me know. They invited me to a party Friday night, special guests, very possibly their connections."

Henry: "That's great. I'll take pictures there also."

Ernie: "Henry, this is some case that you have; you deserve congratulations for putting this together. I'll see you tomorrow."

Henry: "I didn't do this alone, Ernie. Without you it would have never happened. This is a team effort, my friend."

Ernie: "OK, Henry, have a great night."

May 21, 1979

Ernie slept in that morning. When he got out of bed he went down to the kitchen to have some coffee and speak with Teresa.

Teresa: "Good morning, sleepy head."

Ernie: "Yeah, I slept a little late; I have to work again tonight."

Teresa: "You've been working a lot of nights; what's going on?"

Ernie: "Just chasing some snow. We're trying to build the case and then finish, that's all."

Teresa: "Be careful please, I'm tired of seeing blood on you when you come home."

Ernie: "Don't worry; I don't like spilling the blood either."

Teresa: "I know, but be careful, please."

As they were talking they heard a loud crash or bang on the second floor, Ernie ran up and Teresa was right behind him. At the top of the stairs was a small hall with three bedrooms and bath off of that. They checked all the rooms and could find nothing that would make a loud noise. Then Ernie decided to check the attic.

Ernie: "Let me check in the attic."

Teresa: "Oh, the attic"

Ernie: "What did you do Teresa?"

Teresa: "I put some heavy stuff up there."

Ernie opened the attic and lying on its side were three large boxes. The items in the boxes had spilled out onto the attic floor. Ernie stood them all up and refilled the boxes and fixed it so that they would not fall again.

Ernie: "How in the world did you get them up there?"

Teresa: "My mother helped me and we did it."

Ernie laughed: "You're Mother? She's pushing 80 and you let her help you?"

Teresa: "You know her, you can't say no to her when she decides that she is going to help or do something."

Ernie: "Do me a favor. Next time let me know and don't tell her anything about what you're doing."

Teresa: "She really didn't do much, I did most of it."

Ernie: "I understand, but it can be dangerous. She's your mother, you don't see her as getting old, but she is."

Teresa: "You're right, but you weren't here and I wanted to store that stuff."

Ernie: "I wasn't here, so it's my fault? Next time wait for me to do it."

Teresa: "OK, I'm sorry. It wasn't anyone's fault, she just wanted to help. Are you leaving now?"

Ernie: "Yes, off to chase snow. I'll see you tonight."

Ernie kissed his wife goodbye, left the house and drove to Quincy. While getting into the car in his driveway he heard that familiar sound of the mockingbird. He stopped and stood by the car for a few moments admiring the warmth of the 60 degree weather, the beauty of the day and the sounds he was exchanging with the mockingbird.

It was 1 pm as he drove over the Blue Hills just outside of Quincy and Boston in route to Quincy. At the top of the mountain there was a parking area, an over look. He pulled over at a lookout site and was enjoying the view of the valley, trees and animals in the area. After a few minutes, He left that area and drove over to the Quincy office where he met with Detective Henry Griswold and some of the other men in the unit.

Henry: "Hi. Ernie"

Ernie: "Hi, Rick, hi, Carl; Henry."

Rick: "This case looks good, Ernie; should we use some electronics tonight at this party?"

Ernie: "No, I don't think so, but there is one possibility of a problem, I could use some back up in case someone at this party knows me as a cop, it's always possible. This girl that works at the police station may know who I am. Althhough I almost never go to the station and never go to the records office. It could happen that she will know me?"

Rick: "No problem—you're covered, we'll have plenty of people around the area. What time?"

Ernie: "9 pm should be OK, Rick."

Jack: "Henry will have cameras there. I'll rig a long range listening device that I can use from across the street. That will help us cover you."

Ernie: "Will anyone be able to detect the listening device?"

Rick: "No, it will be like a walkman, I'll appear as if I was listening to music and I'll have my dog with me so it looks like I'm walking him if anyone gets hinky; this small device will record as well. I'll have the recorder in my pocket."

Captain: "Sounds good to me."

Ernie; "Captain, I'm going to write some catch-up reports and when this case is over, I will need a short break."

Captain: "Yes, I don't blame you, take whatever time you need."

Ernie sat at a desk and began his report when the phone rang. Carl answered the phone and handed it to Ernie.

Jean: "Hi, Detective Lijoi?"

Ernie: "Yes, who is speaking?"

Jean: "This is Jean your friend"

Ernie: "Jean, from the Charles Pub?"

Jean: "Yes, you remember, it's been quite a while."

Ernie: "Yes, how are you Jean?"

Jean: "I'm fine, but I was wondering if you could take a few moments and speak with a friend of mine?"

Ernie: "Sure, what's the problem?"

Jean: "Her boy friend beat the fucken shit out of her and she's in the Mass General Hospital, Boston."

Ernie: "Shouldn't the Boston Police handle it?"

Jean: "I guess, but I trust you and I told her that she can trust you."

Ernie: "OK I'll speak with her, but I may have to turn the case over to Boston."

Jean: "Whatever you decide is OK with us."

Ernie: "I'll meet you in an hour at Charles Pub."

Jean: "OK, I'll see you there."

An hour later Ernie pulled up in front of the pub and Jean was standing there. She got into the car and was happy to see Detective Ernie Lijoi who she directed to the Massachusetts General Hospital room 704.

Jean: "Chicken, this is Detective Lijoi, the man I told you about. You can trust him, he's OK."

Ernie: "Chicken, that's a strange nick name? Why Chicken."

Chicken: "Think about it, it's what I love to do."

Ernie: "Love to do?"

Chicken: "Yes, gobble, gobble."

Ernie looked at her in a strange way.

Chicken: "I love to suck cock, so I make a living out of it."

Ernie: "Yes, I get it. What's your real name?"

Chicken: "Oh, it's Sonia Levin, I'm 29 years old, I was born on June 20, 1950 in Roxbury, Massachusetts and I live at 2939 Washington Street, Roxbury. I live alone right now; my phone number is 555-2982."

Ernie was looking at a black female, 5'5" tall slightly heavy set, pretty with long flowing black hair and very dark eyes; she had a tattoo on her right wrist of a chain and heart wrapped around the wrist. This girl knew the ropes. Sonia, answered Ernie, as though she was being booked.

Ernie: "What is it that you want me to do, Sonia?"

Chicken: "Please, call me Chicken. My boyfriend, Leroy, is a very large heroin dealer. You can't miss the bastard, he wears a full length Sable Coat with a large white hat. He's always dressed in a complete suite with an open collar shirt. He got fucken pissed at me the other day because I didn't bring in enough fucken money. I told him that I would call the cops if he hit me again. What am I supposed to do if there are no guys out there that want blow jobs? I don't fuck for a living, I suck."

Ernie: "OK, so what do you want from me?"

Chicken: "You're the cop, bust him."

Ernie: "I can arrest him for assault and battery. Did he use a weapon?"

Chicken: "Yes, he hit me with the clothes hanger, the wire type and he threw a toaster at me then hit me on the head with it."

Ernie; "That ups the charges to A&B by means of a dangerous weapon, but that will not put him away for long, if at all."

Chicken: "What do you suggest?"

Ernie: "What's your boy friend's name?"

Chicken: "Leroy Watkins, he lives in Roxbury, Boston."

Ernie: "How old is he?"

Chicken: "He is about 32 years old, 5'9" tall 195 pounds—that's all I know."

Ernie; "That's OK we will get more from you when you're better. What kind of a heroin or operation does he have?"

Chicken: "Yeah, that's where we can fuck him, take his heroin and put his ass in jail."

Ernie; "You're vicious. If I help you out with this you have to be honest with me. No bull shit, I'm no idiot, the moment I smell a rat I'll shut down and walk away."

Chicken: "No, no bull shit. I want him away for a long time."

Ernie: "OK then we will be friends and we'll speak once you are feeling much better. I will put a completed case together."

Chicken: "What should I do?"

Ernie: "Be your loving self unless you see danger then contact me. Hang in there, get well first and then start your information gathering. Anything can be useful. Call me when you get out of the hospital. Here is my information, memorize it, so that your pimp doesn't find it."

Chicken: "OK, I will."

Ernie: "Jean, you ready to go?"

Jean: "No I'll stay for a while and keep her company, I'll call you later."

Ernie: "OK, I have to get back to the office."

Ernie left and drove his car back to the Quincy office. He was in a conversation with Detective Jack Wade when Detective Carl Robinson walked into the office.

Carl: "Hi Ernie did you get that message from Boston?"

Ernie: "No what message?"

Carl: "Here it is; they want a call from you."

Ernie; "OK, thanks."

Ernie made the call: "This is Ernie Lijoi, Quincy, who am I speaking with?"

Bob of the Boston police narcotics unit: "Ernie, its Bob Hendrickson."

Ernie: "Hi, Bob; what's up."

Bob: "I just wanted to give you a heads up on that angel dust case you did for us."

Ernie: "What happened?"

Bob: "We turned Jimmy, who was the main dealer. He gave us a bunch of small cocaine dealers as well as one good-size dealer; I just want to run the names by you before we close down which will be in about two weeks"

Det. Hendrickson stated all of the names on the list and came to one very small dealer that Ernie recognized. The name was George Oplas."

Ernie; "Bob, how large is Oplas?"

Bob: "Oplas is about the smallest we have, I wasn't even going to bother with him, but I have another guy on his block that is good-sized so I thought I'd throw him into the mix. Why?"

Ernie: "You're sure that he's that small?"

Bob: "Yeah, I'm sure, I'm still not totally convinced that I should take him down and search the whole house which is registered to his mother-in-law who was married to a retired Boston police officer."

Ernie: "I know the family and they are close to me. I know the owner of the house and I knew her husband who was a Boston police officer. He has passed on and his wife is a real wonderful lady. I would hate to see you guys destroy her house. It would kill her. As long as this guy is so small, that you weren't even going to take him, maybe I can take care of it and you take him off of the list."

Bob: "Ernie, normally I would say sorry, I can't do that, but in your case he is all yours for now. If I hear anything again I'll do him and nothing will stop me."

Ernie: "I hate to even ask, but I owe a lot to the in-laws and they are very old. This guy is married to one of the daughters and lives with them. I bet his wife and family, know nothing about his dealing drugs."

Bob: "OK, he's yours."

Ernie: "Thanks Bob, I'll handle it. If he fucks up again, he loses, twice. You charge him with all of it."

Ernie contacted a friend of his, a man that he had known for many years to advise him about the problem of his brother-in-law George Oplas.

Ernie; "Juno?"

Juno: "Yeah, who's this?"

Ernie: "Juno, it's Ernie."

Juno: "Ernie, it's good to hear from you, what's up?"

Ernie; "We have a problem."

Juno: "What problem?"

Ernie; "Look we have been friends for a long time and I am sorry to tell you this, but your brother-in-law George Oplas has been doing enough dealing to become visible to everybody."

Juno: "Dealing? Dealing what?"

Ernie: "Dealing cocaine."

Juno: "That mother fucker, I'll kill him."

Ernie; "No, don't do that."

Juno: "What do you want me to do, Ernie?"

Ernie; "Speak with him and make sure he stops. Get him some help, a doctor. This is a warning from me as a family friend. Your mother, who I love and respect dearly, will die if someone comes in and takes the house apart looking for illegal drugs."

Juno: "Yes, you're right, especially when my father was a policeman. It would kill her."

Ernie: "Speak with him and make sure he stops. Do it quietly, but firmly. If you feel he needs more direction, I'll be happy to come over to the house and speak with him. I would rather he did not know for sure that it was me telling you about this, but if it has to be, I'll live with it."

Juno: "Can you hold off the search warrant while I get him straightened out?"

Ernie; "I have all ready stopped the warrant and the arrest, for now. I can guarantee you that this is the only time that I will do anything like this. I have never done anything like this before and will not again. If he does not stop and he gets busted, don't come looking for help from me. I will turn you down flat. What I am doing does not eliminate the evidence; it simply goes into limbo for now. If he continues on this path I'll go out of my way to get him put away for several years."

Juno: "Ernie, thank you for myself, my mother and for my sister who he's married to, we will take care of it. I guarantee you."

Ernie; "People get addicted to a point where they are selling to take care of their own needs are in very deep trouble. Don't guarantee anything, just do your best. If he doesn't straighten out, I'll know about it."

Juno: "I will take care of it."

Ernie: "OK, see you this weekend at the cook-out. As a matter of fact, why don't you invite him and your sister. You and I will talk. If you need help with him I'll talk to him then."

Juno: "Thanks, Ernie, I really appreciate this."

Ernie: "See you then."

Ernie ended his day with the call to his friend.

That weekend the subject of drugs never came up and as far as Ernie knew, the problem of Juno's brother-in-law was taken care of. A lot of uncomfortable problems were avoided.

Chapter 9

The Pipers Party

Friday May 23, 1979

Ernie walked into the office, went to his desk and be-gan doing some paperwork, when Henry came over.

Henry: "Hi, Ernie."

Ernie: "Hi; what's up?"

Henry: "Ernie, I made that statement to my wife. The one you use once and a while, 'I'm just chasing snow and she asked me: "what does that mean?' I thought about it and said because cocaine is white we call it snow, but I'm willing to bet that you have more than that in mind when you say it?"

Ernie: "No not really, cocaine is white, heroin is most-ly white, Crack (which is cocaine) is white and speed is white. Those are the four most dangerous, although not the only dangerous drugs out there, these days. That's why I sometimes feel as though I'm just chasing snow and that's why I use that expression."

Henry: "I knew you had more to it. Are you ready for that party at Piper's house tonight?"

Ernie; "Yes, is everyone else ready?"

Ernie: "Guys, if we are lucky we I will meet the gun dealer at this party, The Feds will love that gift, after we're done with him. I may meet the girl that does the gun papers for Piper so that he can buy the guns from here in the station. I only hope she doesn't know me."

Jack: "Ernie, it would be great to arrest them all at once, but it's a long shot."

Ernie: "All we can do is, give it our best shot. Hey, let's see what happens? I'm going to do some paperwork then get out of here. I will be at the party around 10 pm, is everyone ready?"

Detective Carl Robinson asked: "What kind of a signal will you use, in the event of trouble, Ernie?"

Ernie laughed: "I'll try and throw something or somebody through a window or through a door, you'll know."

Detective Rick Bradshaw: "Ernie, don't forget that I have the electronic listening device. I should be able to hear most of the conversations, maybe mixed at times, but I'll concentrate on your voice."

Ernie: "OK, why don't I have a statement like; those fucken Quincy cops stopped me for speeding down the road."

Rick: "That's perfect. You say that and we will come in."

Ernie: "We're all set; Gerry, will you do me a favor?"

Ernie was speaking with Detective Jerry Gibson the fingerprint expert.

Jerry: "What do you need?"

Ernie: "I'll leave a report on a Leroy Watkins of Roxbury. He's supposed to be a heroin dealer; will you see what you can find out about him for me?"

Jerry: "No problem, leave me the report and I'll work on it this afternoon."

Ernie: "Thank you, that will save me some time. If he turns out to be a good case we may work with Boston on that Watkins guy."

Ernie did his reports, left the office to head home to re-lax for the day before Pipers party that night. While driv-ing, he chuckled a little; because he saw himself as the pied piper bringing all the sick animals into a party. He was sur-prised that none of the detectives joked about that or brought it up. He guessed that they were concerned for his safety. This party could turn out to be a very hairy situa-tion.

Ernie decided to take a very long way home and drive through downtown Boston. He wanted to take a look at the area where the heroin dealer Leroy Watkins hung out.

As Ernie approached the corner of Charles and Wash-ington Street in Boston, he saw a black man wearing a long Sable Coat and white hat dressed to the tees. This man an-swered the description of Leroy Watkins and was standing with three girls, two white and one black, all beautiful, all dressed in a provocative fashion.

Ernie drove past him and stopped about a half block away went to the trunk of his car and took out his camera. He began taking pictures of the buildings and in the pic-tures he made sure to get a few of Leroy Watkins and the girls with him. He wanted the pictures to confirm that he had the correct person when he spoke with Chicken again.

After he took the pictures he started back to Quincy in-stead of going home and went to the office where he saw detectives Henry Griswold and Jack Wade talking.

Ernie: "Jack I have some pictures of a person that I think is Leroy Watkins with some girls in Boston; can you develop them? I would like to show them to his girlfriend Chicken when we see her next."

Jack: "No problem I'll do it this afternoon. Give me the film."

Ernie left the office again and this time went to his home in Dedham where he tried to take a nap and fell asleep for a few hours.

That evening, he had dinner with his boys and Teresa. The oldest boy, Joe, spoke of hockey, his first love, the plays that were made by the team and went on talking.

Ernie could see his mouth moving, but didn't hear all that he was saying because of his concern about the upcoming case. He smiled as he looked at his sons. Ernie's thoughts changed to seeing his sons watching TV and talking about a hockey game. He smiled and thought how nice it would be to have a hockey game as his only worry.

After the boys left the kitchen, Ernie spoke with Teresa about his plans.

Ernie: "Teresa. I may be late tonight. I may not be home at all until tomorrow some time. We are going to try and close this operation if everything goes as planned."

Teresa: "Make sure you call me and let me know you're all right."

Ernie: "I will as soon I can, unless I am coming home early."

Ernie went in to watch TV with the boys and talk about sports. At 9:30PM he left the house.

At 10PM Detective Ernie Lijoi using the guise of Eddie Pannoni, gun and drug dealer walked in to 1923 Walker Street, the home of Ralph Piper and Arthur (Pigeon) Pidgeoni.

Present in the room were Ralph Piper, Pigeon, two women and four other men. One of the men was very military looking; Eddie picked this military-looking person out as being a good possibility for the supplier of the guns from the local armory, if anyone in that room fit being military, this guy was number one. Ralph Piper came right over to Eddie and welcomed him.

Ernie: "Piper, there's not too many people here?"

Piper: "No not yet, we wanted to have a quiet time with top people early, the real party will start after 1am."

Ernie: "I'll be on the road by that time. I hope?"

As they walked across the living room, Eddie could smell the marijuana floating in the air. Ernie had a good look at the two girls at this party and was certain that he did not know either of them. He hoped that one of them was the Police station contact and that she didn't know him. He also observed that on the large round coffee table, in the living room, were over 100 lines of a white substance that Ernie believed to be Cocaine.

On a couple of end tables were bowls filled with what appeared to be marijuana joints and one bowl had a red "X" on the side.

Ernie: "What is the "X" for Ralph?"

Piper: "Those are laced with blow and the ones in the dining room they are laced with "H", help yourself."

Ernie: "No, First of all I have a long ride ahead of me. Secondly, if I start ingesting this stuff I'll start eating my profits. Third, you know that I try and stay clean, my business comes first, but I'll take a couple for after I get to NY tonight."

Piper: "Eddie, let me introduce you to a couple of friends of mine."

Piper: "Rosa, this is Eddie a close friend and a very smart man."

Rosa was a short girl 5"3", slightly heavy, very pretty with black hair and brown eyes.

Piper: "Eddie, this is Lulu Bell, an old friend from years back. She got that nickname from my mother. Her real name is Lucille Picotalli and my mom loved her name and called her Lulu Bell all the time."

Lulu Bell: "Hi, Eddie, he's right. I miss that lady. she was kind to all of us."

Piper: "Just as your Mom was Lulu. This guy is going to be a good friend, Lulu, so take help him out if you can."

They walked away from Lulu and Eddie asked; "What can she do for us?"

Piper: "Nothing, Eddie. She's a good friend and a lot of fun."

Ernie: "Then she is not a dealer or anything like that?"

Piper: "No, she is an old friend. Here's Dorothy we call her Dot, she is a very important person in my organization."

Ernie: "Dot and Rosa, it is my pleasure to meet you. The two of you are beautiful angels, in the mist of many devils, me included."

After complimenting the two girls, Eddie made a mental note of Dot, an Italian female, 5'5" tall, long black hair, green eyes very pretty and well built.

Dot: "Devils? These guys are good guys."

Ernie: "Oh, sorry. Then I can be the only devil. Want to play in my fire?"

Ernie laughed and so did the girls.

Dot: "You are a devil, I like him, Ralph."

Piper: "That's good because I expect he will be around a lot in the future."

Dot: "We'll look forward to that."

Piper: "Come-on, Eddie, I have another special guy I want you to meet."

Eddie followed Piper across the room to the military-looking man who was standing next to the fireplace with a drink in his hand. This guy was a white male, 5"10" tall, very large- boned but still slender, wearing clean and neat clothing. The military dress line in his shirt ran straight down the center of his body and clothing. He stood straight and tall, he had light brown hair and hazel eyes, this man was military and would be easy to find at a later date.

Piper: "Eddie, let me introduce Warren Schuler, my main man, a good friend and partner."

Piper: "Warren, This is Eddie who is expected to be one of our top customers. If the deals work out right, we all stand to make a lot of money through him."

Ernie: "I haven't even given you an order yet."

Piper: "Yes, that's true, but because of the way we met and the way you speak about what has happened, I believe you and who you have indicated that you represent."

Ernie: "Thank you for those kind words, Ralph."

Ernie put out his hand to shake with Warren. "Hi, Warren, Ralph seems to like you."

Warren shook Ernie's hand: "He has a lot of confidence in you, Eddie."

Ernie: "Ralph, can I speak freely in front of Warren since he's your supplier?"

Piper: "Sure go ahead."

Ernie: "Guys, I spoke to New York today via phone. I didn't have to mention guns, they mentioned them to me and gave me a list of what they would like to have."

Piper: "I knew you would come through, Eddie. What are we talking about?"

Ernie: "I know what they're looking for but I think most of it is untouchable by you guys. They need eight M249's and eight M16's, plus, twenty-five 9mm hand guns."

Piper: "Can you get them, Warren?"

Warren: "Eddie, That can all be had, but it will take about a month to put that much together and deliver it here. You take it from here; we have plenty of the 9mm hand guns and about half of what you need right now, so it will take a little time for the rest."

Ernie: "Good. Now all I need is my blow and I'm ready for New York."

Warren: "Blow, Eddie? I stay away from that stuff. The military does not like that kind of shit."

Ernie: "Yeah, Warren, I understand. By the way what's your rank and what branch are you with?"

Warren: "I'm with the Army and I'm a Captain in Supply for the entire East coast."

Ernie: "I see that's why you're able to hide things and get them out."

Warren: "You know all you need to know Eddie. You're a nice guy, but I have said enough about me, the less you know the better."

Ernie Smiled: "Warren, you and I are going to get along terrifically. We seem to have the same philosophy, to the letter."

Piper: "Eddie, we'll discuss money and that stuff later, Warren doesn't want to get involved with that end of the business. He has enough on his mind with getting us the supplies."

Ernie: "That's fine"

Piper and Eddie walked away from Warren to the other side of the room.

Piper: "I don't want to discuss prices and orders in front of him, Eddie; he may decide to go independent and then I'll have to make an effort to stop that kind of interference."

Ernie: "That's fine with me. I wouldn't do business with him unless you're involved anyway. I don't care about your politics and I'll do as you wish."

Piper: "Good, what will they pay?"

Ernie: "One thousand dollars each for the hand guns and three thousand dollars each for the assault rifles. That's very good money, all cash, that's fifty seven thousand dollars. I suggest that it would be to our benefit, to show good faith business practice and save them a couple of thousand. We can offer them their entire order for fifty five thousand dollars. What do you think?"

Piper: "That sounds fair to me; how often will they ask for an order like this?"

Ernie; "I would say, about every six months. They destroy all of the weapons that they use. They have to replace those weapons. That destruction creates orders for us to make money. How does that sound."

Piper: "I will give them anything they want. I knew that this would work out perfectly."

Ernie: "I agree, this is some deal were getting into, Ralph. All I have to do now is put my blow order together and I'm all set to report back to New York."

Piper: "Eddie, Let's go and speak with Pigeon, he's down in his lab finishing up a rush order for some blow."

Ernie: "Wow; a lab in the house? Ralph, that's great and easy to do whatever you want."

Piper: "Yeah, it's helpful."

They went through a doorway and down a flight of stairs to a large room broken up into two rooms by a wall that someone put up. Ernie didn't see anyone as he scanned the two rooms. On one wall was a 30 inch wide dresser that he knew had the gun room behind it and that was about it.

Piper went into the second room and over to the far side wall and slightly pushed on the wall. A section about the size of a normal doorway popped forward a few inches. Piper pushed that section of the wall to his left and the section of wall slid over opening up to a third small room. This third room was the lab and Pigeon was just cleaning up after getting his blow ready for delivery.

This third room was a very well ventilated room about 10 feet long by 8 feet wide with two long tables and bags of heroin and cocaine stacked on one table, the other had two scales and cutting materials. In the far corner was a safe that looked like a gun safe over six feet high, four feet wide and three feet deep which is probably where he kept his money and stored the drugs when he wasn't working on them.

High in one corner was a camera scanning back and forth on its hanging arm constantly viewing the entire room. Below it was a television and on it was a view of the entire area just outside of the lab room where they were standing. The picture changed to the first floor of the house and another change to the exterior entrance, a very elaborate system and important to know about for Ernie and the men on his team.

Ernie: "Man, you guys like secret rooms, don't you?"

Piper: "Hey, in this business we need all the protection we can get."

Ernie: "Yes, I can see that you take advantage of all of the newest gadgets."

Pigeon: "Hi, Eddie good to see you; Ralph you should not have brought him in here, not yet. You understand, Eddie, don't you?"

Ernie: "Yes I do, but I'm here now."

Pigeon: "I guess it's all right."

Ernie: "So this is your private lab, Pigeon?"

Pigeon: "Yes, here I can do almost anything you like including mix up a load of crack or heroin. I can do grass mixtures, (bombs) or any of the hundreds of combinations. There's a buyer for everything these days."

Ernie; "Yes I've been hearing a lot about that crack. I don't have a big call for it, but I am ready to make up as much as I need when the call comes."

Pigeon: "You'll get plenty of calls in time. It's just catching on. That shit, crack, is as bad as heroin. The addiction is unbelievable and harder to break."

Ernie: "I heard that there were a lot of heart attacks with the crack."

Pigeon: "I heard that also and I believe it's from an allergy to blow (cocaine). It's amazing how many people are allergic to the blow, especially if they use the crack form."

Ernie: "I see. I still have to learn about that drug, crack especially."

Pigeon: "No problem Eddie, I'll teach you what you need to know."

Ernie: "I see you have very good ventilation here."

Pigeon: "Yeah, that's to make sure no one gets overdosed and in case I decide to spread out into speed."

Ernie; "You're going to set up a speed lab?"

Pigeon: "I'm thinking about it."

Ernie; "You better think hard; I've seen two speed labs blow up and take a whole house and one took a neighbor's house with it."

Pigeon: "Yes, that's exactly what bothers me."

Ernie: "I have to get going. I want to be in New York by morning. I have a meeting with the family. We'll settle the deal on those weapons as soon as I see them, they're expecting me."

Piper: "Don't you want to take the guns?"

Ernie; "No, I have to go and collect the money first. We want to get paid before we hand over the guns. By that time, maybe you can gather the rest of the guns I need."

Piper: "Yeah, I like your thinking Eddie. We must be paid first; I'll push for everything that you need. When will you be back?"

Ernie: "I have a lot to do this trip but now that I have a blow connection here, it saves me some time. I have to put together all of my orders and then get enough stock for three months supply which I estimate will be fifty keys. There's only one question; how much are you going to charge me?"

Pigeon: "Eddie. I'll take care of you, don't worry."

Ernie: "Pigeon, you're a good guy, but business is business and I must know a price."

Pigeon: "We're talking about 50 keys?"

Ernie: "Yes."

Pigeon: "I can do them for twenty five thousand each; how does that sound?"

Ernie: "Twenty would sound better."

Pigeon: "Eddie, I don't haggle, I don't cut the drugs that I sell. I like you, but I don't reduce the price."

Ernie: "Pigeon I have to sell this to my people who front the cash for me, we have to do something."

Pigeon: "I'll tell you what I will do for you and only you. Don't tell anyone that you meet around here. I will give it to you for twenty four thousand dollars cash and when you buy 100 keys or more I will drop to twenty three thousand per key."

Ernie: "So, we are talking about one million two hundred thousand dollars for fifty keys. That's good, now I can sell the New York people on this deal without any problem."

Pigeon: "One question Eddie, are you going to travel with all that cash?"

Ernie: "No, these people have what I call banks all across the country. These are actually offices that they use for business in every State. Once I confirm that they agree with the deal, they release the money or give the OK and I can pick it up. In this case, they will probably tell me to use one of the Boston offices if not Rhode Island."

Pigeon: "Have a good trip and give us a call when you get back."

Ernie: "Do I have your phone number?"

Pigeon: "Yes I gave it to you at the lounge and you wrote it down then put it in your wallet, but here take one of our cards."

Ernie: "Thanks, I'm off, see you guys is a week or two."

Eddie (Ernie) left the house. His mind was overflowing with information. He sat in his car for a few minutes making notes before he left the area and before he forgot any important statements. He drove for a few blocks and the other detectives were right behind him.

He pulled over into a supermarket parking lot and went behind the building to be out of the public eye and the other detectives followed him.

Henry: "Ernie, how'd you do?"

Ernie: "We have enough to put Pigeon and Piper out of business for a long time. I got the gun suppliers, both of them. I met this girl named Dot who works at the station and then I met the soldier, a captain in the Army who is supplying the serious weapons."

Henry: "That's great. Then everything is OK?"

Ernie: "Yes, I set it up so that we can close it anytime we like, let's talk Monday"

Henry: "See you then."

Henry got on the radio and told all of the detectives that the case was cleared for the night. He also told them that they would all meet on Monday for further information.

Chapter 10

Main Man

Sunday May 25, 1980

Ernie, Teresa and the boys spent the weekend in Maine. It was a beautiful spring weekend, the best so far that year. The temperature was in the 60's. There was a slight mist of rain in the early mornings, as though the night had just finished it's morning shower and was opening up to nice warm sunshine day.

Ernie and the boys did quite a bit of fishing. Ernie was very proud of the fish that he and the boys caught especially the 8 pound trout that they caught in Togus Pond, Augusta, Maine. The pond was a small pond of 700 acres next to his house. The 8 pound trout is an exceptionally large fish for a small pond.

While telling a neighbor in Maine about the trout, the neighbor told him that he read in the News Paper that the state had just stocked the lakes in the area, including Togus, with large fish up to ten pounds. This information blew the wind out of his 8 pound trout story. Ernie decided to keep the part about the state stocking the lake to himself.

Monday May 26, 1980

Ernie arrived at the office and observed the detectives getting ready for a raid.

Ernie: "What's up?"

Henry: "We've been trying to get a hold of you all weekend."

Ernie: "Sorry, I was in Maine, great fishing this weekend; what's going on?"

Henry: "Jack has a warrant for a guy that's dealing cocaine. This guy owns two guns. The suspect lives in the Neck area."

The Neck is an area of Quincy, which is filled with private and multiple dwelling houses containing good people who are trying to make a living, raise a family and going about their lives in an honest and trustworthy fashion. The subject that Jack was after was not a lifelong Neck resident.

Captain: "Ernie, can you team up with Henry and he will fill you in? We're ready to go."

Detectives Ernie Lijoi and Henry Griswold drove over to the assembly area.

Ernie: "Who is this guy, Henry?"

Henry: "His name is Petri Anderson and he's a minor dealer of Cocaine; grams, quarter ounces and up to one ounce—no higher. He has a reputation for being a vicious bastard. From what we hear, he always carries a gun and he's always pulling it on people that he disagrees with."

Ernie: "What is this, a fucken disease? I've heard about another guy that does that same thing."

Henry: "Well, we have a plan to get him. According to our information he should be sleeping right now. We should be safe from the gun problem."

They all met about two blocks from the house that Petri Anderson was living in to go over the strategy for the raid. Captain Richards was in charge.

Captain: "The first thing is that we must understand there are two guns on the premises. Secondly, our warrant is for guns and drugs so that gives you access to all storage areas in the house and any storage area outside on the property."

Henry: "Do we know where his bedroom is?"

Jack: "Yes, here is a layout of the house; he should be in the back bedroom."

Captain: "Is everyone ready?"

No one answered.

Captain: "Ernie, you take the back door with Henry. Jack, you're with me on the front door. Jerry and the rest of you will cover the windows and side until we're in and the house is cleared. I want to try and be as quiet as possible. I don't want to wake this prick before we're ready, if we don't have to."

The men surrounded the house while the Captain, Detective Jack Wade and Detective Jerry Gibson knocked lightly on the front door and announced themselves, no answer. The Captain, announced the detectives again, no answer. He tried the door and it swung opened. The three men walked into a living room where a black female was asleep on the couch.

They woke her with whispers, very quietly apologizing for interrupting her sleep and asked where Anderson was.

Girl: "Who is Anderson? Who are you?"

Captain: "I am Captain Richards, Miss, where is the man that owns this house?"

Girl: "Oh, you mean Petri; he's in his bedroom. What's going on?"

While the Captain was talking with the young girl in the living room, Ernie and Henry walked into the kitchen where they were about to unlock the back door and let the other men into the house when Ernie saw Chicken standing at the sink.

Chicken: "Hi, Detective Lijoi."

Ernie: "Chicken, what the hell, you doing here?"

Chicken: "This guy is a good customer."

Ernie: "Stay here, Chicken, we have to check on your customer. Jack, keep an eye on her."

The detectives walked down the hall, opening the doors in the hall which led to empty rooms. In the last bedroom they opened the door and found a white male in bed, sound asleep. This subject was believed to be Petri Anderson and a .44 caliber handgun lying next to him. This man was out like a light; nothing was going to wake him. Petri Anderson was a medium size man about, 5'7" tall, with light colored hair on his head, and dark eyes. Henry grabbed the gun, two men stood Petri Anderson up and the captain spoke with him.

Captain: "Mr. Anderson, Do you understand me?"

Anderson looked, shook his head and started to fight with Jack who was holding him, but gave in quickly.

Captain: "Are you Anderson?"

Anderson: "Yes, who the fuck are you guys?"

Captain: "Mr. Anderson, we are the Quincy Police and I have a search warrant for your residence and an arrest warrant for you."

Anderson became alive and alert at that moment; he took the paperwork and looked at it.

Jack: "Mr. Anderson Do you have a permit for this gun?"

Anderson: "Yes, Sir I can show you it's in my wallet."

Jack: "That's OK, my men will get it. Do you have any other guns?"

Anderson: "Yes, in that dresser there is a Smith and Western .38 cal and a 12 gage shot gun."

Jack: "How old are you Mr. Anderson?"

Anderson: "I am 35 years old. Why?"

Jack: "I need the information for the record. Go with Detective Griswold, he will take you into the living room and you stay there until we're finished."

Ernie; "Captain he seems like he's a reasonable person right now."

Captain: "Ernie, I bet it is because he is afraid of what we may find."

The men searched the entire house including the attic and all of the bed rooms, kitchen, dining area and living room. In the kitchen they found several ounces of marijuana in the top shelf of a wall cabinet. In the bedroom they found a few grams of cocaine when Ernie and Jack lifted the mattress and the Box spring off of the bed revealing a hidden safe under the bed.

Ernie: "Henry, bring Anderson in here."

Jack: "Mr. Petri Anderson, guess what we found."

Anderson: "That was there when I bought the house, I didn't put it there."

Ernie: "We don't care who put it there, we want it opened."

Anderson: "I don't know what's in there."

Ernie: "What are you trying to do? Set up your defense strategy already? We're going to find out what's in there, one way or another."

Anderson: "Detective Lijoi, I heard someone call you by that name. I've heard of you, I've heard you are a very fair man, can I make some kind of a deal, here and now?"

Ernie: "You're talking to the wrong man, this is not my case, it's Detective Jake Wade's investigation. You can speak with him if you like."

Anderson: "No, I'll wait."

Jack: "My Anderson, you're under arrest, in case you haven't figured that out, for possession of illegal narcotics. You have the right to remain silent, the right to an attorney, if you cannot afford an attorney, one will be provided for you by the courts, the right to have an attorney present during questioning. Do you have any questions?"

Anderson: "No I know that stuff; I just want to make some kind of a deal. I have responsibilities; I can't go to jail."

Ernie: "Mr. Anderson, I want you to know that because of the narcotics charges we are confiscating your guns. Do you wish to have an attorney present before you speak with us?"

Anderson: "No, I'll get an attorney if I need one. Take what you want, but I can't go to jail."

Ernie: "You should have thought about that before you started dealing drugs."

Anderson: "Yes, I guess you're right Detective Lijoi."

Ernie: "Do you want to give us the combination to the safe or do we call someone in?"

Anderson: "OK, on one condition."

Ernie: "We are listening."

Anderson: "I get to sit down with you and the guy in charge later and try to work something out"

Ernie: "We can do that, but you will have to get your attorney to come in or sign a release indicating that you understand your rights and still wish to speak with us."

Anderson: "The combination is 8-right, 20-left and 56-right, it will open."

Ernie stayed with the prisoner Petri Anderson while Detective Jack Wade opened the safe. In the safe they found eight ounces of cocaine that could represent as much as eighty thousand dollars in street value after cutting, a pound of marijuana and thirty thousand dollars in cash and a United States Passport in the name of Petri Anderson. Everything in the safe was confiscated and placed into evidence bags and taken back to the station as evidence.

Anderson was being cuffed by Ernie when he saw that all of his money and drugs were being bagged for evidence he fell to the floor and went completely limp and said; "You fucken guys have no heart, I have to pay bills and I owe on that heroin."

Ernie: "Heroin? I thought it was cocaine. It's very white and has cocaine constancy."

Anderson: "No, one ounce is heroin. I'm fucked, he'll kill me and I even had his girl here, blowing me."

Ernie walked out into the living room: "Chicken, did you make this delivery?"

Chicken: "No, but I was with him."

Ernie: "Leroy?"

Chicken: "Yes, he brought it; I didn't know a thing about it until we got here."

Ernie: "Why did you stay behind?"

Chicken: "Leroy told me to wait here after Petri made a few jesters indication that he wanted me to stay a while. Then Petri told me that he wanted a bow job. That's what I do."

Ernie: "We're going to take you back to the station. We'll talk there."

Chicken: "OK, I'll go with you."

Ernie went back into the bedroom and asked the Captain to come out so that they could speak privately. He informed the captain of what he found out and what he told Chicken.

Captain: "Good. Then we don't need this jerk."

Ernie: "He still has a blow connection that Jack could cut into."

Captain: "Not without your help; Jack's a photography expert."

Ernie: "That's not a problem; I'll give him all the help I can."

Captain: "Good, let's clean this up."

The Captain went back into the bedroom.

Captain: "Jack, take him and the girl back for booking, then you and Ernie interview them both, but it appears that the girl is not associated with this, she's a hooker that he hired. Ernie will fill you in later. The rest of you men clean up the evidence and lock up the house when you leave. I'll see you all back at the office later."

Petri and Chicken were booked at the station. Chicken's paperwork was taken by Detectives Lijoi and Wade to protect her. She was working with them in this case and in the case against Leroy Watkins. They would hide the fact that they knew her personally. Later they will have time and opportunity to speak further with her privately.

The two detectives took Chicken, who lives in Roxboro, Massachusetts, to be questioned. She was a light-skinned black female, 5'5" tall slightly heavy set, pretty with long flowing black hair and very dark eyes; she had a gold colored tattoo on her right wrist of a chain with hearts, wrapped around the wrist. Detective Lijoi had taken a liking to the girl that called herself Chicken because she had the guts to speak up instead of just taking the beatings like most girls did in her business.

Ernie: "Chicken, have a seat."

Chicken: "You guys arresting me?"

Ernie: "No, I have all of the paperwork completed, but we didn't assign a number to your booking. We want it to look like you've been booked so that you are protected. This paperwork can be destroyed, deleted or possibly filled against you at a later date. That all depends on how the cases turn out."

Chicken: "What are you going to do?"

Ernie: "I will hold it for now and see how things go with this Leroy case. If you're as innocent of the drugs as you say, we will drop all charges."

Chicken: "Our mutual friend, Jean will tell you I don't mess with drugs, but I can't control what other people do."

Ernie: "I understand, but we have a district attorney that we have to answer to. You were on the premises where the drugs were being stored. Don't worry, as long as you are honest with us, we will be fair with you."

Chicken: "OK, what do you want from me?"

Ernie: "I want everything you know about Leroy Watkins."

Chicken: "That's easy; I told you I wanted to get that bastard for beating me. Since I was in Quincy, I was going to call you today when I left Petri's house and ask for that meeting you suggested."

Ernie: "Now's your opportunity to fill me in. Simply answer the questions, add anything that you like and be honest. If you don't know, tell that you don't know."

Chicken: "Just ask and I will answer your questions."

Ernie pulled out a file and showed her the pictures that he took of Leroy Watkins while he was in Boston.

Ernie showed her some pictures: "Is this him?"

Chicken: "Yes, that's him with his other two bitches."

Ernie: "What can you tell me about him?"

Chicken: "He lives in Roxbury, Boston, at 1998 Warren Ave, 32 years old, 5'9" tall, 195 pounds. Leroy is a very large heroin dealer. You can't miss the bastard—he wears a full length Sable Coat with a large white hat and is always dressed in a complete suite with an open collar shirt."

Ernie: "OK, that all checks out against his past record. What kind of a car does he drive?"

Chicken: "He drives a brand new Cadillac Eldorado blue with a white top."

Ernie: "When does he do his pickups?"

Chicken: "I don't know, but he disappears every month on the first and is back on the third and dealing heavy after that."

Ernie: "Is there anything else you can tell me right now?"

Chicken: "He has two guns and is always carrying a gun."

Ernie: "What kind of guns?"

Chicken: "I don't know? A handgun like yours and a smaller one like that," as she pointed to a 9mm hand gun.

Ernie: "They are both 9mm like this, just one is smaller."

Chicken: "Yes I think so; I really don't know anything about guns."

Ernie: "Can you get a ride home from here? It will be better if we don't take you."

Chicken: "Yes, I can call Jean. She will come and get me."

Ernie: "OK, you call her with the phone in the other room and you can go, but I will be in touch with you later about the Leroy case. When you are ready, I will walk you out."

Chicken: "Will you take care of my charges on this thing?"

Ernie: "I will speak with the District Attorney on your behalf."

Chicken: "Thanks"

They escorted her out to the front office where she met her ride. Ernie put her through a normal release process and then they let her go free.

Ernie: "Jack, what do you say to getting something to eat and some cold drinks before we interview Petri Anderson?"

Jack: "Sounds great to me, I'm hungry."

The two detectives left the station and went to the square to eat at a restaurant that they both liked.

Ernie: "You know, Jack, this guy Anderson falling to the floor like that was strange. I was reminded of an incident when I was just a kid of about 12 years old."

Jack: "What was that?"

Ernie: "As a boy, I watched a neighbor go through an exercise related to his manhood right in front of the apartment building where he lived, down the street from my apartment building."

Jack: "What did it involve?"

Ernie: "He was of Indian decent and his father had a blanket laid out in the front yard with a fake fire in the middle. My friend, Robert, was dressed in Indian type pants with a headdress on. He did a dance around the fake fire which was very interesting to watch. After about twenty minutes the dance ended and my friend Robert fell to the ground the same way that Anderson fell."

Jack: "That must have been interesting."

Ernie: "It must have been the way that Anderson fell. I haven't thought of that incident since it happened in the 1950's."

Jack: "Yes the mind can bring back memories from any incident at times."

Ernie: "I guess so."

The two detectives finished lunch and went back to the station to interview the prisoner. Mr. Petri Anderson was taken into the interview room and cuffed to the table which was bolted to the floor. Just outside of the Interview room Ernie and Jack discussed Petri Anderson.

Ernie: "Jack this is your case so why don't you take the lead on the interview, I knew Chicken; that's why I spoke with her."

Jack: "Ernie, if you don't mind, I would appreciate it if you do it, because you know how these people think and you're ahead of them most times. I don't have the experience, but I'm learning."

Ernie: "OK, Jack, if that's what you want."

Detectives Ernie Lijoi and Jack Wade walked into the room.

Ernie: "Good afternoon, Mr. Petri Anderson. My name is Detective Ernie Lijoi and this Is Detective Jack Wade. Have you been given a decent lunch?"

Anderson: "Yes, they gave me some shit to eat. Who the fuck is hungry with all this going on?"

Ernie: "Yes I understand. Would you like a cup of coffee?"

Anderson: "Yeah, I would."

Ernie: "By the way, you remember that I gave you your rights at the house, do you want me to repeat them for you?"

Anderson: "No, I'm familiar with them."

Ernie: "Then you know that you have the right to have your attorney present during this questioning and any other interview."

Anderson: "Yes, I know and I don't have to talk etc, etc. I understand."

Jack left the office for about 5 minutes to get some coffee from down the hall for himself, Ernie and Petri Anderson the prisoner.

Ernie: "Here's some coffee, relax and enjoy it. Mr. Anderson, if you wanted to talk with us, now's your chance. We already told you what your rights are. If you sign this paper you will indicate that you understood your rights and that you are willing to speak with us without an attorney being present."

Anderson: "Yes, I will sign it. Look, I can give you the locations of two bodies. I can tell you who has the weapon that did them and I'll give you the guy that did them."

Ernie: "We are listening."

Anderson: "No, no, your turn, Detective Lijoi; your turn to give me something."

Ernie: "I guess we are done here, Jack, let's go call someone to take him back to his cell. Have him transported to the County Jail."

Anderson: "Wait a minute; didn't you hear what I said?"

Ernie: "Yes, we heard you, but we act on evidence not supposition, not words that don't prove anything."

Anderson: "What do I have to do?"

Ernie: "Give us what you have for information. We will check it out; if it's good information then we'll speak to the district attorney and he'll speak to the judge."

Anderson: "I'll tell you some of what I know then you tell me what you can do?"

Ernie looked at Jack, raised his eyebrow and shrugged his shoulders. Jack answered Anderson.

Jack: "We're still listening. Are you sure you do not want your attorney present?"

Anderson: "Yea, fuck my attorney. I don't need him right now. All he'll say is for me to be quiet and not talk to you guys. In the end I'll talk with you anyway."

Jack: "Then we'll listen for a short time." Jack looked at Ernie with a look that said; please take this over.

Anderson: "Ha-ha, I have a supplier, my main man for blow, heroin and smoke. He is a black guy and lives in Roxbury. He wears a full length sable coat with a wide brimmed white hat; he's always in a suit. He also runs about seven girls in his stable that he uses to bring in the side money from the street, as well as move the drugs."

Ernie: "Yeah what is this guy's name and what about these murders?"

Anderson: "I'm getting to that. He was in 'Nam and made connections there for his goodies."

Ernie: "Vietnam? He was in Vietnam?"

Anderson: "Yes, the other world, I was there also. That's where we met, but I didn't have the connections that he had. He learned the language and they loved him for it."

Ernie: "How old is this guy?'

Anderson: "I believe he is 32 years old, same as me."

Ernie: "What's his name?"

Anderson: "I'll give up his name, but then you speak with the DA."

Ernie: "OK, we'll give you that much, remember this interview is being taped."

Anderson: "Yeah I know. His name is Leroy Watkins. He is actually, a very nice person as long as you don't cross him."

Ernie: "Why are you telling us all of this information?"

Anderson: "I want you guys to protect me. My life will be on the line. I'd like to get no time at all in jail or at least a very short stint in jail. I want a protected area and I want to get out of this area as soon as I am released."

Ernie: "Why do you ask for a protected area? Are you afraid of something?"

Anderson: "Yes, look at me, I'm puny. If I'm not in a protected area, I'll wind up as some one's bitch, for one thing. The other being that I need protection from Leroy— he has long enough arms to get me in jail."

Ernie: "I'm sure that your protection can be arranged, but we already know about Leroy. You have to come up with stuff that we don't know to keep us interested. You're not telling us anything we don't already know. You'll have to do better than that; what about those murders."

Anderson: "You know about Leroy?"

Ernie: "Yes, we know about him, I have a file two inches thick on him. He will not do you any good. What about the murders that may help you?"

Anderson: "That gun you took out of my drawer— when you test it you will find that it is connected to two murders. Leroy gave me the gun to get rid of last week."

Ernie: "That's interesting, but what we have is a gun with your prints on it and in your home, no others, unless you will testify to his giving you the gun for destruction."

Anderson: "Leroy asked me to get rid of it for him and I was waiting until I went up to New Hampshire and I was going to drop it in a lake up there."

Ernie: "We will check on it, but you may have to testify to what you just told us."

Anderson: "Get me a deal and I will, or else I'll forget what I said."

Ernie; "What is Leroy's connection to the two dead people and who are they?"

Anderson: "They were people that owed him a lot of money, in the twenty-five thousand dollar range. They refused for some reason to pay him after a long time. He shot them and buried the bodies."

Ernie: "He must have had help?"

Anderson: "Yes, he has a bunch of guys that are on his payroll. He calls them his organization and has a name for them; 'The Country Boys'."

Ernie: "Do you know their names?"

Anderson: "No"

Ernie: "Where did he bury them?"

Anderson: "Do you know where the Zoo is in Franklyn Park off of Blue Hill Avenue?"

Ernie: "Yes I'm familiar with the area."

Anderson: "Along the back wall, behind all of those bushes, is where he buried both of them."

Ernie: "When did he shoot them?"

Anderson: "One was about six months ago and the other was a week ago."

Ernie: "I'll talk to the DA. You and I will speak again. The District Attorney may want to speak with you and your lawyer at some point."

Anderson: "That's fine"

Ernie: "In an effort to protect you, we will put you through the entire process and send you over to the jail. It will look better for you. After I speak with the DA, I'll have a better idea of exactly what we can do for you."

Anderson: "Thank you, at least you're trying to protect me."

Detectives Lijoi and Wade left the room and signaled to the guard officer standing outside the room that he could take Petri Anderson away. Once in the hallway they decided that they will have to speak with the Captain as well as the DA now that they had this information.

Jack: "Yes, it's getting late; let's speak with them in the morning?"

Ernie: "That's fine with me, Jack, I'll see you then."

Chapter 11

Guns and Drugs

Tuesday May 27, 1980

At 7 am Ernie telephoned Captain Richards at his home to let him know about what had happened at the interviews.

Captain: "That's a good job Ernie. It would be great to find the bodies and clear those cases, not to mention the families of those dead guys. You're in Dedham, right?

Ernie: "Yes, up the street from the DA's office."

Captain: "I'll run by the office, pick up Jack and meet you at the Mug and Muffin in Dedham Square and we can all go over to the DA's office together. I have to see him on another matter as well."

Ernie: "OK, I'll see you at the Mug, What time?"

Captain: "In about an hour and a half."

Ernie; "I'll be there."

Ernie drove up to the square and on the way saw two boys about fourteen years old standing on the street corner, smoking. Normally he would not pay attention to this, however this time, he observed one boy pass the lit object to the second boy after taking a toke (drag).

Ernie pulled up to the boys, got out of the car walked over to them and they froze when he flashed his badge. He took the marijuana cigarette and patted them down and found two more marijuana cigarettes. He ordered them to get into the car.

He drove to the Dedham Police station and handed the two boys over to the desk sergeant with the evidence. Ernie asked the Desk Sergeant to contact their families and to put a good scare into the two boys. He then left the police station and went over to the Mug and Muffin in Dedham Square.

While having a cup of coffee and waiting for Capt. Richards and Detective Wade to arrive, Ernie thought about those two boys. It brought to mind two other boys that he caught the same way long ago.

1974 MBTA POLICE:

Patrolman Ernie Lijoi was working for the Massachusetts Bay Transit Authority Police department. He was assigned to the South Boston train station for the day, where he watched for pickpockets and other criminal activity.

While on duty he noticed two young boys that were 14 years old smoking marijuana and passing the joint. Ernie approached them and they froze. He took the drugs from them and took them into custody, called for a car and transported them back to the MBTA Police Station.

As he walked into the station with the two boys' one of the other men—a black police officer—started hollering at Ernie: "Why are you picking on these two children? Is it because they're black?" He went on and on trying to incite Ernie into an argument about taking the boys into custody. Ernie knowing that the man had recently been very ill did not reply, went on with his work involving the two boys. Ernie contacted the parents of the boys and requested that they come to the station.

He locked the boys up in a juvenile cell and when the parents arrived he let them speak with the boys. Ernie later took the parents into another room and explained to the parents that they can take their sons home but asked them to watch the kids and advised them as to symptoms of drug use and what to look out for. He told the parents that he didn't want to officially arrest the boys, just put a scare into them in hopes that they would get the message about drugs.

The parents were very upset with the boys for using the drugs, thanked Officer Lijoi for his interest in the boys and promised that they would keep them in line. One of the fathers asked if they could call on Ernie in the future if need be. He assured them that he would be happy to help out anytime.

The parents asked if they could leave the boys in jail while they went out for dinner, giving the boys more time to think. Ernie agreed. The parents went into the boys and said goodbye that they would do what they could to help them, but it would take time if they could do anything at all. The boys were obviously scared. The parents went out to eat for two hours then returned and took their boys home.

The black officer that degraded Ernie later came over to him and apologized for his conduct using the excuse that he has been ill and was not well yet. Ernie told him not to worry about it, but to try to have more confidence in his friends.

That case was over in one night. By 11 PM that evening, the boys and their families were at home safe. Ernie never heard from them again.

Back at the Mug and Muffin;

Ernie was finishing his second cup of coffee and his recollections as the Captain and Detective Wade walked in, sat with Ernie and ordered coffee. Their discussion went directly to the district attorney.

Captain: "I spoke with the DA, Ernie and he said to come right up. Finish your coffee and we'll walk over to his office."

The three men finished up at the coffee shop and walked over to the DA's office where they met with Assistant District Attorney John Hageman. John took a lot of notes from Detectives Lijoi and Wade regarding the information on Leroy Watkins and his associates.

Hageman was made for his job, 5'9" tall, well-built, balding on top and very curious about every aspect of every case. He always had a million questions, smart questions that led to the heart of the case. Each time a cop spoke with him, the cop would learn from him how to draw out additional subject matter during questioning.

Hageman stated that he would do what he could for Anderson, but he would have to speak with Anderson's attorney. Detectives Lijoi and Wade thanked him and left the office.

Jack: "Captain, you have some other business with Mr. Hageman; we'll wait over at the coffee shop for you."

Captain: "OK, men, I will not be long."

A half hour later Captain Richards came into the coffee shop, he and Detective Wade left for Quincy. Ernie drove home first then went to the office to organize the cases of Arthur Pigeoni—a/k/a Pigeon—and Ralph Piper.

Ernie arrived at the office and went right to work on the information for the reports that were required by the Court. Ernie spread out his notes all over his desk. As he finished one section he would tear that note up and go on to the next and on and on until he completed as much as he could without getting any of the facts confused.

Ernie was well-organized, although if someone was looking at his desk they would think he had a complete mess on his hands. He did that on purpose so that no stranger that happened to be in the office could put any two facts together and make heads or tail of them.

Ernie was finishing up the reports and most of the men were back in the office, finishing up their daily reports. Ernie called the men together. He asked that everyone pay attention to him so that they could discuss the upcoming raid.

Ernie: "Guys, I would like to call Pigeon or Piper—whichever one is there—and confirm the deal for tomorrow during the day. Can all of you men be available at that time for a raid? There will be a lot of things to do."

Jack: "Ernie, they may get hinky, doing it during the day?"

Ernie: "They may, I think that I can handle them or any complaints that they may have about doing this during the day. Daytime, will be much better for us to hit them. They own guns and probably carry them, especially during a deal. At night we can have serious problems with innocent bystanders possibly being injured. We can control the situation much better during the day and much easier. Let's be very careful."

Henry: "What about that guy Piper? He's a dangerous guy, I'm told."

Ernie: "I'd put money on the fact the he and Pigeon both carry 9mm hand guns. That's why we have to be very cautious."

Jack: "What type of cover do they have?"

Ernie: "I have never seen anyone with them, but we must be aware that someone is covering a deal of this magnitude. Does anyone have any more questions?"

There was no reply, from any of the detectives in the room.

Ernie: "Since there are no more questions from any of you, we can move forward. As long as the call that I'll make in a few minutes goes all right, I'll take it that we agree to meet here in the morning and start the endless paperwork."

Ernie picked up the telephone and dialed the Ralph Piper residence; the phone rang several times and Ernie was just about to hang up when someone answered..

Ernie: "Hi, this is Eddie, who's this?"

Pigeon: "Pigeon, I was down in the lab working on your project."

Ernie: "That's good, Pigeon; do you have the whole 100?"

Pigeon: "I thought you wanted 50."

Ernie: "I did, but I got authorization for 100 and I have all cash for you."

Pigeon: "You have two million three hundred thousand dollars in cash?"

Ernie: "Yes, and I hope you don't mind large bills. that's all I could get."

Pigeon: "That's great; I can have your order ready for you in four hours. I just have to do the packaging up."

Ernie: "No, not tonight. I'm still in New York. I'll drive up there early in the morning. I'll go and pick up the money at the bank, first. I'll see you around noon, if that's OK with you?"

Pigeon: "Good, then I can get some rest."

Ernie: "Pigeon, how about Ralph's stock? Is it ready?"

Pigeon: "Yes, we have all of it for you."

Ernie: "You have it there in the house?"

Pigeon: "Yes, we keep everything here for all of our projects."

Ernie: "Great, that'll make it easier to do the deal. I'll see you tomorrow at your house."

Pigeon: "Around noon, I'll tell Ralph so that everything will be ready for you."

Ernie hung up the phone and decided that it was too late to start the affidavit for the search warrant. Ernie explained to the other detectives the conversation that he just had with Pigeon. He finished up as much of the paperwork as he could and left the office for the day.

All of the men agreed to meet in the office at six in the morning which should give them enough time to get set up on the house and complete all of the paperwork required by the court to obtain the search and arrest warrants.

Wednesday May 28, 1980

Ernie walked into the office at 5:30 am ready to start on the Ralph Piper and Arthur Pigeoni affidavit for arrest and search by helping Detective Henry Griswold do the paperwork. As he entered the office he noticed that someone was present by the full coffee cup on one of the desks.

Henry walked in from another room: "Hi, Ernie."

Ernie: "Hi, Henry, you're here early."

Henry: "Yes, I knew you would be here, that's why I came in early; Ernie, could you do me another favor?"

Ernie: "What do you need?"

Henry: "I am not as familiar with the structure of an affidavit as you are, I was wondering?"

Ernie jumped in.

Ernie; "Henry, that's why I came in early to help you out and maybe get a head start. I'll be happy to put it together for you. You can learn the same way I did, by helping and watching."

Henry: "Great. Thanks, I was a little ashamed that I am not very up on those affidavits, but my specialty is firearms and that's where I put my learning skills."

Ernie: "No problem, I'll do the affidavits, you learn from me and the next case we'll do them together. You can help by putting the reports in order by date so that I can use some of them to get the facts. There was a time, Henry, prior to working with the men here, when I didn't know much about doing a search warrant either. When I asked, a certain detective for assistance, I was refused. I was taught by the DEA agents that I worked with, who were happy to teach me. I'm more than happy to teach you."

Henry: "Wow, I didn't know that. Who was it that refused to help you?"

Ernie: "It's not important. That person knows who he is. Maybe he learned from his mistake, although knowing him, I doubt it. He was a very jealous man—unlike the rest of his family who were very nice people."

Henry: "I can guess, but, that's OK. I understand that you don't want to say anymore."

Ernie sat down at the desk and began his affidavit on the subject Ralph Piper and Arthur Pigeoni for a search warrant and body warrants, as well as their two gun suppliers including the girl that worked at the police station.

Ernie: "First of all, Henry, I was getting confused for a moment; too many cases. I thought that this was Jack Wade's case. I must be starting to get old. Secondly, did anyone chase down this 'Dot' girl that works in the station?"

Henry: "You're not getting old, just too many cases and yes, I have a file on Dorothy (DOT) Tomasalli here."

Ernie: "Did anyone follow up on the soldier Warren Schuler, Piper's supplier of guns from the military?"

Henry: "No, we'll find him this morning while you're working on the paperwork."

Ernie: "Sounds good. If you need help with that, I have some ATF agents that would love to get in on that part of the case."

Henry: "Let's see what we can do first."

Ernie; "OK, it's your case, your decision."

Henry: "Ernie, would you prefer that we turn that part over to the Feds?"

Ernie: "No, they will have to be brought in at some point because it's the military. But for now I agree with you. I think you're correct in your judgment on that point, at least until the case is proven, then we can turn the entire thing over to them."

Henry: "Thanks."

Ernie started by reading the report over to refresh his memory and then began writing the affidavit.

Affidavit for Search and Body Warrants
For Mr. Ralph Piper and Mr. Arthur Pigeoni both Quincy Residents

My name is Detective Ernie Lijoi Sr., I am a Police (Narcotics) Detective with the City of Quincy, Massachusetts and I have been a Police Office for a period of time in excess of ten years.

During those years I have been responsible for the arrest of a number of people which exceeds 100 persons for narcotics, weapons and other violations of the criminal code of the Commonwealth of Massachusetts.

On Monday April 14, 1980 Detective Henry Griswold contacted this officer due to information that he received regarding a person offering weapons for rent and for sale and further that this person who was identified as Ralph Piper was frequenting a club in Quincy known as the Bomb Room.

In addition to the information from Detective Henry Griswold, this officer received information from an informant who stated that a person know to the informant as Pigeon was offering narcotics for sale.

This informant described the subject Pigeon as having the tattoo of a pigeon on his arm and a scar on his nose and further that the subject frequented the Bomb Room in Quincy.

This officer was familiar with the subject Pigeon in that this officer played pool with the person answering to the name Pigeon and with the same tattoos and scar on his nose.

This officer, Detective Ernie Lijoi, Sr., took the information of Detective Henry Griswold and the informant. This officer, working in a deep cover capacity went to the bomb Room to follow-up on this information in an undercover capacity.

After spending some time playing pool in the lounge commonly known as the Bomb Room, this officer became acquainted with Mr. Ralph Piper again, due to the use of the pool table and the convincing that this officer was a visitor from out of state.

During conversations with Mr. Piper, this officer was able to instill in Mr. Piper confidence in this officer as a drug dealer and gun runner from New York City, visiting area friends. With this stated confidence Mr. Piper offered to sell weapons and drugs to this officer.

In that effort Mr. Piper took this officer to his home located at #1923 Walker St. in Quincy which is located in the vicinity of the Bomb Room.

We traveled to his home in a 1978 red Cadillac which was later found to be registered to his partner Mr. Arthur Pigeoni at #1923 Walker Street, Quincy, Massachusetts.

The two subjects, Mr. Pigeoni and Mr. Piper both live in the residence of #1923 Walker street, Quincy, Massachusetts.

While in his home this officer observed numerous weapons both automatic and semi-automatic weapons which Mr. Piper was offering to this officer for sale at various prices depending on the type weapon.

In addition while in the home this officer was offered the opportunity to purchase extremely large quantities of cocaine and heroin from Mr. Piper's partner, a man know to this officer as Arthur Pigeoni AKA "Pigeon".

Mr. Pigeoni and Mr. Piper at separate time showed this officer two separate hiding places in the cellar, one for the guns and one for a laboratory and work area to breakdown the drugs and for storage of the drugs.

These two storage areas were connected to the house through hidden doorways that were made for each separate room in the basement walls.

These doorways led to the rooms which were tunneled out of the dirt that was leaning against the house substructure and were about six feet below ground along side of the supporting substructure of the house.

In view of all of the information stated herein this officer is requesting search warrants for the entire premises of #1923 Walker St. in Quincy including any and all storage areas and/or out buildings and any and all vehicles.

In addition this officer is requesting a body warrant for Mr. Ralph Piper and Mr. Arthur Pigeoni for Illegal possession of dangerous weapons, the sale of dangerous weapons and illegal possession and distribution of ammunition and illegal narcotics.

Please review the attached affidavit for Mr. Arthur Pigeoni of the same residence believed to be a dealer of narcotics in excess of fifty kilos in any one or more transactions and the partner of Mr. Ralph Piper.

Additional charges to be filed at a later date after consultation with the District Attorney.

Respectfully Submitted,

Detective Ernie Lijoi SR.

Summary of an Affidavit for Body Warrants

Application for body warrants for the following subjects: Mr. Arthur Pigeoni, Mr. Ralph Piper, Miss. Dorothy (DOT) Tomasalli, all Quincy residents and Mr. Warren Schuler, a member of the United States Armed Forces.

My name is Detective Ernie Lijoi Sr., I am a Police (Narcotics) Detective with the City of Quincy, Massachusetts and I have been a Police Office for a period of time in excess of nine years.

During those years I have been responsible for the arrest of a number of people which exceeds 100 persons for narcotics, weapons and other violations of the criminal code of the Commonwealth of Massachusetts.

Ernie went on to do the second affidavit for a body warrant. One for each of the suspects involved. A total of four body warrants and one search warrant covering all the aspects of the house, car and any all storage area to make sure he covered everything.

By 11 am Ernie finished up with all of the affidavits and walked out to the main room in the office to speak with the other detectives.

Ernie; "Henry asked me to do the affidavits for this case. I just finished them and I'll go down to the court."

Jack: "Ernie, we have been putting together a plan of sorts. We were thinking that to avoid suspicion we would have a couple of guys go down early and hang out in the area of the house. We'll walk into the area and keep cruisers and cars out until you are safely inside and give us some signal."

Ernie: "What do you have in mind for a signal?"

Henry: "Once you are inside, we'll get as close as we can. We'll see if we can see through the windows; you have to come out for the money so when you do, we will close in. All you have to do is the old signal of adjusting your cap."

Ernie; "Henry, that's exactly what I had in mind; I'll wear this red cap. Why don't you and I go up for the warrants and everyone else can get set up on the house and the area early?"

Ernie and Henry took all of the affidavits, went to the Quincy District Court and they spoke with the Clerk of Courts regarding the warrants. Ernie answered all of the questions and the warrants were issued.

Ernie: "Henry, what about that serviceman, Mr. Warren Schuler? What did you come up with?"

Henry: "All we have to do is call Colonel Roberts at the armory. He'll have him there waiting for us when we are ready."

Ernie: "Good, that's one down, three to go; the girl can wait until we are finished at the house."

Henry: "Yes, she's working right now and has no idea what's going on."

Ernie; "Great, I'd like to walk in on her and see what she says."

Henry: "We'll arrest her later today, before she quits for the day."

Ernie: "Let's go back to the office and I will make the call to confirm the deal and time."

Ernie and Henry went back to the office and upon arrival received a call from Agent Jesus Martinez who was in Arizona.

Jesus: "Ernie, it's Jesus."

Ernie: "God forgive me, I have sinned; nice of you to call from heaven."

Both Jesus and Ernie laughed.

Ernie; "What's up, Jesus?"

Jesus: "We finally put a small deal together with your friend."

Ernie: "Are you speaking of the southerner with my name?"

Jesus: "You got it and I would like to speak with you about the case."

Ernie; "How urgent is this conversation?"

Jesus: "We can wait."

Ernie; "Give me your number and I will call you tomorrow or Monday at the latest."

Ernie and Jesus spoke for a couple of moments and Ernie explained that he was in the middle of serving some warrants. Jesus understood and the issue was put off until a later time.

Ernie dialed the Piper residence.

Ernie: "Hello"

Pigeon: "Eddie?"

Ernie: "Yeah, I'm ready to play. You guys all set? Who's this, Pigeon?"

Pigeon: "Yeah, It's Pigeon; we'll be ready in about an hour, its 2pm now, how's about three for the deal?"

Ernie; "I will be there around three this afternoon; I want to get in and out so I can leave for New York right away."

Pigeon: "No problem, we'll help you load, once we settle up."

Ernie: "I'd appreciate the help. See you then."

Ernie and Henry contacted the other detectives, then contacted Captain Richards and advised him as to what was going on and what time the deal was to take place.

The Captain made arrangements to place a couple of cruisers near the area of the house and required that they do not use sirens or lights. He told them what was going on. They were to do back up once the detectives were inside of the house.

At 3 pm Detective Ernie Lijoi Sr. made another of his usual conversions to Eddie Pannoni and drove up to the driveway at #1923 Walker street, Quincy, Massachusetts.

Eddie exited his 1978 white Thunderbird and walked to the door of the home where he rang the bell.

Piper: "Come on in, Eddie."

Piper opened the door. Eddie could see Pigeon standing in the dining room with Eddie's completed order spread out on the dining room table.

Ernie; "I see you guys are ready for me."

Pigeon: "Eddie, it's always good to see you especially when you're bearing cash; just count up the keys and check the guns so we can close this deal. We'll help you load this stuff into your car"

Ernie: "Thanks I appreciate that; I'll check it all out now."

Eddie checked the guns by making sure they had firing pins, mechanisms and that the movement was tight and secure then went over and counted the 100 kilos of cocaine. The entire order checked out to be as planned, a perfect order.

Ernie: "It all looks good to me; you didn't cut this cocaine, did you, Pigeon?"

Pigeon: "No, I wouldn't do that."

Ernie: "Good because there would be too many repercussions from New York; you don't want them after you."

Pigeon: "No, I want to keep you as a customer. I expect to be doing many deals with you later; I'll be as honest as possible"

Ernie: "OK, I think it all looks perfect to me. I'll get your money from the car. As I said, I hope you don't mind all large bills?"

Piper: "Are you kidding me. They spend better then small bills," as he joined Pigeon in laughter.

Ernie walked out to the car, opened the trunk, took out his brief case and adjusted his hat. Piper and Pigeon were watching Eddie. They observed the detectives approaching the house.

Men came from everywhere. The first man at the door kicked it in. He was Detective Rick Bradshaw, the electronics expert. As the door swung opened a gun shot rang out and he went down. Rick had been shot.

Then a second and a third shot rang out as the other men were struggling to get Detective Bradshaw out of harm's way. They grabbed his legs and just pulled him behind them as they moved out of the way of the door to the house.

Ernie was at the trunk of his car and pulled out a megaphone. He began speaking with the two men inside of the house.

Ernie: "Ralph, Arthur, we can settle this without any more injuries."

Piper: "It wasn't us that shot at you guys; it was our cover man from the living room."

Ernie: "Do you guys want to keep this idiocy up or stop it now and we'll work this out?"

The detectives could hear Ralph Piper yelling to a third party in the house. He called that person, John. John later turned out to be John Burnski of Quincy resident who was hired by Ralph Piper to cover the deal for any rip off.

Ernie; "Ralph this is Eddie. Just tell him to knock off the shooting and throw his weapon out."

John: "Talk to me, asshole, not him, I'm the one that shot your man."

Ernie: "OK, John, is it?"

John: "Yes, John. I thought it was a rip off so I shot the first face that I saw and didn't recognize, after you went out."

Ernie; "Well you're in luck because he was wearing a flak jacket. You may have busted a few ribs and knocked him out, but he'll be OK. No one has been seriously hurt or killed yet."

John: "What am I looking at?"

Ernie: "John, if someone dies because of your craziness, you could be looking at murder. That's a capital crime. Right now you're looking at assault and battery with dangerous weapon, a lot less serious charge."

John: "As long as Arthur and Ralph go along, I'll walk out."

Ernie; "Good, Arthur and Ralph—are we in agreement?"

Pigeon: "Yes, we're in agreement. Look, we didn't want anyone hurt, we can't be charged with that shooting."

Ernie; "We'll go over all of that, don't worry. Let's end this craziness before someone gets hurt worse. John, I want you to throw the gun outside of the door, then walk out with your hands on your head and walk out backwards, Ralph and Arthur, the same goes for you two men."

John came to the door with the gun over his head, he threw the gun out then turned and put his hands over his head and walked out backwards. The other two men followed and all three were taken into custody.

The ambulance pulled up and took Detective Rick Bradshaw to the hospital for treatment. The prisoners were transported to the police station for booking.

A couple of the detectives entered the house and took all of the obvious evidence into custody, marked it and transported it back to the station as evidence.

The other detectives including Detectives Ernie Lijoi Sr. and Henry Griswold began a complete search of the house.

Upon completion they confiscated fifty 9mm hand guns and 100 rifles of various types from the gun storage room in the cellar. In the lab room they found the safe in the corner as described in Ernie's reports.

Ernie: "Shit, I forgot about that safe, maybe it's unlocked?"

Henry walked over to the safe tried the door and it was locked.

Detective Lijoi went up to the first floor of the house and dialed the police station and asked for the booking desk. The booking sergeant placed Pigeon on the phone with Ernie.

Ernie: "Pigeon, this is Eddie, I need the combination to the safe."

Pigeon: "If I give you the combination, will I get some sort of a break here for being cooperative?"

Ernie: "Pigeon, it's a combination; I can get someone down here to open it. I get the numbers from you which keeps things friendly or the hard way which could be harder on you later. All I can tell you is that I can add to my report that you gave me the combination."

Pigeon: "OK, just remember I am helping not hurting; the numbers are 7 right, 15 left, 84 right then back to zero and it will open."

Ernie; "Thanks, you did the right thing."

Ernie returned to the lab where he applied the numbers that Pigeon gave him to the safe and it opened easily. Inside the safe was found four hundred and fifty thousand dollars in cash and 140 kilos of cocaine along with 5 kilos of heroin and 25 pounds of marijuana. All of the evidence was bagged and tagged and transported to the Police Station.

Once back at the police station two detectives were sent over to the Quincy Armory to relieve the commanding officer of Mr. Warren Schuler, who was brought in quietly.

Ernie and Henry checked with the hospital to find out how Detective Rick Bradshaw was doing. They were advised that he was fine just a couple of broken ribs. He would be kept overnight for observation and released in the morning.

Ernie and Henry went down to the clerical office where each of the girls in the station worked and had their own cubical to work in. They observed Dorothy (DOT)

Tomasalli working at her desk and not paying attention to her surroundings.

Detective Lijoi walked over to her desk.

Ernie; "Hi, Dot."

Dot: "Eddie, what are you doing here?"

Ernie: "My name is Detective Ernie Lijoi."

Dot: "I don't understand. You're Eddie aren't you?"

Ernie: "Yes, I'm Eddie when I work, but now I am a Quincy Detective and you're under arrest."

Dorothy Tomasalli was taken into custody and booked on charges of theft, selling stolen property and possession of stolen guns.

The police department accountant was called in to do an audit of her records for the purpose of building a stronger case.

The arrest of the woman "Dot" Dorothy Tomasalli ended the day for the entire unit and the men agreed to meet in the morning. Each man would do his own report at that time.

Dorothy Tomasalli was eventually fired and received three years in the county jail for women.

Chapter 12

Chicken

Thursday May 29, 1980

Ernie was up early and happily thinking about Detective Rick Bradshaw and how great it was that he didn't get seriously injured in the gun fight during the raid. He thought to himself that it could have easily been him that was shot. As he walked down the stairs to the first floor of his home he said out loud to himself: "Teresa would be very upset, if I got shot again."

He had breakfast and coffee with Teresa his wife, they spoke of the children and some friend that Teresa had invited to dinner for Sunday afternoon.

The old friends that they invited Mr. and Mrs. Robert Spatski, two very nice people and a pleasure to be with at anytime; Teresa said that she was going to prepare chicken, spinach and potatoes to be followed up with homemade lasagna. Teresa told Ernie that he would have to make his Volcano desert for everyone.

The Volcano, as Ernie called it, was a piece of cake baked in a special small pan then taken out so that a slot, created by the shape of the pan, was on the top then the slot was filled with caramel, a scoop of vanilla ice cream over the caramel, a hard chocolate, covering with raspberry syrup to top off the chocolate, whipped cream and a cherry on top. This desert was a mixture of cake, ice cream, caramel sauce, raspberry sauce and chocolate shell that Ernie saw in a restaurant, tried it, loved it and figured out how to make it. Everyone loved that desert.

Ernie agreed to the menu and asked if it was enough food. Teresa replied, "We'll be eating lasagna for a few days." Ernie laughed and left for the day.

The day was warm, around 60 degrees, the area, outside of the house was quiet with one exception. As Ernie walked out the door of the house he heard the mockingbird singing a joyful song. Ernie whistled back, the same tune. The bird repeated the tune and as Ernie walked to the car the symphony went on.

About 25 minutes later Ernie walked into the office and he was early, but not earlier then Rick who was sitting there making out reports on the shooting and the raid.

Ernie: "What the hell are you doing here? I'm happy to see you, but shouldn't you be home resting after taking a bullet like that?"

Rick: "Maybe, but I was tired of staying in that hospital, they can't do anything for ribs anyway, so I left, signed out and came here for a little while to make sure I helped you with the paperwork."

Ernie: "Man, go home, rest; there are plenty of us to do that. Enjoy a few days off. Shit, you were shot!"

Rick: "OK, I'll take some of the forms with me and fill them out at home."

Ernie: "Are you OK? Did this affect you psychologically?"

Rick: "No, I'm just bored. I like to keep moving. Hell, this could have stopped me forever, so I'll keep going."

Ernie: "OK, I understand, but no, take the time and rest. When you're feeling better, I'll stop by your home to see you, maybe Monday. Don't worry about this crap. The guys and I will do the preliminary and evidentiary reports for the court this morning. I'll leave the rest until Monday."

Rick: "Thanks Ernie, I'll see you on Monday." Rick left the office and traveled to his home.

Ernie sat down at the desk and started his preliminary report for the court to go along with the affidavits that he submitted. This report would be enough until the trial came up in a few weeks. As Ernie was finishing up with the preliminary reports, a call came into the office from Captain Richards.

Captain: "Ernie, are you alone?"

Ernie: "Jack and I are here right now, what do you need?"

Captain: "Good, Take Jack with you and go down to the park on Hancock Street. Some kids found a dead female. See what you can figure out and get back to me. The Medical Examiner is on the way."

Ernie: "On our way!"

They arrived at the park and were directed to the body of a black girl who was not readily identifiable because she had been beaten so badly.

Ernie; "Look at her arm, Jack."

Jack: "Yeah, I'm looking."

Ernie: "Do you see that gold-colored tattoo on her right wrist of a chain and heart wrapped around the wrist?"

Jack: "Yes, I see it; maybe it will help with identification."

Ernie: "Yes, it does. This is Chicken, my informant."

Jack: "That girl you said you liked? She had spunk, you said."

Ernie: "Yeah, she was ballsy, that's probably why she's dead."

Jack: "What do you think, Ernie? Her pimp?"

Ernie: "That's a definite possibility, but if she got killed the way I think she did; this is a message for me."

Jack: "What kind of message?"

Ernie; "Stay the fuck in Quincy and out of Boston. He may be making this a personal thing. We'll find out, that's for sure."

Jack: "I see how you're thinking, but how do we confirm something like this?"

Ernie: "She was obviously thrown here, from a moving vehicle. She must have had a fight with him and mentioned me. He killed her and threw her here on our turf indicating a message to stay out of Boston."

Jack: "Sounds logical, but we would have to prove it."

Ernie: "Yes, that was his mistake. By dropping her here in Quincy, he invited us into a case that we may have turned over to Boston. If I'm correct in my assumptions, he made a big mistake because this body puts that case right in our laps. I have another person who knows most of what goes on with Chicken. They are good friends."

Jack: "What kind of a person would do a thing like this?"

Ernie: "The person that did this is a real sick bastard. I could be wrong, but I doubt it. I think it's Leroy Watkins, her pimp, heroin dealer and cocaine dealer. He's a major guy in the Roxbury, Boston area. He is also believed to be involved with at least two murders and suspected of several others. She was helping us out with the case."

Jack: "You seem to know him well, Ernie."

Ernie: "Jack, he made a major mistake murdering this girl and involving us like this. I liked Chicken, she had something special, all I can call it is guts or spunk. She obviously, did not deserve to die, especially not like this. I have two people we can talk with and maybe with a lot of work we can find out the truth about him and this murder."

Jack: "Ernie, what's BCI (Bureau of Criminal Investigation) doing here?"

Frank: "The captain asked us to come down, Ernie, and assist you guys; I guess there was no one around and free to cover."

Ernie was speaking with Frank Deloso a homicide detective from the Quincy homicide unit. A heavy-set man, 5'9" tall, 45 years of age, balding and well-dressed the same as all the Homicide Detectives dressed, nothing like the narcotics unit who dressed appropriately for each situation.

Frank: "Did you guys draw any opinion on this case?"

Ernie: "No, Frank, not one I'm willing to discuss at this time, but we'll look into a few things and if we come up with something we'll let you know."

Frank: "You do that, let us know, this is obviously a homicide case. While you chase your little drug dealers, let us know if you come up with anything."

Ernie: "You're a funny guy, Frank."

Ernie and Jack left Chicken's body to the Homicide Unit. They left the area and returned to the office where they wrote a report indicating their suspicions as a starting point for the investigation into the death of Sonia Levin, a/k/a Chicken. While at the office they began setting up a plan to look into Chicken's death.

They contacted the Captain and told him all that they knew and surmised from viewing the body and searching the area around the body. After they received approval from Captain Richards to follow up on the case he told them to keep him and Boston Police in the loop on the Chicken case. Ernie told the other man in the unit about his belief and the connection of the dead girl, Sonia Levin, to the drug dealer Leroy Watkins. As Ernie was finishing up his conversation with the men the telephone rang.

Jesus: "Ernie?"

Ernie: "Yes, Jesus, you must be psychic. I was just going to dial you to complete our discussion from last Thursday. Sorry I couldn't get back to you sooner."

Jesus: "No problem, this fucken Ernesto is busting my balls saying that he wants to cooperate, but wants to speak with you and work with you."

Ernie: "He's out of his fucken mind; there is no way that I'll go back into Mexico. I'd love to visit just for relaxation, but that's it."

Jesus: "What would you think about taking a short trip here and speaking with him?"

Ernie: "As long as you guys are paying for the ride I'll do it as a friendly gesture, but I'm not going back to Mexico."

Jesus: "I don't expect you to go to Mexico, but remember, this guy still sees you as his brother Eduardo. Is there anything interesting going on there?"

Ernie; "We just came back from a body that was placed very carefully. I think it was done to send us a message, big mistake on the killer's part."

Jesus: "That sounds very interesting, anything my guys can do to help?"

Ernie: "Not at this time, but if I am correct in my assumptions, I will be calling on your people down the road."

Jesus: "Any time, just let us know; your flight is already approved, you know the process. When can you be here?"

Ernie; "I will be there tomorrow say around 2 pm if I can catch that flight."

Jesus: "OK, call and let me know for sure. I'll meet you at the airport and we will go from there."

Ernie: "See you then." Ernie hung up the phone and spoke with Jack.

Ernie: "Jack, I have to go to Arizona for a couple of days on that Mexican case."

Jack: "I'll start my report on Sonia Levin, Chicken, and start looking into Leroy Watkins. I should have some info when you get back."

Ernie: "OK, let's keep this in the unit until we confirm a few things. We don't want to look like assholes to the Homicide unit if we are wrong."

Jack: "I agree. They can be pricks sometimes, but they don't mean any harm."

Ernie: "I know, just a game they like to play, but they do think of themselves as the elite of the department."

Jack and Ernie laughed. Ernie began to type his reports and realized that he should contact Captain Richards about his trip to Arizona. He dialed the phone.

Ernie: "Captain"

Captain: "Yes, Ernie?"

Ernie: "I spoke with Agent Jesus Martinez and he wants me to go to Arizona for a sit down with Ernesto Adelanto, the Mexican drug lord that we arrested."

Captain: "What do they want you to do?"

Ernie: "Not sure, He's asking to speak with me. I told them I'm too busy to go back to Mexico."

Captain: "Good, you're better off; when will you be back?"

Ernie: "In a couple of days; in the mean time, Jack will do some research on Leroy Watkins. He'll confirm that the girl is Chicken via finger prints, etc. When I get back we'll start the case moving and find out if he killed her."

Captain: "Didn't you say that he beat her face in, extremely badly, when you saw her in the hospital? I think I read that in one of your reports?"

Ernie: "You are 100% correct and that is what added to my suspicions."

Captain: "Good, just keep me advised and take the rest of today since you will be on duty for a few days in Arizona."

Ernie; "Thanks Captain, I'll see you in a couple of days."

Ernie and Jack left the office, went to the coffee shop and discussed the coming events. They talked about who would do what and when. Jack was excited since this was his first murder case and wanted to double check everything to be sure that it's all done correctly. After they left the coffee shop Ernie headed home for the day knowing that he would be on a plane to Arizona by this time the next day.

Ernie: "Hi Teresa"
Teresa: "Hi, what are you doing home so early?"
Ernie: "Do you want me to leave?"
Teresa: "No, I'm happy you're here, silly."
Ernie: "Want to go for lunch somewhere, Teresa?"
Teresa: "Yeah, I'd love that; how about Tahiti's?"
Ernie: "Sounds good to me."

The couple spent some time around the house, changed clothes and that afternoon went to the Tahiti's Chinese Restaurant for lunch.

Ernie: "I have to go to Arizona for a couple of days."
Teresa: "When do you leave?"
Ernie: "Tomorrow morning"
Teresa: "Is this another case?"

Ernie: "No, just a cleanup. The guy that we arrested wants to speak with me before he says anything. I'm surprised that the Feds are agreeing, but he has a lot of good intelligence that they can use. I agreed to help them out, if I can."

Teresa: "Just be careful."

After lunch they returned home and Ernie went out to his garden to work breaking up the soil so that the roots can breathe and the plant can get plenty of nourishment.

Ernie made arrangements for his flight that afternoon and contacted Agent Jesus Martinez in Arizona to advise him about his flight to Arizona to meet with the DEA and the drug lord Ernesto Adelanto, a/k/a 'The Surgeon'.

Ernesto Adelanto is referred to as 'The Surgeon' because of his swift skill at killing, maiming and disfiguring those that opposed him over the years.

Friday May 30, 2009

Ernie arrived at the airport in Arizona and Agent Martinez was there to meet him. They immediately drove to the Arizona offices of the Federal Drug Enforcement Agency (DEA) where Ernie was put through the normal process of checking his weapon before entering the building. They traveled up to the DEA offices and Jesus poured them both a cup of coffee.

Ernie: "Wow, this coffee is strong."

Jesus: "Oj, sorry, I should have warned you. I like it very strong, childhood thing I guess."

Ernie: "No problem' I wasn't expecting it, that's all."

Jesus: "Ernie, this guy, Ernesto—to my best knowledge—does not know your real name and I suggest that we keep it that way as long as possible."

Ernie: "I'm fine with that. When do we see him?"

Jesus: "They're bringing him in to the interview room right now."

The two men walked down the hall and entered a small office that had a desk, a few chairs and a large glass one-way mirror so that you could see in from the next office to the interview room.

Jesus: "There he is. He looks a little beat."

Ernie; "Jesus, that's what jail will do for you. Do you have any idea what he's looking for from me?"

Jesus: "I'm not sure. Let's play it by ear for now, Ernie, and see how it goes."

The two men walked into the interview room, Ernie and Jesus sat opposite Ernesto along the long gray table that Ernesto was handcuffed to. That table was bolted to the floor.

Eddie: "Ernesto, nice to see you again."

Ernesto: "Eduardo, you are a son of a bitch, but for some reason I do not have a lot of hate for you. That does not mean that I would not kill you if I had the chance."

Eddie: "Ernesto, I pray that meeting never comes to pass, since I have always liked you as well. Why do you want to speak with me?"

Ernesto: "To tell you what I just said and to say that I have long arms."

Eddie: "I understand, is that all?"

Ernesto: "They want me to give them information about the other four lords in my area of Mexico and I am sure they want my labs."

Eddie: "They don't need your labs, but they could use help with the other lords in the cartel."

Ernesto: "What do you mean, they don't want the labs?"

Ernie looked at Jesus for direction as to whether or not he should tell Ernesto what he knows about the labs and Jesus nodded his head in an indication of, yes go ahead.

Eddie: "Ernesto, your labs are gone; as we speak the Mexican and United States governments are working together to close them down, every one of them."

Ernesto: "You're crazy they will never find them."

Eddie: "You underestimate the United States and, in this case, the DEA."

Ernesto: "You know where they are, you were able to track yourself and figure out where they are?"

Eddie: "Let's just say that technology is a wonderful thing sometimes."

Ernesto: "You'll never find the others, the ones that you did not see."

Eddie: "Again you underestimate our abilities, but possibly you're right, that's another matter. What about helping these men?"

Ernesto: "I want to work with you, let me out. I'll take you back to Mexico and introduce you to all of them. You can do your own thing, of course. I will help as much as I can."

Eddie: "Sorry that's out, Ernesto. I cannot go back there. I am tied up with other cases. Why don't you work with agent Martinez, he speaks your language?"

Ernesto: "I want to work with you."

Eddie: "Ernesto, I will be happy to listen to whatever information you want to tell us along with Agent Martinez right here in this building, but I cannot go to Mexico at this time."

Ernesto: "Did anyone ever tell you that you look like my dead brother?"

Eddie: "Yes, I recently found that out."

Ernesto: "I like working with you."

Eddie: "Look, I cannot go, I will not go. Take one of the men here or just forget it and do you thirty-plus years."

Ernesto: "I was thinking that you could eliminate, many of those years for me, if I worked with you."

Eddie: "No way, you may save some time, but only five or ten years. I really shouldn't comment on that because it's Agent Martinez who will be making the recommendations, not me."

Ernesto: "I am finished talking. I will think about this conversation for a while. Eduardo, be careful, be very careful."

Eddie: "Are you threatening me, Ernesto?"

Ernesto: "I never threaten, you have observed that."

Eddie: "You are saying that you will in fact kill me or have me killed?"

Ernesto: "I did not say that, but do be careful."

Eddie: "You're trying to put a fear into me, Ernesto. I don't live that way."

Ernesto: "Be careful, my friend."

Eddie: "I am always careful, but then you must be careful also, isn't that true?"

Ernesto: "Why would I have to be careful?"

Eddie: "You must remember you have many lives on your hands from the narcotics that you have supplied to the United States, from the chasers of snow, from sheer greed and from defiant neglect. The government in this country is opposed to you, your ways and what you stand for."

Ernesto: "No one will take my life, not in the United States; you people are too soft for that"

Eddie: "I don't know about that, but there are a lot of men in prison. A lot that do not respect drug dealers of your caliber, those men have children and grandchildren. Think about it."

Ernie and Jesus got up and left the room.

Eddie: "What do you think, Jesus?"

Jesus: "I think he is a lost cause, but I would be careful if I were you. If you see anything suspicious contact the local DEA office right away."

Eddie: "OK, I'll keep that in mind, thanks."

Jesus: "It's still early do you want to fly back tonight or tomorrow morning?"

Eddie: "I'll go in the morning. Where do I sleep?"

On the way out of the building Ernie told Jesus that he sees Ernesto as a spoiled child who must have his own way, no matter what the results. He is a very powerful and dangerously spoiled child.

Agent Jesus Martinez agreed with Ernie and added that this Ernesto may get a much needed education in our prison system.

Agent Jesus took Ernie out for dinner and a couple of drinks then dropped Ernie at the hotel and stated that he would pick him up in the morning and take him to the Airport.

Chapter 13

The Sleaze Bag

Monday June 2, 1980

Ernie got out of bed walked over to the window over-looking the back yard and admired the sun glittering off of the morning dew on the grass, the birds singing and the vegetables sprouting on the vines in the garden.

After showering he went down to the kitchen and had breakfast with Teresa and the boys. His son Joey asked if anyone had anything special in mind for his birthday. Ernie asked what he would like to do. Little Ernie started to answer the question, but stopped. Joey said he would like to go fishing. Ernie was all for that and the plans were made to go to Hale Reservation in Westwood, Massachusetts, a couple of towns away from the house, where they would fish, swim and cook out for the day.

After breakfast Ernie left for the office. He walked to the car; the familiar sound of a singing bird was heard. It was his friend the mockingbird. Ernie whistled and the bird replied with the same tune. The tunes went back and forth between them for a couple of minutes after which, Ernie drove off with a smile.

He arrived at the office and the other detectives asked what was going on. Ernie looked at them like they were crazy; he didn't know what was going on or what they were asking about.

Detective Jack Wade took the lead in the conversation saying that the answering machine in the office is full and the station telephone operator has another twenty massages for Ernie.

Ernie was still at a loss.

Ernie: "Who were the calls from?"

Jack: "Some girl saying that she needed to speak with you, she sounds worried and anxious to us."

Ernie: "Funny, funny guys, let me listen."

Jack: "We're not kidding Ernie; here listen to this girl's voice."

Female voice on the phone: "I am trying to get in touch with Detective Ernie Lijoi, it's very, very important." The tone was very scared and worried.

Ernie: "Jack, are they all like that?"

Jack: "Yes every one and sometimes she sounds a little desperate."

Ernie: "Jack, you don't know who that is?"

Jack: "How would I know, I have no pregnant women chasing me."

Ernie: "That's Jean; I bet she wants to talk about Chicken's death or has some information for us."

Jack: "Oh, yea, I remember her. You mentioned that we should speak with her. I like the pregnant women idea better." All the men in the room laughed.

Ernie: "You guys are funny. I bet that she's probably wondering what happened to Chicken, since she hasn't seen her all week end."

Jack: "You're probably right. By the way, why didn't you want to tell Frank, in BCI, that you knew who the victim was?"

Ernie: "I wasn't totally sure. Not until you guys confirmed who she was with her prints, and I heard Jean's calls. We'll let Frank know today and save him some leg work. Why don't you call him, Jack?"

Jack picked up the phone and dialed.

Jack: "Frank?"

Frank: "Yeah?"

Jack: "It's Jack Wade, Narcotics. Listen, the female victim from the park is nick named Chicken, her real name is Sonia Levin, 29 years old, born on June 20, 1950 in Roxbury, Massachusetts and lived at 2939 Washington Street, Roxbury alone, phone number is 555-2982. Black female, 5'5" tall, slightly heavy set, pretty with long flowing black hair and very dark eyes; she had a tattoo on her right wrist of a gold chain and heart wrapped around the wrist. That tattoo was the first thing that we noticed and recognized. We wanted to be positive before we said anything. "

Frank: "I had a feeling you guys knew something."

Jack: "We weren't sure until today; we'll do some follow up on it if you don't mind?"

Frank: "No I don't mind at all. We're happy to have the help, just keep me in the loop."

Frank: "There's one more thing, not public knowledge at this time. We think that this murder may be a message for Ernie and our department to stay out of a certain dealer's business."

Frank: "I understand that you can't say who this idiot is at this point, but at some point, you'll have to let us in on that part of the case. If you need anything, let me know."

Jack: "Will do and thanks for the offer to help." Jack hung up the phone.

Jack: "Ernie we're all set, he even offered help if we need it."

Ernie; "Yeah, I expected that. He's OK just likes to fool around a lot."

Jack: "What do you think we should do?"

Ernie; "Let's go find Jean and do an interview, we're apt to learn a lot from her."

Jack: "Where could she be now?"

Ernie: "She should be finishing up her work in Boston about now, we'll find her."

The two men drove into Boston and down to the area known as the Combat Zone, an area frequented by many people from all walks of life. All of the major stores are located in that area. The historic sites are located around the outer edge, like the Boston Commons, The State House, and the Old Grave Yard, all of which is part of the world-renowned Freedom Trail. As they drove by the State House Ernie looked over and began to chuckle a little.

Jack: "What's so funny, Ernie?"

Ernie; "You're not aware of it, but the original State Charter from the 1600's was stolen out of the State House a few years ago. I recovered it two years later during a search warrant. I almost threw it out thinking, at first, that it was simply a toy of some sort, but I took it as part of the search. Had it not been for the District Attorney himself, Mr. DeHunter, I would have given it back. He identified it as the original State Of Massachusetts Charter from the 1600's. I never could figure out why the thief wanted it or was going to do with it. That document was too well known to be of any value to him."

Jack: "You mean Mike O'Reilly, the famous art thief?"

Ernie: "Yeah, what's even funnier is that the turnkey in the lockup, the officer that introduced me to the informant, refused to have anything to do with the case. I asked him several times if I could mention his name or the fact that he introduced me to the informant who happened to be locked up at the time, he kept saying no. He told me that he was not interested at all in any drug case. After I found the State Charter and did all of the reports, excluding his introduction, according to his wishes, he turned around and complained because he was not involved. I later found out that he did it because the city was going to give me an award for recovering that document. Instead, because of his complaints, they gave the award to him. I guess an award was more important than his honor: factual story, Jack."

Jack: "What a fucken sleaze bag. Who was that idiot?"

Ernie: "Doesn't matter, water under the bridge, not important now, that's why I laugh."

Jack: "I guess not."

Ernie: "Jack, look over there in that coffee shop, having coffee. Isn't that our friend Jean Rufford?"

Jack: "Let's go and speak with her."

They parked the car and walked into the coffee shop, sat down and ordered coffee and a roll. Jean saw them and came over to their table.

Jean: "Hi, guys. Ernie, I've been trying to get a hold of you all weekend."

Ernie: "Looking as lovely as ever. Jean, how was your night?"

Jean: "Slow night, only did a few hundred."

Ernie: "Why did you want me, Jean?"

Jean: "Two reasons, have you seen Chicken, we have been worried about her?"

Ernie: "Who's we?"

Jean: "Me and the other girls."

Ernie; "I have some bad news for you, sit down."

Jean: "What's wrong?"

Ernie: "We found her dead. Her body was thrown into a Quincy park, last Friday night."

Jean: "That son of a bitch Leroy; was she beaten to death?"

Ernie: "It looks that way."

Jean: "She was arguing with him Friday. She got so upset that she threatened to call you, right to his face. I knew that she was wrong in saying that to him. In this business we expect to have bad things happen, but not murder, Chicken was a good girl," as she hung her head and began to cry for her friend.

Ernie: "We're very sorry about her loss. You're going to have to come into the office so that we can get all this down officially."

Jean: "OK, but there is something else I need to talk to you about."

Ernie: "What's that?"

Jean: "There are five girls in my group and we have been talking, we want you to take our money each night and invest it for us."

Jack and Ernie looked at each other, then at Jean as a million different thoughts went through their heads. They both laughed at her, as though she was joking.

Jean: "I'm not joking, you're honest, we can trust you to handle the money and then if everything works out we can all retire in five years. You'll get a nice percentage."

Ernie: "Jean, that's a very nice gesture. I appreciate your confidence, but I am a police officer. Even if I wasn't a police officer, I could never do anything like that. I don't want to do that. I appreciate your friendship and that's as far as it goes. Let's go over to the station and discuss the Leroy case."

Jean: "Hey, I didn't think you would accept, but I gave it a shot."

They drove Jean across Boston, across the town line, to the Quincy Police station. They entered the station and went directly to the interview room where they discussed the Leroy Watkins case.

Ernie: "Jean, I can't show you any pictures of her body. He beat her very badly; you wouldn't recognize her, anyway. Let me get the recorder set up so that we can type out this conversation later." Ernie left the room for a while.

Jack: "Jean, I'm Jack. Do you remember me?"

Jean: "Yes I do; do you work with Ernie all the time now?"

Jack: "No, I happened to catch this case with him so I'm learning in reality, but if there is anything I can do for you let me know. How about a cup of coffee?"

Jean: "Yes, that would be nice."

Jack: "Oh, here's Ernie, I'll get us all some coffee."

Ernie: "OK, Jean, as soon as Jack gets back we will talk."

A few minutes later Jack walked in with Captain Richards.

Ernie: "Jean, this is Captain Richards, he works with us."

Jean: "Hi, Captain, nice to meet you."

Captain: "It's my pleasure. I'm very sorry for the loss of your friend.

Jean: "Thank you, Captain. She'll be missed."

Captain: "Ernie, let's talk privately for a moment." The two men walked to an outer office.

Captain: "I have an old friend in Roxbury who happened to be on the corner the other night when Leroy Watkins was there talking to another man. My friend heard

Watkins telling the other man that; 'those Quincy cops will not be back here anymore.' Leroy said to the other guy that he left a gift for Quincy and as long as they are smart enough, they'll stay away from his business."

Ernie; "Captain, will he testify?"

Captain: "He can't, not at this point anyway. He was just warning us about that guy Watkins."

Ernie: "Will you write it up for us, Captain?"

Captain; "Of course, but be sure you guys are careful, he's definitely nuts. Those drugs are getting to him." Pointing to Jean he asked: "Is she goanna be any help to us?"

Ernie: "I think so, her heart is in the right place and she's a smart girl."

Captain: "Call if you need anything."

Ernie; "Thanks, Captain, I will."

Ernie: "Jean, let's try again." Ernie began the interview: "Present in the room is Jean Rufford, Detective Jack Wade and speaking is Detective Ernie Lijoi. We are here to interview Miss. Rufford regarding the death of Sonia Levin, a/k/a Chicken."

Ernie: "Jean, you know Chicken, Miss Levin?"

Jean; "Yes, we've been friends for a long time."

Ernie: "Then you know her associates as well?"

Jean: "Yes, most of them."

Ernie: "What does she do for a living?"

Jean: "She works the street like me."

Ernie; "You mean she's a prostitute?"

Jean: "Yes, I guess so."

Ernie; "Is that your chosen profession?"

Jean: "Yes, do we have to discuss that?"

Ernie: "No just background, that's all. You are originally from New York and now live in Jamaica Plain; is that correct."

Jean: "True, your honor."

Ernie; "Come on Jean play nice. Did Sonia have a pimp?"

Jean: "Yes, Leroy."

Ernie: "What's Leroy's last name and where is he from?"

Jean: "Leroy Watkins from Roxbury. He's always talking about his experiences in Viet Nam."

Ernie: "That's Roxbury, a section of Boston?"

Jean: "Yes, you know where Roxbury is."

Ernie: "Yes I do, this tape is for the Court some day and I must be as precise as possible."

Jean: "OK."

Ernie: "Jean, do you know where Mr. Watkins lives? Can you describe the house? Will you describe Mr. Watkins for us, please?"

Jean: "Yes, I've been there a hundred times with Chicken. Do you know that place they call the Flume in New Hampshire?"

Ernie: "Yes, been there many times with my family."

Jean: "You know you walk between the walls, several hundred feet tall along the 60 foot wide stream to the top where the stream begins, beautiful area."

Ernie: "Yes, I do. What about it?"

Jean: "You go up Malcolm X. Boulevard to King Street and take a left. His house is at the end of the road and when you are in his home and look back down King Street, Leroy always says that it looks like the Flume, he's a little nut's I think."

Ernie: "Do you know the house number?"

Jean: "No, but it is a blue house with white trim and the only single family home there. All the rest are tall apartment houses going up to his house."

Ernie: "I see. Can you describe him?"

Jean: "Oh, you can't miss that asshole. He wears a full length Sable coat white and a white hat. He's about 35 years old, 5'9" tall, about 195 pounds. Leroy is a very large heroin and cocaine dealer and is always dressed in a complete suit with an open collar shirt."

Ernie: "Do you know where he gets his heroin?"

Jean: "All I know is that he talks about his Asian connection, Fraido Lucasie, who controls the heroin for this area from the Asian market. Leroy calls Fraido his friend."

Ernie: "He speaks freely about this man, Lucasie, an old army buddy?"

Jean: "No, he only speaks about him when there are people around that he trusts, like the girls. He trusts us."

Ernie: "Interesting. Jean, is there anything else you would like to tell me at this point, anything at all?"

Jean: "Yes I wish you would take me up on my offer."

Ernie: "Come on Jean, be serious."

Jean: "I heard that he shot a few people and buried them down by the Zoo in Franklyn Park. He's threatened the girls with that a couple of times. He says; 'If you're not careful, I'll put you in Franklyn Park like those other guys'."

Ernie: "He makes those kinds of treats?"

Jean: "Yeah, he also says; 'you girls had better produce or you will visit my friends at the Zoo'."

Ernie; "How many bodies are there?"

Jean: "I heard that there are six bodies there, but I don't really know, I never saw any of them."

Ernie: "Is there anything else?"

Jean: "Are you interested in guns?"

Ernie; "Yes, why would you ask that? You know I am always interested."

Jean: "He has a lot of hand guns in his house."

Ernie; "Thanks for that, How about cover? Does he have people working for him?"

Jean: "Yes, he has four men, three black guys and one white guy. They're all nice unless you cross Leroy or try to bother Leroy."

Ernie; "OK, I understand; do you know their names?"

Jean: "Yes, Herbert is the white guy; Guyton, Shan and Perry are the black men; as I said. all nice guys."

Ernie: "OK, anything else?"

Jean: "No, I don't think so."

Ernie; "Jack do you have anything?"

Jack: "No, you covered all that we could for now."

Ernie; "We'll drive you home or wherever you like, Jean."

Jean: "OK."

Ernie: "Make sure you don't lose your cool and say anything to anyone about our meetings."

Jean: "No I'm not like Chicken. She had some temper and would say things just to get someone upset. That's probably what got her killed."

Detective Ernie Lijoi Sr. and Detective Jack Wade took Jean to a very late lunch then drove her home. They decided to call it a day. In the morning they would advise the homicide squad and later interview a second party with some information that may help them with the case.

Tuesday June 3, 1980

During breakfast with Teresa, Ernie and the two boys discussed the upcoming fishing trip and what was needed; what fish they may catch and how many they would keep.

It was decided that they would fish for bass and keep one or two to cook up for dinner.

After breakfast Ernie left for the office. The weather was so mild and warm with clear skies which made driving to work more enjoyable

The squirrels were out running and playing and their tails had thinned for the summer. The horses in the blue hills had lost their extra winter hair and the mockingbird was still singing with the same repertoire that Ernie had learned from the bird.

Once Ernie arrived at the office he began typing reports and after a few moments Detective Jack Wade walked in. The two detectives talked and decided to interview Petri Anderson after they have coffee.

They went for coffee. At about 10 am they arrived at the county jail where Petri Anderson was held as a prisoner on narcotics and weapons charges.

Jack: "Hi Petri, how do you like your accommodations?"

Petri: "You know better than to even ask that one."

Jack: "Yes, I understand."

Ernie: "Have you thought anymore about Leroy Watkins?"

Petri: "No, why would I think about him? Now, my girl—yes, I thought about her."

Ernie: "You said that he gave you the gun to get rid of, do you remember telling us that?"

Petri: "Yes I did say that and it's true."

Ernie: "But we can't prove it, the guns were in your possession, with your prints on them and they came up as stolen guns."

Petri: "Look, I am a drug dealer, I'm not vicious, I'm not a thief and I'm not a killer."

Ernie: "The thing is we believe you. The problem is proving to a court that what you say is true."

Petri: "I don't know what I can do in here to help clear it up or prove that what I say is the truth."

Ernie: "What if you were outside, say on bail? What could you do then?"

Petri: "Maybe I could cut you into him. Can you walk the walk, talk the talk?"

Ernie: "I have been chasing snow for many years so don't worry about me. It's you we're here to discuss."

Petri: "OK, then if you can get me out of here, this is what we'll do. I'll throw a party and cut you into him, then I am out of it."

Ernie: "Petri, any suggestion will be listened to. If we get you out, I call the shots. If that isn't good enough for you, we'll drop the idea here and now. If we move forward and you give us a problem outside we'll send you back."

Petri: "Say I agree to do this for you, what can you guys do for me?"

Ernie: "I would have to speak with the District Attorney, however, I have never seen a case like this where he did not do all he could for the man being charged as long as he cooperated to the fullest. What it comes down to is doing ten years if you don't cooperate and doing maybe three years or less if you do, which is only one year with good time. Of course, these are just estimates; the DA and the courts will make the final decision."

Petri: "I want my cash back, the money that you took out of my safe, thirty thousand dollars."

Ernie: "Good luck with that. It will not happen unless you do something spectacular for us and then they may use it to pay your attorney's fees, but you'll never see that cash again."

Petri: "I can ask."

Ernie: "Yes you can, but you are better off having your attorney handle that for you."

Petri: "I'll have to think about this."

Ernie: "That's the smartest thing you've said, ask the turnkey to contact us when you decide."

The two detectives left the county jail and proceeded to Boston to take a look at the residence of Leroy Watkins, on King Street in Boston.

Later that day, they contacted Detective Frank Deloso of Homicide to discuss the case.

Ernie: "Hi, Frank."

Frank: "Men, what did you find out about this girl, Sonia Levin, a/k/a Chicken?"

Ernie: "I think we have quite a bit for you, but we must keep it low key for a while."

Frank: "Explain, please"

Ernie: "We have two informants that can and may be willing to testify. It appears that Leroy Watkins killed her and several others over time. We have a gun that should come back to two murders once we dig up the bodies. He is a major narcotics supplier working directly under and with the Asian mafia and his primary drug is heroin."

Frank: "That's all good, but how does Sonia tie in?"

Ernie: "Sonia Levin was one of his girls and an informant of mine and wanted to get Watkins because she was tired of him beating the shit out of her and putting her in the hospital. I was told that he beat her to death because she threatened him with me. She had a bad temper."

Frank: "That's all well and good, but it is not fact."

Ernie: "No not yet, but I have someone that will cut me into him. We'll take him down for everything once I get into him good enough."

Frank: "That sounds good, Ernie; I've always wanted to work one of your cases with you."

Ernie; "Thank you, Frank, let Jack and I continue on our end and we'll keep you posted."

Frank: "Great, I'll wait to hear from you."

Ernie; "Don't forget, this must stay quiet. It's my informants life that we're talking about here, not to mention my safety."

Frank: "Done."

Ernie and Jack left the area and received a call to return to the County jail.

Ernie; "Jack, I live in Dedham where the jail is. Why don't I go see Petri and go home from there? I'll see you in the morning."

Jack: "Ernie, that sounds good to me, I'm done for the day anyway."

The two men left the office and drove away in different directions. Ernie arrived at the jail, went in to speak with Petri Anderson and find out if he decided to help.

Ernie: "Petri."

Petri: "Detective, I will help you, but you must understand it will not be easy to cut you into him. Leroy is a very suspicious person."

Ernie: "Would your friends, dealers and suppliers assist you in raising some money to defend yourself?"

Petri: "Some would help, but I have money put away."

Ernie: "I realize that, most of you guys have a defense fund these days."

Petri: "Yes, you have to have it or rot in jail."

Ernie: "Will they come to a party at your place?"

Petri: "Sure they would. I'll tell them the reason for the party. I need to raise money for defense. Please, remember, I'm not turning in everybody, just Leroy Watkins."

Ernie: "I don't want everybody. I want the head of the snake, Watkins. You have to put some trust in me."

Petri: "He is very suspicious, I told you that."

Ernie: "Don't worry, he'll come to me. I want you to run a large party for your customers and your suppliers to raise defense money and I will take it from the party on."

Petri: "I'll do my best for you."

Ernie: "OK. I must speak with the District Attorney to confirm all of this. I'll be in touch with you soon."

Petri: "I'll be here, I'm not going anywhere."

Ernie left the jail and called it a day.

Chapter 14

The Murder

For the next few days Ernie worked with the district attorney doing reports on Petri Anderson. Preparing the paperwork for the courts, arranging to place the reports in sealed files until the case is completed. After a few days with all of the other work that the district attorney had to do they finally accomplished their goal and Petri Anderson was released on personal recognizance to work with the detectives.

Ernie made arrangements to meet with Anderson on Thursday afternoon at the Braintree Motel which was a safe place to meet and keep the informant anonymous.

Ernie: "Have you gotten the party set up?"

Petri: "Yes, and Watkins says he'll be there. Wait until you see how he shows up."

Ernie: "Here's our back story; I am from New York, an old friend of the family, you haven't seen for many years. A well-known dealer in the New York Area of Brooklyn, my name is Eddie Pannoni, say it."

Petri: "Eddie Pannoni, That's pretty good, and I don't really know what you do; all I know is what you tell me."

Ernie: "That's correct and that's your biggest protection."

Petri: "Sounds good, the party will start around 8 pm, but Leroy won't be there until nine o'clock. He likes to make a big entrance. He's the king and wants everyone to know it."

Ernie: "OK I'll be there at 8 pm; you introduce me to Leroy as Eddie Pannoni. I will take it from there."

Friday June 6, 1980

The entire team met at the office at 7 pm and everyone was advised of the case as it stood at that time. The detectives were pleased with the way that the case was forming. They wanted, very much, to cooperate in every way.

Ernie spoke to all of the detectives in the unit and made arrangement for them to do surveillance of the party. He asked that they take vehicle plate numbers throughout the night and cover him in the event that things go wrong.

Detective Jack Wade, the photography expert, would get pictures of everyone that entered and left the home while Ernie was at the party. This information would create a mountain of intelligence for later use.

The men left the office, to set up on the Petri Andersons house. Ernie left the office about a half hour after the detectives, giving them enough time to be in position when he arrived.

Shortly after 8 pm Ernie arrived at the house. The front door was opened; he walked into the living room. There were a few people in the room, but no visible signs of drugs or guns with one exception.

A white male, about thirty years old with dark black hair and blue eyes was sitting on the couch smoking from a long glass cylinder which had a tube connecting him to the cylinder. He would take a drag and sit back for a short while then exhale; this was known to Ernie as a hashish pipe or a bong.

With this pipe they usually smoked Hashish (more commonly called hash). This is a potent form of cannabis produced by collecting and processing the most potent material that female marijuana plants naturally generate as part of their growth cycle. When this product is completed and ready for use, it's a jelly like form of brown or black substance.

As Ernie scanned the room he saw Petri Anderson talking with a female in the adjacent dining room, who was unknown to Ernie. He looked over and saw Ernie, waved a gesture for Eddie to join him.

Ernie: "Hi, Petri."

Petri: "Eddie, I want you to meet Nancy Izetti from Boston and a great person to know."

Ernie: "Hi, Nancy; your last name is Izetti? I grew up with an Izetti family in Brooklyn back in the day."

Nancy: "That's possible I have family in both New York and New Jersey."

Ernie: "Isn't it a small world? We must sit down and talk sometime. I bet it's the same family."

Nancy: "Yes, let's do that and soon."

Ernie: "We'll talk."

Petri: "Eddie, come with me. I want to show you something."

Eddie followed Petri down a hallway into a bedroom at the back of the house.

Petri: "That was pretty good, Eddie. I think you'll be OK when Watkins gets here, but he's not a broad and not so easy to talk with."

Ernie: "Don't worry, just do as I instructed and you'll be OK. I've done this a hundred times before."

Petri: "Most of the people here are just smaller dealers, my personal dealers and friends. The only interest for you is Leroy Watkins. I wish you the best of luck with him; just keep me as far out of it as you can."

Ernie: "You worry too much, my friend. We've done this many times. I know it's easy for me to say that, when you're in the hot seat, but try and believe that we will do all we can to protect you."

Petri: "I have confidence in you, Eddie."

They left the bedroom and went back out to join the party. As they entered the living room a large black man wearing a white fur coat, a white hat, and shinny suit, about 32 years old, 5'9" tall, 195 pounds walked in the front door with two other men and four girls. All eyes were on this man in the fur coat. He attracted and seemed to enjoy the attention. Ernie took this as a clue to his personality. This man was Leroy Watkins he answered the description perfectly.

Watkins walked over to the couch where other people were sitting and just stood there looking at them until they left the couch, then he sat down and spread his arms out for his girls to sit with him. As an Arabian King may direct his harem without a word.

Petri went to the liquor table and made a drink, brought it over to Watkins and sat opposite him. Watkins took the drink and shook his head in an expression of thank you.

Petri: "How's things, Leroy?"

Leroy: "Petri, you disappointed me."

Petri: "How did I disappoint you?"

Leroy: "By getting busted, that's how."

Petri: "That's nothing, I can handle that, I may do a year or two, but that's all."

Leroy: "We'll see."

Petri: "I want you to meet a guy I knew in New York he is top notch."

Leroy: "Who is he, what does he do?"

Petri: "In New York he is at your level, but I think there was some trouble. His name is Eddie Pannoni."

Leroy: "OK. I'll meet him."

Petri: "Eddie, come on over here."

Ernie walked over to the couch.

Petri: "Eddie, I want you to meet Leroy—a good and trusted friend."

Ernie: "Leroy, nice to meet you," as Ernie put his hand out to shake.

Petri: "I have other guests so I'll leave you guys for a moment."

Ernie: "Leroy, you made quite an entrance, chasing everyone off the couch, I had to laugh."

Leroy: "You think I'm funny?"

Ernie: "Man, I come from Brooklyn; I see that kind of shit every day."

Leroy: "I may get to like you, Eddie. Sit down, join me."

Ernie; "Let me get a drink first."

Eddie walked over to make a drink and Nancy Izetti walked over, grabbed his arm and asked for a drink. Ernie made the drinks for both of them and then he and Nancy joined Leroy.

Leroy: "What's your business, Eddie?"

Ernie: "I satisfy the wants and needs of the public at large."

Leroy: "Man, that's perfect. I'm going to steal that statement and use it myself."

Ernie: "Be my guest."

Leroy: "How about a bomb?"

Leroy was offering Ernie a marijuana joint laced with heroin. Ernie decided to use a fear of addiction as an excuse.

Ernie: "Sorry, buddy, but I never use, I am afraid of getting addicted, if I do, there goes my business and all my profits."

Leroy: "I knew I was going to like you. What brings you to this part of the country?"

Ernie: "Two things: First; Petri needs some financial help because of the arrest. Second; there were some major problems down in New York. You may have seen it on the news, it was a fast story, but it destroyed my business for a little while. All because of a guy that got busted and became a rat; that rat is being taken care of as we speak. I wanted to be sure that I was far enough away, that I had plenty of witnesses. All you guys are witnesses to the fact that I am here right now and not in New York."

Leroy: "I got the impression you were a smart operator by the way you presented yourself. We must talk sometime."

Ernie: "No, I'm sorry, I'm not interested in doing business with you, not unless we can have a private conversation right now to clear the air on a very particular point."

As Ernie spoke and finished the statement he looked over at Petri in another part of the room which Watkins picked up on.

Leroy: "I think I know what you're getting at. Yes, let's talk in the back bedroom."

The two men left the living room and went down the hall to the bedroom. Petri noticed them get up and walk down the hall.

Petri: "Eddie do you guys need anything want me to get you something?"

Ernie: "No, Petri, We just want to use your bedroom to talk privately, if that's OK?"

Petri: "Yea, sure go ahead, if you need anything just let me know."

Ernie: "We'll be fine Just business talk, that's all."

Ernie: "Leroy I originally came here to make a new contact because of what is going on in New York and then I find out that Petri got busted. I would rather wait than deal with anyone now. He's an honest guy, I believe that he can be trusted, but why take a chance?"

Leroy: "I agree, Eddie, but I do trust him as long as you do. Just out of curiosity, what kind of weight do you do Eddie?"

Ernie; "I do about a hundred Keys of blow and two to three "H" every couple of months."

Leroy: "Don't worry about Petri. I will take care of him and he will cause no problems."

Ernie: "Look with all due respect, I don't deal with people in this situation."

Leroy: "What situation?"

Ernie: "One of your people just got busted, I cannot take the chance that you go down and my money or product goes with you."

Leroy: "I'm telling you; I'll end his career."

Ernie: "What are you saying?"

Leroy: "I'll tune his clock so that he no longer runs at all."

Ernie: "That's no good, if you mess up it will just make him madder and he will defiantly turn on you."

Leroy: "Then I'll fucken bury him and that will be that, he's a minor dealer anyway."

Ernie: "Bury him, do you mean kill him, end his life?"

Leroy: "Yes, you sound surprised."

Ernie; "No, but are you sure you want to go to that extreme?"

Leroy: "I don't fuck around; you will learn that about me."

Ernie: "Why would you kill him, if he already spoke to the bulls, you would be the number one suspect?"

Leroy: "Yes that's true, but I like doing my own work."

Ernie: "I'll take care of it."

Leroy Watkins looked at Eddie as though he could not believe what he had heard Eddie say.

Leroy: "How much would you want to handle it for me?"

Ernie: "Not much; a key of heroin along with my order."

Leroy: "Now, why would I pay for something I can handle and enjoy doing?"

Ernie: "I'll tell you what, I will handle it; forget the heroin, this time."

Leroy: "Why would you do that for me?"

Ernie: "Doing things like that is a big part of my business, but because we will be working together this one is on me, call it a gift and once you see my work; you will be willing to pay in the future."

Leroy: "When would you do it?"

Ernie: "He will be gone by tomorrow afternoon so be sure that you are around a group of witnesses all day, and you'll read about it in the papers once they find him."

Leroy: "This I have to see."

Ernie; "Read the Sunday paper."

The two men left the bedroom and returned to the living room where they re-joined the party. While sitting in the living room; Leroy reached into his pocket and pulled out a card which he handed to Eddie. "You call me or stop by the house anytime, brother."

He then stood up in the living room and made an announcement: "This man, Eddie, is my people and he will be treated as such from now on."

Eddie got up and shook Leroy's hand. As they sat down Eddie told Leroy that he would call him on Monday and they should be able to talk then. Leroy looked at Eddie and answered that he is available whenever Eddie is ready. Eddie walked over to Petri.

Ernie: "Listen, Petri; remain sober tonight. Do not over do it."

Petri: "What are you talking about?"

Ernie: "I will be back after the party is over. I'll explain later, we have a lot to do. I'm in a good position with him."

Petri: "OK, whatever you say."

Ernie: "One more thing, if you get the chance, tell him that I am Black Hand."

Petri: "Those are murderers!"

Ernie: "Exactly, say I was raised into an Italian tradition, but keep it short and don't say much just teasers; try to end the party early."

Petri: "OK, you got it."

Eddie went back to the couch area and said his goodnight to Leroy and everyone else. Nancy Izetti came running over to Eddie, grabbed his arm and wanted to know if she was going with him.

Ernie: "No, honey, not tonight; give me your number and I'll call you."

She put on a sad face like she was being cheated out of something. Eddie smiled at her and said goodnight then took her phone number and left the house. He went directly to the office. All of the detectives started coming into the office right after him.

Ernie: "Jack, did you get plenty of pictures?"

Jack: "I got plenty, including that big guy in the fur coat."

Ernie: "Here is the phone number of one of the girls named Nancy Izetti. I'll look at the pictures and point her out. This is Leroy Watkins' business card with all of his information."

Jack: "That's great—you got next to him."

Ernie: "Yes, and he is as crazy as a bedbug. To stop him from murdering Petri Anderson, I told him that I would do it. We have to set up a murder that looks like a suicide with plenty of pictures. The pictures are to be given to the papers for release in the Sunday paper. Can you do that, Jack?"

Jack: "Not a problem, but when?"

Ernie: "I told Petri Anderson to end the party early so that we can come back. We just have to wait. Can one guy sit on the house until that party ends and notify us when the last person leaves?"

Henry Griswold stood up and said he would take that assignment.

Ernie: "Let's go and have some coffee and I will explain everything. Buy the way, men, I promised my son's that we would go fishing tomorrow. I am going to leave the set up of the murder to you guys, any objections?"

Henry: "No not at all, have a good time."

Jack: "Ernie, one question, once we set up this whole murder thing, what do we do with Petri?"

Ernie: "Take him over to the county jail and have him incarcerated under special protection and a different name. He is to be kept from mixing with the population."

Jack: "He's gonna be pissed about that."

Ernie: "Explain to him that he can stay out in the public eye, but Watkins has him marked as a target. This is the
best way to get Watkins and protect him at the same time."

Jack: "OK, are you coming with us to the house once
he cleans out the party?"

Ernie: "I think I better, he trusts me and I can speak to
him. I'll leave the rest to you guys."

Just then the radio started blasting, "November 3 to 7."

Ernie replied knowing that November 3 is the call sign
for Detective Henry Griswold.

Ernie: "November 7 standing by."

Henry: "The tank is emptying out, the big fish left; I
think we will be all set in a few minutes."

Ernie: "On our way."

They all arrived in one car and Ernie went into the
house to make sure no one was there except Petri Anderson.

Ernie: "Hi, Petri, you OK?"

Petri: "Yeah, I'm Ok. Let me in on what's going on?"

Ernie: "Watkins has a bullet for you because of your
arrest, lucky you."

Petri: "That motherfucker, I'll fix his ass, I'll testify
against him."

Ernie: "Not if you're dead. We'll have to kill you and
put you away first."

Petri: "Kill me? What the fuck are you talking about?"

Ernie: "I told Watkins that I would take the contract on
your life. Now, we'll set up a fake murder, I'll get the
guys." Ernie walked to the front door and signaled for the
men to come in.

Ernie: "Jack, you're the photographer, you set it all up
so that it looks realistic."

Jack: "Mr. Anderson, please sit here and droop your head to the left."

Petri: "Like this?"

Jack: "Yes I have a bullet-hole sticker to place on your head and here is plenty of ketchup I am going to pour it on you."

Petri: "OK"

Jack: "That looks good. Now I will take some pictures and then you can clean up."

Jack: "Ernie we're finished, I'll take him to the jail and then I will be done for the night."

Ernie: "Petri, do what Jack says; we will come in and see you from time to time until this is over."

Petri: "OK, Detective, I am counting on you guys."

Ernie: "Don't worry, we have it."

Ernie left the house and headed home.

Saturday June 7, 1980

Ernie's family got up early; he took the family out for breakfast. Later they loaded the car with fishing gear, food for a picnic and drinks. At 10 am they were off to Hale Reservation in the town of Westwood a couple of towns west of Dedham.

They pulled into the gate at Hale Reservation, drove down the long narrow road to the lake, parked the car, got out and looked around.

Stretched out in front of them was a small lake that was used for fishing and swimming. To the right was a cliff about 40 feet high that led to a small inlet on the other side. Straight in front of them and across the lake was a small sandy beach which was netted off from the rest of the lake so the snapping turtles could not infiltrate the swimming area. The lake was surrounded with many different types of trees.

The family worked together to set up the picnic area and the boys went into the water for a dip. After they came out of the water Ernie asked if the boys want to go over to the inlet area and fish for a while. The boys agreed, so they took the fishing gear and walked over to the other side of the lake, up over the cliff and down the opposite side to the lake inlet area. They had been fishing for a while when Ernie looked at the two boys and asked if they wanted to hear a story that he wrote and they agreed. The two boys enjoyed Ernie's stories over the years.

The Fisherman

It's a beautiful summer day along the southern coast of the United States – just a hint of a cloud in the sky and the air as warm as the water splashing against the feet of the fisherman walking along the beach, looking for a place to throw in a line and catch dinner.

Ah, there's a spot – some rocks to sit on, a place to put his gear and a back rock to rest against. This has been a long-anticipated day.

The Fisherman, John Altrick, is about 66 years old. He has spent his entire life serving the public. He has seen a lot and has just as many stories constantly running through his mind, yet he has no one to tell them to – no family left except for those who are much younger and uninterested in an old man's thoughts. So he goes fishing and wraps himself in his own memories.

John puts his equipment down and sets himself up for the first cast with some shrimp as bait. He throws the line out and sits back to rest while he waits. Then, a strike. A small Tarpon starts jumping in and out of the water. He thinks it's too big, he can't handle it. He fights with the fish and the line breaks. He pulls in the line – new hook, new sinker, new leader, new shrimp – and throws it back out.

A half-hour passes, an hour, then suddenly he hears a squeaking noise out of the silence of the water. He looks around, but sees nothing. He pulls in the line, puts on new bait, then throws it out again. He sits back and rests, enjoying the view of the ocean.

A dolphin about 10 feet off shore – squeak, squeak – this must be what he'd heard earlier. He's just sitting there, relaxing against the back rock, when the dolphin stops in the water, hangs his body as they sometimes do, and looks right at John. This seems odd. John thinks that the dolphin is looking for some food, so he throws in a few shrimp. The dolphin doesn't move.

"What would you be waiting for, Mr. Dolphin?" John asks with a smile.

"You, Mr. Man," answers the dolphin.

John looks around; there must be someone in the rocks playing a game on him, a kid or someone. He doesn't see anyone and laughs, "I must be dreaming."

John looks back at the water and the dolphin is gone. He pulls in the line, re-baits and throws it out. Looking over the water, he spots the dolphin, stopped and hanging in the water. *This is really something. I'm dreaming, but I'm completely awake.* He pinches himself. He feels it. He's awake.

"Mr. Dolphin, what can I do for you?"

"We can hear your thoughts. We will listen to your stories."

This is nuts, I am speaking to a dolphin. There are dolphins that can talk, though. Maybe this one got loose from somewhere, some training facility. "How is it that you can speak, Mr. Dolphin?"

"I cannot speak, Mr. Man."

"But, I hear you."

"I hear your thoughts, Mr. Man, and I allow you to hear mine. You think I am speaking, but I'm not."

"I have never heard of such a thing in my entire life, Mr. Dolphin."

"It is a rare gift that I give you, Mr. Man."

"But, why me?"

"We enjoy your stories, Mr. Man. Every time you come here, we wait for your stories."

"We?"

The ocean starts bubbling in front of John. One by one, heads of dolphins pop up, their bodies hanging in the water. They all look, silently, towards John.

I cannot believe this. There must be a ventriloquist around here or something, or someone doing this, playing this game on me.

"What is a game?"

"A game is an activity that people participate in – together or on their own – for fun and enjoyment." He finally gives in and says out loud, "Who is here doing this? You've played a great joke, and you win. I'll tell you the stories if you come out and show yourself."

No reply. No one comes out from the rocks or any-place else. John shakes his head and then hears, "Make game, tell story."

He does not know what to make of it, so he lays back, watches the dolphins and begins telling stories. There is the story of the soldier, starlets, cats, the story of the model, the story of the fish. They love the story of the fish, and on and on for what seems like hours of pleasure for John.

After each story, the dolphins squeak and squeal and John begins to be able to recognize when they think a story is great. He is running out of stories and thinking about going home for the day.

"Fish story, make game."

John tells the fish story again – a story about a fish that gets separated from the school. He is a lost baby fish for a long, long time. After many seasons of light shining through the water, he is found by his original school. Because of his education through living on his own and having to learn all of the tricks of survival, he becomes the leader in that school.

Suddenly, John feels something touching his right leg. He looks down and there are five youngsters sitting there in front of him, looking up at him.

"Hey, mister, you were asleep," one of the children said, "but those stories you told, were wonderful. Can you tell us the fish story again?"

The boys caught a bunch of catfish and pickerel. They enjoyed the story and the day.

Sunday June 8, 1980

Ernie was up early and walked up to the center of town to buy the Sunday Globe from the news store in the square. He tucked it under his arm and walked back home.

Ernie spread the paper out on the kitchen table, poured himself a cup of coffee and began to look through the paper. Page 4 top of page there was an article with the picture of a man that appeared to have shot himself.

The picture appeared with an attaching story which read that a Mr. Petri Anderson appeared to have committed suicide sometime early Sunday morning.

"Detective Jack Wade stated that investigation showed that Mr. Petri had recently been arrested on narcotics violations. According to the note that was found with the body, Mr. Petri Anderson had a tremendous amount of shame and did not wish to face the world any longer."

This picture and the associated story were telling the dead man's history and background which was enough to make Ernie happy about the Watkins Case. This gave him a tremendous amount of credibility for his next meeting with Leroy Watkins which he planned for Monday.

Chapter 15

The Green Farm

Monday June 9, 1980

Detective Lijoi arrived at the station early so that he could get reports completed on the cases that he had been working. All of the men walked in one by one and were talking about the suicide of Petri Anderson and discussing how well it all went.

One of the men asked Ernie how his weekend went. Ernie told them about Hale Reservation and how he and his family enjoyed the past Saturday fishing, swimming and just relaxing. They all wanted to know exactly where it was and what the hours of operation were so that they could take their family. Ernie offered to go and get some brochures and bring them into the office for all of the men to read.

They began to listen to the answering machine which was set up so that anyone could leave a message anonymously if they wished.

Call number seven was the voice of an older man who stated that he had been walking in the woods off of Faxon Park Road down by the Penn's Hill area, not too far from Echo Lake and observed in the middle of the woods about a quarter acre of marijuana plants growing or at least that is what he thought they were.

Henry: "That sounds very interesting. Who wants to take a stroll in the woods?"

Jack, spoke up first and asked: "Why don't you and I take it, Ernie?"

Ernie: "OK, let's go, but I have to call Watkins later."

The two detectives went over to the area that was described by the voice on the machine and walked around for about an hour. They were getting ready to quit when an older gentleman approached them.

Joseph: "What are you men doing here?"

Jack: "Quincy police Sir, we received a call about this area. Who are you, sir?"

Joseph: "That was me, but I am too old to get involved, my name is Joseph Vergo."

Ernie: "No problem. If you don't mind, please, show us what you observed. Then go on your way so you're not seen with us."

Joseph: "Thank you, men; it's over here."

The two officers followed Joseph for about five minutes and they came up on an opening in the trees. Standing straight, full and tall in front of them was about two hundred or more marijuana plants. The flowers were just getting to the stage where you could collect them and make some very potent marijuana with this little green thumb.

After the field was located the officers called the Station via radio and asked for assistance from the Highway department. Jack asked them to meet just outside of the park. By the time they walked out of the small forest the supervisor from the Highway department was waiting for them.

Ernie: "Hi, Jim, how are you?"

Jim: "Good, Ernie, what's up?"

Ernie: "Do you remember when we had that body in the woods a few years ago?"

Jim: "Yes, we cut a beautiful road to get in overnight. That was some job."

Ernie: "We need something like that here; I'll show you where we have to get into with trucks and cruisers."

Ernie and Jack took Jim, the Highway department supervisor, back to the location and advised him that they would be placing an officer there all night. The officer would remain until the Highway department was finished and the police department could get the marijuana plants out. They would later be burned at the incinerator in the next town, named Braintree.

Jim: "Not a problem, we will start this afternoon."

Jack: "Thanks for the cooperation. Jim."

Ernie called the Station again and asked for someone to be assigned at that location with a cruiser. He also told them that the detail would last until the completion of the job. Ten minutes later a cruiser pulled up and the officer was taken back to the marijuana plants. The officer was happy to take care of it.

There was normally another way of handling such a situation. They would wait until the owner showed up to cultivate and or feed the plants, but they had too many things going at that time and figured that they would simply do a clean up this time. If the farmer wanted to do it again they would be notified and go after him or her at a later date.

Ernie and Jack arrived at the office where they discussed the continuation of the Leroy Watkins case and the next move. It was decided that Ernie would contact Watkins and make arrangements for a large buy which should close his operation down. They would do a buy bust and arrest everyone that showed up. Ernie had to get Watkins to agree to come into Quincy. Ernie dialed the number that he had for Leroy Watkins and spoke as his guise Eddie Pannoni.

Ernie: "Hello, is Leroy there?"

A female voice answered the phone and spoke with Eddie.

Female: "Who is this, please?"

Ernie: "This is a friend, Eddie."

Female: "Oh, Mr. Eddie. We have been waiting for you to call, but Leroy just ran out for about an hour can he call you when he gets back?"

Ernie: "That's OK; I'm on the road, I'll call back in an hour or so from a pay phone."

Female: "Listen; if you want you can come over and spend the time with me. I am beautiful, you'll have plenty of fun."

Ernie: "Who are you?"

Female: "I'm Sheila, I work for Leroy."

Ernie: "That sounds very interesting, but I have some commitments I must take care of, I'll call back, Sheila, and take a rain check."

Sheila: "Any time, Leroy says whatever you want you get. I'm available anytime for you and if you don't like me, there are other girls."

Ernie; "Thanks for that, some other time."

Ernie hung up the phone and turned to Jack who heard the conversation and asked if Ernie wanted to go and get some lunch. They went to a restaurant on Quincy Avenue in Quincy near the Weymouth line that was known for its fish chowder. This restaurant made it nice and thick and extremely enjoyable.

On their way back to the station after lunch they were stopped at a light at the intersection of Quincy Ave and Potter Drive when Ernie and Jack noticed a car in the parking lot across the street that was parked and facing out, toward the street.

What attracted them to this vehicle was the fact that the driver was obviously smoking, what appeared to be marijuana.

The subject driving the car was later identified as Jerry Swashly, a white male, 5'9" tall, 165 pounds, dark hair and eyes of Braintree, Massachusetts the next town south of Quincy.

The detectives decided to pull into the parking lot and watch the car for a few minutes because it looked like he was waiting for something or someone.

Their curiosity paid off, a white male about 5'8" tall with a blue coat came out of a house on Potter Drive walked across the street carrying a green gym bag and sat in the car that the officers were watching.

This subject was later identified as Robert Paussie, a white male, 22 years of age, 5'8" tall, 155 pounds who lives at 222 Potter Drive and has been suspected of dealing in marijuana and cocaine.

The officers called for assistance and pulled up to the car. The two men were surprised and simply gave up.

In the gym bag the detectives found two pounds of marijuana and one ounce of cocaine, the two subjects were arrested and taken to the station. Also found in the car was several thousand dollars in cash.

While speaking with the men, Paussie stated that he lived at 222 Potter drive with his parents and asked the detectives not to bother them. He stated that they knew nothing about his operation, he only lives there with them and has his own room.

After their discussion Detective Lijoi and Wade went to the residence of the parents to advise them about their son, in an effort to stop this dealing before it goes too far and to save the parents some heartaches.

The officers explained the case to the parents who were completely unaware and shocked by the fact that their son was dealing cocaine and marijuana. The parents were thankful to the officers for stopping their son from a degrading life in illegal narcotics and pledged to get the boy some professional help.

The detectives requested permission to search the room of their son, Robert. The parents agreed. During the search they found another pound of marijuana and a very small amount of cocaine which they showed to the parents and took with them, as evidence.

The officers decided to let these two prisoners stew for a few days until they had more time to speak with them.

It was getting late in the day and Ernie still had to speak with Leroy Watkins. They returned to the office where Ernie telephoned Leroy Watkins.

Watkins: "Speak."

Ernie: "Hi, this is Eddie."

Watkins: "Eddie, my man the número uno, (number one) you are unbelievable."

Ernie: "I take it you read the newspapers?"

Watkins: "I sure did, you are number one with me. We will have a long and great friendship."

Ernie: "Were you around witnesses all day Saturday and Sunday?"

Watkins: "Plenty of them. Don't worry about that."

Ernie: "Good, I'm sorry I couldn't call earlier, but I had some important business to take care of."

Watkins: "That's OK; I left word that I am available whenever you want to speak with me."

Ernie: "Good, thanks. Can we speak tomorrow in person?"

Watkins: "Sure, you can just come on over and we'll talk."

Ernie: "See you around one in the afternoon, is that OK?"

Watkins: "I will see you then."

After the detectives logged in the evidence and wrote a preliminary report on the arrests they decided to call it a day.

Tuesday June 10, 1980

Ernie arrived at the office and started working on the reports for the Leroy Watkins case in an effort to get his reports up to date.

Detective Jack Wade attended the preliminary hearing for the arrest of Robert Paussie and Jerry Swashly at the Quincy district court. The case was called and Detective Wade was asked to testify about the evidence that was confiscated and the reason that the detectives did not get a search warrant for the house. Detective Wade answered the questions and the Court was satisfied that the evidence was obtained under the law with the permission of the parents.

Later the District Attorney wanted to know why Detective Lijoi did not attend the hearing. Detective Wade explained that Lijoi was working in a deep cover capacity and could not take the chance of jeopardizing his cover by appearing before the court. "If you want him, we'll have to ask the court to put the actual trial off until the deep cover case is complete."

Attorney: "I will need him, as an expert witness, for the trial. Will he be available?"

Jack: "Detective Lijoi should be available by then; this case shouldn't take that long."

Attorney: "Keep me apprised of his availability, if he is not available, I can continue the case for a while."

Jack: "I will do that."

Detective Jack Wade left the court house and returned to the office.

Ernie: "How did it go, Jack?"

Jack: "Ernie, the DA wants to make sure that you will be there for the trial."

Ernie: "When will that be?"

Jack: "In a month."

Ernie: "We should be finished by then, but I don't know why he needs me; it's a small case."

Jack: "Who knows what their thinking is. He says that he needs you as an expert witness."

Ernie: "That's fine with me. Look, I have to call Watkins shortly; I'm going to play it by ear with him for a while."

Jack: "Whatever you decide is OK with me."

Ernie picked up the phone and dialed the Watkins number.

Ernie: "Hi, this is Eddie. Is Leroy there?"

Sheila: "Yes, Eddie, this is Sheila, we spoke yesterday."

Ernie: "Yes, Sheila, nice to speak with you again, but I should talk to Leroy."

Sheila: "OK, hold on."

Ernie could hear Sheila call Leroy to the phone and say that Eddie is a real gentleman and that she wants to meet him.

Leroy: "Hello, Eddie."

Ernie: "Yeah, man, you gonna be there for a while?"

Leroy: "Yeah, you're getting all my women excited man, you must have the magic."

Ernie: "Man, all I got is me/ I don't know nothing about magic."

Watkins: "Come on over, we'll talk."

Ernie: "On my way—give me a half hour."

Ernie hung up the phone, looked at Jack and Jack seemed worried.

Jack: "Should I get a couple of cars to cover your meeting?"

Ernie: "No, this should be easy. It's just negotiate and celebrate the deal meeting. I'm not worried."

Jack: "OK whatever you say, but he is a nut and can blow up at anytime over any little thing."

Ernie: "I'll be fine; I'll be back as soon as I can."

Ernie left the office and went to Leroy Watkins' home where he parked and walked up to the front door.

The two guards, on the front steps, stopped Ernie: "Who the fuck are you, man?"

Ernie: "I'm Eddie, a friend."

Guard: "Oh, yes he mentioned you, arms up."

The two bouncers searched Eddie and found his Glock, model 17, 9mm handgun, tucked away in his belt against the small of his back.

Guard: "Sorry, Eddie, we will have to hold this while you are inside."

Ernie: "As long as I get it back when I leave."

Guard: "No problem, go ahead in. He's expecting you."

Eddie entered the building which had been converted to a very large single-family home with three stories. On the first floor was a large living room, dining room, kitchen and a game room. All of the bedrooms were on the second and third floor. The house was very nicely done and there were five women walking around or sitting in different areas of the first floor, all were half dressed and all of them came over to greet Eddie as he entered.

Behind the girls was Leroy Watkins who simply said, "Go sit down," and all of the girls complied with his wishes. Leroy walked up to Eddie and put his hand out to shake hands.

Watkins: "Man, you're OK. Anything you need is OK with me."

Ernie: "Leroy, I'm surprised, you don't show me any hospitality at all."

Watkins: "What the fuck are you talking about? You can have any girl here any drug, just about anything after what you did."

Ernie: "I'm talking about my greeting at the door. I was searched, my gun was taken away. I was treated like a piece of shit off of the street. That's not being courteous."

Leroy walked over to the window and yelled out to the two men guarding the house.

Leroy: "Hey, you guys come in here right now."

He no sooner told them and the door opened, the two guards walked in. Leroy looked at Eddie and winked then approached the two guards.

Watkins: "Didn't I tell you assholes that this guy Eddie is a friend?"

Guard: "Yes."

Watkins: "Then give him his piece back and don't ever bother him again when he comes to see me."

Guard: "OK, if that's what you want. Here's your gun, Eddie, sorry we bothered you."

Watkins: "Eddie, are you happy now?"

Ernie: "Yes, I don't like being treated like a piece of shit off the street."

Watkins: "I don't blame you. Tell me all about what you did and how you did it."

Eddie sat in the living room for a few minutes answering questions and telling the fictitious story about how he killed Petri Anderson and made it look like a suicide.

Ernie: "I see you have a pool table in the game room."

Watkins: "Yeah, I need the relaxation, do you play?"

Ernie: "I play a little, not as good as I should."

Watkins: "Common let's play a couple of games."

Eddie and Leroy played several games of pool; Leroy was a good shooter and had a good eye for the game. They split the games even.

Watkins: "Eddie you played very well. I thought you said that you were only a fair player?"

Ernie: "Leroy, I am better off saying that then saying I can play and then looking bad; anyway I rarely run across a guy that can play as well as you."

Watkins: "You're good with me, Eddie. Can I get you something, a joint some blow or a needle?"

Ernie: "I thought I told you, I make it a habit not to put my profits up my nose or in my arm."

Watkins: "That's right you did say that, I give you credit for being able to stick to that."

Ernie: "If I didn't we wouldn't be talking."

Watkins: "What do you mean?"

Ernie: "I would never have done Anderson for you; I would have been more interested in getting a free fix. Let's face it, when you're hooked, the drugs come first, before anything else. I don't have to tell you that."

Watkins: "I agree. You sure are good at taking care of things."

Ernie: "Thank you; I appreciate your appreciation of my work."

Watkins: "Is there anything I can do for you?"

Ernie: "As I told you I need a new supplier if you're interested."

Watkins: "What are we talking about?"

Ernie: "I need Grass, heroin, speed and cocaine, all the snow."

Watkins: "What kind of weight do you move?"

Ernie: "First of all I would have to make arrangements for transportation to New York for distribution, if we can come to an agreement."

Watkins: "Don't worry about that, we will come to an agreement."

Ernie: "Assume I can do 10 bales of grass, 50 keys of cocaine and two keys of heroin."

Watkins: "How often would you need that?"

Ernie: "That would be a small load. I would double that order after three months, assuming that the product is good and accepted well on the street by my customers."

Watkins: "When you say double do you mean double every three months?"

Ernie: "No, I would double the order and it would stay at that level then I would need to reload every three or four months."

Watkins: "I can do that without any problems. When do you want it?"

Ernie: "Let me do this; I am leaving tonight for New York. I'll put some numbers together and when I come back, I'll call you with the exact quantities that I need and we can put it together."

Watkins: "Let me have a number where I can reach you, Eddie."

Ernie: "I'll give you a secure number when I get back, after the first deal is completed."

Watkins: "OK, I can respect caution."

Ernie: "No, I'm not being cautious with you. I'm being protective, making sure no one else knows who you are, only me."

Watkins: "Good. Thank you for that."

Ernie: "It is my pleasure to be certain that you are safe and I would expect the same protections from you."

Watkins: "No problem, my friend. Here take this with you and you will see how well I will treat you." Leroy handed Eddie a glassine bag, one quarter filed with a white substance that turned out to be cocaine and another glassine bag inside the first with a smaller bag of white substance which turned out to be heroin. Both substances were later tested in the lab to confirm what they were.

After the conversation Eddie took the bags, left the house and drove back to the office where he bagged the heroin and cocaine that he was given as a gift and turned them in as evidence, sat down and made a few notes for his report. Detective Wade was there waiting for him. Ernie told Jack all about the meeting, saying that they would have to have a meeting with all of the men before he actually made a buy or even set up a buy.

It was decided that they would begin the next day on setting up the approach and surveillances needed to make sure that no one is hurt when that buy goes down. They left the office and Ernie drove home.

It was a beautiful June day as Ernie drove past a group of children running through a sprinkler on a lawn. This scene reminded him of his childhood in Brooklyn, New York.

Brooklyn 1950's

Ernie grew up with his friends in Brooklyn. Summers were extremely hot in the city which made for an uncomfortable day, hard to run around and play games like kick the can on the corner or even stick ball in the streets.

One hot summer day Ernie was standing in front of one of the Italian clubs on Dean Street around the corner from his house. An elderly man walked out of the club looked around at the all of the kids standing in the area and realized it was too hot for the kids to play.

The elderly man went back into the club and a moment later came out with a sprinkler cap for the fire hydrant (commonly called a Johnny Pump) and a wrench.

He walked over to the fire hydrant, unscrewed the side cap and replaced it with his cap which had holes in it. He then placed his wrench on the top screw of the Hydrant and began turning.

The elderly man turned the top screw several times and suddenly the water was sprinkling everywhere. Within seconds all of the kids were under the sprinkling water and the day quickly became a cool fun day.

After that day the kids learned how to get the water and after that day it seemed like everyone had a wrench to get the water running.

One day they got the water running and did not have a sprinkler head to put on the hydrant so one of the boys got hold of a short piece of wood. He placed it under the 6 inch wide fountain of water coming from the hydrant and slanted it upward. They now had their shower and took turns holding the wooden control.

Ernie arrived home. He spent time in the garden and then with Teresa and the boys after dinner.

Chapter 16

The Deal

Tuesday June 10, 1980

Ernie had coffee and toast at home then went out to the garden to check his plants. He checked the timer that controlled the watering, a Sears product that he purchased for twelve dollars that goes on the water spout and controls the water to the garden. Everything looked good.

After the garden he went to his car and while walking across the driveway he heard his friend the mockingbird, they whistled back and forth for a very short while and Ernie had a smile to carry him through the day.

He arrived at the office and some of the men were already there, the rest were coming in. They all sat around and made some plans to take down Leroy Watkins.

The first thing was for Ernie to notify the Boston Police Narcotics unit of his case and have them file for a search warrant based on Ernie's information which would be an easy thing for them to do. Ernie's information has been reliable in the past. The fact that he has worked with the Boston Police in the past and the fact that he is a deep cover detective working in close with the criminal element will seal the warrant for Boston.

The next stage would be to find a good place to meet Watkins and transfer the narcotics, a place that would be safe, out of the public eye and presented few obstacles.

The third stage would be to assign every one of the detectives so that each man knew where they were going and exactly what to cover, although these men were experienced at this type of work.

The last stage would be to order the drugs and convince Leroy Watkins that the location they picked would be the best one.

After all the decisions, the rest of the day was spent doing evidence reports, case report. Then Ernie contacted Detective Frank Deloso of the Quincy homicide Division to inform him of the case progress. Frank offered any and all the help that Ernie might need. Ernie told him that he would get back to him if necessary.

He later contacted Detective Bob (Robert) Hendrickson and Detective Thompson of The Boston Narcotics Unit to inform them about the case and the warrant issues.

Ernie: "Hi, Bob."

Bob: "Ernie, how are you?"

Ernie: "Doing good, Bob, thanks; do you remember that heroin dealer we briefly spoke of, named Leroy Watkins?"

Bob: "Yes, I remember that guy. Why? What's up?"

Ernie gave Hendrickson all of the information he needed for the search warrant of the house and filled him in on where the case was at that time.

Detective Hendrickson offered any assistance that Quincy may need at anytime and thanked Ernie for all of the information. He asked to be kept informed of what is going on and how the case progresses.

Ernie: "Bob, there are aspects of the case that you will have to handle; I'll go over them when we do the search warrant."

Bob: "Anything you need, Ernie, all you have to do let us know."

It was agreed between the two men that Ernie would stay in contact and confirm when the buy goes down so that Boston can follow up with the search warrant.

After the telephone call Ernie sat down at a desk to do his report on his conversation with the Boston Police detectives. The day ended, the paperwork was completed. He was ready for the last few stages of the case, the buy bust, the house search and the search for the bodies at the Franklyn Park Zoo in Boston.

Thursday, June 12, 1980

Everyone arrived at the office early to be sure that they didn't miss any part of this case or the set up for the close of the case. They were all ready to work on closing the case in a safe way.

Ernie contacted Leroy Watkins via telephone. He woke Leroy up.

Ernie: "Sorry about that, man. Is it OK if I come over at about eleven this morning?"

Leroy: "If anybody else but you woke me, he would be a dead man. You're lucky we are good friends."

Ernie: "Thank you for calling me a good friend. Is eleven OK?"

Leroy: "Yeah, I'll be up by then."

Ernie: "See you then."

All of the detectives were present in the office, Ernie called them together.

Ernie: "I'll meet Leroy at eleven this morning and I will set up the buy at the quarries here in Quincy. I need you guys to go up there and get good layouts and surveil-lance locations."

Henry: "No problem, Ernie, consider it done, but what if he doesn't want to go there because it's Quincy?"

Ernie: "I'll tell him that it's Braintree, not Quincy. At least that's what it looks like on the map."

Henry: "That's thin, he comes from Boston, remember? He'll know the area."

Ernie: "If I can't convince him, I won't push it. We'll be forced to go plan 'B'."

Henry: "What's Plan 'B'?"

Ernie: "Doing the best we can. Actually we will decide that when and if that time comes."

Ernie started out the door when the phone rang and the call was for him.

Ernie: "Hello"

Jesus: "Ernie, this is Jesus."

Ernie: "Ah, Jesus. What can I do for you, Lord?"

Jesus: "You're funny. Your friend, Ernesto Adelanto seems to be getting a bit fidgety. He has been making some remarks that don't really worry us yet, but they could turn into a problem."

Ernie: "What kind of remarks."

Jesus: "Are you sitting down?"

Ernie; "Yes."

Jesus: "He says he would like to kill you."

Ernie: "And you're saying that you don't think that it is not a realistic threat?"

Jesus: "No, but I am going to have a talk with him next week, you just keep your head up."

Ernie: "I'm not worried about myself; it's my family that worries me. I can't be with them all the time."

Jesus: "No, I wouldn't even concern myself. These guys are bad, but it's a business. They don't want you going after their family, so if they go after anyone it will be you, no one else."

Ernie: "OK, I'll keep my eyes opened, thanks for the tip."

Jesus: "I'll keep you advised."

Ernie: "Thanks, Jesus, you're OK. By the way, what happened to the tunnel in Arizona that Ernesto installed underground between Mexico and Arizona?"

Jesus: "We started filling in Ernesto's Tunnel, on the Arizona side. The Politicians negotiated with Mexico to get the Mexican side sealed. The United States paid the bill to have the Mexican side sealed as well, now they are both under concrete."

Ernie; "I bet that cost us a bundle."

Jesus: "As I understand it, the US paid out several million dollars to Mexico to get the Mexican side sealed."

Ernie: "That figures, we seem to pay the world for their problems; get back to me if anything comes of this Ernesto threat."

Jesus: "I will, and don't worry."

Ernie: "I don't worry. I am just cautious."

Jesus: "OK, Ernie, I'll get back to you."

Ernie hung up the phone and advised the other men as to the information that he had just received. All of the men offered their support and time to watch over the family if needed. Ernie thanked them all and left to go visit with Leroy Watkins under the persona of Eddie Pannoni.

An hour later he pulled up to the residence of Leroy Watkins, parked the car and walked up to the front door and approached the two guards.

Ernie: "Hi, men, how's things?"

Guard: "Good, Eddie, he's waiting for you."

Ernie: "OK, see you guys later."

Ernie entered the home and as he went in, he looked up and noticed a skylight in the ceiling allowing the sunlight to enter.

Ernie: "Hello, Anyone here?"

Unknown Female: "Hi Eddie can I do something for you?"

Eddie was approached by a white female with long dark hair, a beautiful face and a body that was perfect which you could see plenty of through the skimpy nightgown she was wearing. With her was another girl, black, just a beautiful and wearing the same type of nightgown and this girl was even more perfect in every way.

Ernie: "No, I'm here to see Leroy."

Female: "You can have your choice or even both of us if you like."

Ernie: "Thanks, but I don't have the time right now, gorgeous."

Female: "OK, but I'm going to think you are gay if you don't watch out."

Ernie; "No, I'm not, but what's wrong with that, if I were?"

Female: "Nothing, I can get you a guy if you like."

Ernie: "There's only one guy I want to see and that's Leroy. What's your name, young lady?"

Rose: "I'm Rose and she is Maria. Sit down; help yourself to a drink. I'll get him; he's in his office down in the cellar."

Ernie: "May I come along?"

Rosa: "No, I have to have his permission to bring someone down there."

Ernie: "OK, I'll just wait for him."

Eddie grabbed a can of 7-Up soda and sat on the couch until Leroy came up from the cellar.

Leroy: "What the fuck is wrong with you, Eddie? You could have played with these two and waited till I was finished."

Ernie: "No one said you were busy; I just want to confirm our deal and let you know where I will meet you."

Leroy: "OK, you want 10 bales of grass, 50 keys of cocaine and two keys of "H", am I right?"

Ernie: "That will be enough unless you can up the blow to 100 keys."

Leroy: "So you want 10 bales of grass, 100 keys of happy and two keys of "H" instead."

Ernie: "Yes, can you do it?"

Leroy: "Man, there ain't a fucken thing I can't do. You realize how much money we are talking here?"

Ernie: "Yeah, we are talking two million, four hundred and fifty thousand dollars cash every three or four months and I expect a kickback with each deal."

Leroy: "Kickback? I thought you were in charge."

Ernie: "I work with people who finance these things constantly for me and take care of the distribution as well."

Leroy: "So you want to fuck your partners."

Ernie: "No, just get what I should, that's all."

Leroy: "Then I will charge you an extra twenty thousand and that's your end."

Ernie: "No, they are not stupid."

Leroy: "How much do you want?"

Ernie: "I'm not greedy, just give me five thousand with every load this size; traveling money that's all."

Leroy: "OK, that's reasonable and I can handle that."

Ernie: "How soon can you be ready?"

Leroy: "I need another hour or two."

Ernie: "Then let's say 4 o'clock in that quarries area at the top of the hill by the fish quarry."

Leroy: "In Quincy?"

Ernie; "No, that's Braintree on the map."

Leroy: "Why there? I don't like going so far from home on deals like this."

Ernie; "In case anything goes wrong the quarries are right there to unload the goods in an emergency. They will sink and no one will find them. Secondly, it is a quiet place no one is there. We can take our time and check the money and the goods."

Leroy: "Eddie, anybody else I would put a bullet in their head and forget the whole thing. Since it's you and it's our first deal, I'll go along with you, but in the future we do the deals here. I will need three hours."

Ernie: "That's fine let's say five pm at the top of the hill in the quarries."

Leroy: "I'll be there with a small van that you can take if you like, just bring it back."

Ernie: "Thank you, Leroy, I will take you up on that. Usually I rent a small van for this type of deal."

Leroy: "How will you take both vehicles out, the one you come in with and a green van?"

Ernie: "I won't, I will be dropped off near there by friends and walk in. Then when you get there, I'll take your van and leave you with the satchel of money, so bring a second vehicle."

Leroy: "OK, that sounds good. I'll have arrangements for a second car to take me out."

Ernie: "I'm gonna leave, so that I can arrange for your cash. We have to count it three times at the bank before they turn it over to me."

Leroy: "Yes. I know how those banks are, so your people have accounts up here?"

Ernie: "They have accounts all over the world. There is no bigger organization then the one I'm with."

Leroy: "Sometime after this deal we have to talk, I have some great ideas that we should discuss."

Ernie: "I am always open to a good deal, my friend."

Leroy: "We will plan on that."

Ernie: "I'll see you at five."

Ernie left the Leroy Watkins house and as he left he again noticed the skylight which reminded him of a particular skylight in Brooklyn, NY where he grew up.

1955 Brooklyn

Ernie was raised at 388 St. Mark's Avenue in Brooklyn during the 1940's, and 50's, a neighborhood controlled by the Mafia. The neighborhood was a safe place to live and raise a family because the organized crime people made sure it was a safe place for all of the people, no matter what their color or nationality. These were all working class people and more interested in making a living then fighting. Different races lived in separate areas; one block would be Irish, one Italian, one black and so on, the only ones that would fight were the kids.

On St. Mark's Avenue across from where Ernie lived there was a factory where they made dresses, gowns and the famous Knox Hats. This building was four stories tall and two stories deep into the ground.

Ernie, a couple of friends and cousins—all about 12 years old—were playing around the building one summer evening when they got the idea of going into the building to sing because of the echo that this area caused when the sang. Later that night they decide to go up to the roof of the Knox building.

This was not strange to them because it was a common thing to go up on the roofs of the tenement houses that they all lived in. Ernie's cousin Lorenzo had homing pigeons on the roof that they all helped train. Sometimes they just hung out on Ernie's roof. In the summer they would throw water balloons down on the kids that passed by. They always found things to do.

The night in question Ernie, Lorenzo, Vincenzo and Antonio—a boy who lived in the same building as Ernie— all went into the building with the idea of singing because the echo was so great in the big hallway and it was a place to get out of the night air, summer and winter. The four boys stayed there singing popular songs for a while and admired their singing ability all by themselves. They were having fun.

They began to get tired of singing and started to investigate the building, up through the stairwell to each separate level. At the top Ernie looked down through the center of the stairwell; the stairs went around in a very large square leaving the center open from the subbasement all the way to the large square skylight on the roof. It had to be over 75 feet because each floor was at least twelve feet high.

They stopped on each floor and looked into the large rooms filled with sewing machines, on some floors people were working a night shift so the boys kept going quietly not really thinking about where they were going, just going. They were having some fun.

The four boys reached the top of the stairs and tried the door; it was not locked and opened onto the roof. They walked out onto the roof and went over to the edge and looked off it was pretty far down to the street.

Ernie: "That's about the same as our house, Antonio."
Antonio: "Yeah"

They walked along the perimeter of the roof all the way around until they reached the large clock which was in a separate tower above the roof on one corner of the building. The clock began to chime 9PM. Time to get home or they would be in trouble.

The boys began to run across the roof stepping on the steel-grated skylights with one step and jumping across them on their way to the exit. They approached the first, stepped and jumped, then the second skylight, the boys stepped and jumped then the third skylight, Lorenzo stepped and jumped, Vincenzo stepped and jumped, Ernie stepped, the steel cage protecting the skylight gave way and Ernie fell through and was stopped in mid air, with six stories under him. He was hanging by the hood attached to his jacket. Ernie looked down and saw that long six story drop below him, then looked up and saw Antonio standing at the edge of the skylight holding onto Ernie's hood which in turn, was holding Ernie in mid air. Antonio was behind Ernie when he fell through and grabbed the hood of Ernie's jacket. He saved Ernie's life, that night.

The other two boys came over and together they all pulled Ernie up and out of the skylight, onto the roof. Then it hit them, they broke the skylight. The four boys ran all the way down to the street and home. The next day they talked about how Lorenzo, Vincenzo and Antonio saved Ernie's life. The fun ended at that point.

Ernie arrived at the office, parked his car and went into the offices. He told everyone about what had happened at his meeting with Leroy Watkins, where the deal would take place and the quantity of illicit drugs involved. The men showed Ernie the plan they set up and where they would be to watch his moves when Watkins showed up for the deal.

Everything looked good. Tthey all prayed it would be safe.

Chapter 17

The Crap Shoot

Evening of June 12, 1980

All of the detectives were in place and it was time for Ernie to go up to the Quarries in Quincy. Detective Jack Wade stayed behind to drive Ernie and the money satchel to the entrance of the Quarries in case the entrance was being watched, then drive around the base of the hill and enter by walking up a back trail.

Eddie began walking up the hill and ten minutes later reached the top and the clearing next to the quarry. He placed the money satchel behind a tree out of site to create a few seconds of confusion if and when he needed it.

After a few minutes, Ernie could see a car was coming up the hill and behind it was a green van; this had to be Leroy Watkins and his henchmen.

The car stopped about 25 feet before reaching Ernie. Two men got out carrying M-16's or what looked like M-16's and those two men jumped behind a tree in a spot that gave them a good clear view of what was going on.

Leroy drove the van closer toward Eddie, got out from behind the wheel of the Van and moved toward the front of the van which placed him between Eddie and his shooters.

Leroy: "Eddie, are you ready to do this?"

Ernie: "Yeah, I'm ready; why all the hardware?"

Leroy: "They treat me like a baby, would not let me come alone."

Ernie: "OK, can I see the product?"

Leroy: "Sure, come on over. It's all ready for you. Look in the van."

Eddie walked over to the van. Leroy opened the side door which revealed 100 keys of cocaine, 2 keys of Heroin and the two bails of marijuana.

Leroy: "I have a question, Eddie."

Ernie: "What's that?"

Leroy: "Why do you buy only two bails of grass?"

Ernie: "I don't sell it. I give the grass away to my multi kilo customers as a gift, those that purchase two keys at a time or more get an amount of grass, sometimes as much as a pound, simply an incentive for my buyers."

Leroy: "That's a great Idea."

Ernie: "You're welcome to it."

Leroy: "Thanks, now what about the cash payment?"

Ernie: "I have it over there, I'll get it."

Eddie walked over toward the tree, adjusted his hat, the signal to move in. He heard a shot ring out; one of Leroy's people saw a detective in the woods, trying to move in closer and fired at the detective. Ernie jumped behind the tree where the money is supposed to be. This tree would be his protection as he returned fire.

Leroy yelled to Ernie: "Eddie there are cops here, you a cop?"

Ernie: "I believe there are, unless they are trying to rob us."

Eddie moved so the Leroy was between Ernie and Leroy's people in an effort to stay safe. Leroy was firing wildly at the trees around them.

Then another shot was fired and Leroy went down, Eddie jumped behind a tree and could hear shots going off and could feel the shots hitting the tree on the opposite side of him. About twenty-five shots went off, then it was quiet. Eddie could not see what was going on but could hear that Watkins was moaning while he lay on the ground. Ernie attempted to return fire, but could not get a good enough shot off.

The shots stopped and the area was quiet. He heard Detective Jack Wade yell, "Ernie, it's all clear, are you OK?"

Ernie ran over to Watkins and tried to help him, Watkins had been hit by his own men who had been trying to shoot Ernie. Watkins was bleeding badly from his chest and Ernie used his shirt to try and stop the bleeding. He yelled to the men that he needed an ambulance.

After a few moments an ambulance arrived and the driver gave Ernie a hospital shirt to wear as they took Watkins up to the hospital where he was operated on. Ernie walked over to take a look at the two men that arrived with Watkins and found that both men had been shot and both were dead.

Jack: "Ernie, do you know these guys?"

Ernie; "Yes, they are the two body guards that were always on the front steps of the house and Watkins balled them out for searching me the first time I went there."

Jack: "They won't be searching anyone else."

The detectives were later told that Watkins would pull through, but they would have to wait a few days before they could speak with him.

Ernie suggested not placing a guard on Watkins room. Ernie wasn't sure that Watkins realized that Ernie was a police officer. He wanted to create a false impression of freedom in case Watkins decided to speak with his partner or supplier. They would get a tap on his phone and wire his room for sound before he came out of surgery. The captain agreed with him.

Ernie and the other detectives took all of the illicit drugs into evidence, marked everything and transported all of the evidence to the station for lock up in a secure holding area.

At the Office:

Ernie contacted the Boston Police department and advised Detective Bob (Robert) Hendrickson that the buy was completed, Leroy Watkins was in the hospital being operated on and the two guards that are usually at the house were both dead.

Bob: "So the house should be fairly easy to enter."

Ernie: "Yeah, Bob, just one thing – the girls will probably be there and when I was there last he was in the cellar and I was not allowed to go down so there must be something down there."

Bob: "Ernie, do you and your guys want to come along?"

Ernie asked the men in the office: "Hey, guys, Bob is going to hit the house. Want to meet him there?"

Henry: "Tell him we are on our way."

Ernie: "Bob, did you hear that?"

Bob: "Yes, I'll see you there."

Ernie hung up the phone. He and the men left the station to go over to Boston and assist the Boston PD at their invitation to search the house.

Once Ernie and the other detectives arrived it was decided that Ernie should go in first since he is known by the girls. Ernie entered the house and one of the girls was standing a few feet away from the door, she looked up. "Eddie, where's Leroy?"

Ernie: "He's in the hospital."

Rosemarie: "Who are these men?"

Ernie: "They are detectives, stay calm; they have a search warrant."

Rose: "You ain't no, fucken cop, are you? You working with them?"

Ernie: "How many girls are here?"

Rose: "Three of us, here come the other two now."

All three girls were placed in the living room and the detectives began their search, they found nothing on the main floor except some very small quantities of white powder, believed to be Heroin after looking at the girl's arms. The girls had needle marks all over their arms and legs.

The detectives found the entrance to the cellar and walked down the stairs. As they reached the bottom they could see two large tables, then one of the men found the light switch.

The light went on and there were over 100 bales of marijuana against one wall, two tables were set up one for heroin and one for cocaine to package and cut. There was cutting powders on a shelf against another wall which were used to cut the potency of the heroin and cocaine. There were stacks of packaging papers and bags on another shelf.

This was a small factory with a safe which was against the farthest wall from the stairs. Ernie walked over to the safe, tried the handle and the safe was unlocked.

Ernie opened it and inside were stacks of money that was later counted out. The total came to five hundred and ninety thousand dollars in cash and a record book, all of which was taken as evidence.

Bob: "This is going to take all night, putting this together, marking and transporting."

Ernie: "Bob, any plans for the girls?"

Bob: "No not really, they're just caught up in this garbage."

Ernie: "How about taking them to the drug center, maybe they can help them?"

Bob: "Whatever you want to do, Ernie. is OK with me. I will charge them with possession and that's about it, your guy Leroy Watkins will take the hit for all of this."

Ernie: "Good, thanks. We'll talk to them together and then send them off, maybe we can turn this into something good."

Bob: "OK, let them sit for a while until we get this straightened out."

Hendrickson made a few calls to his department to get the ball rolling and to get some more assistance at the house, then went with Ernie to speak to the girls.

Bob: "Hi girls, we need your names, dates of birth and where you come from and now live and I want to see some identification."

Rose: "I'm Rosie Roberts, we all live here I'm from Texas. I came up here looking to get into the entertainment business. I guess I did that OK."

Bob: "How old are you, Rose?"

Rose: "I was born September 15, 1960 I'm 20 years old."

Ernie: "Do your parents know where you are?"

Rose: "Yes, I send them money from time to time."

Bob: "And you, Miss, your name?"

Joanna: "I am Joanna Harris, I was born June 30, 1958, I'm 22 and I come from West Virginia."

Bob: "And you'll be 23 soon?"

Joanna: "Yes."

Bob: "And you, Miss?"

Shirina: "I am Shirina Brown, I am 19 years old, my birthday is April 4, 1961 and I come from Connecticut."

Ernie: "Your parents know where you are?"

Shirina: "No, and I don't want them to know."

Bob: "OK, Shirina, you're of age."

Ernie: "Girls, Detective Hendrickson is going to charge you with possession and we would like to take you to the drug center to see if they can help you withdraw, if you agree."

Shirina: "What if we don't agree?"

Ernie: "Then he will still charge you. He will book you and you will be placed in a cell until your trial; your choice."

The three girls talked together for a minute then agreed to go to the drug treatment center for help.

Ernie: "Just one more thing, girls; I want the names and ages of the other two girls so that we can help them also."

Rose: "I don't think we should do that."

Ernie: "That's part of the deal, take it or leave it."

Rose: "One is Rosemarie Sanchez, she is 23 years old and from here is Massachusetts, the other is Anny Grapolis, 22 years old, also from Massachusetts."

Ernie: "OK, thank you, girls. A car will be here soon to take you to the Center. One point: don't think you can fake it at the center. If you do not cooperate, we will simply move forward with the drug charges."

Ernie and Bob left the girls with a uniformed man and walked down to the basement.

Ernie: "Bob, that's two parts of this completed."

Bob: "Two parts?"

Ernie: "Yes, the buy bust and the house search."

Bob: "What else in there?"

Ernie: "I thought I told you, we have some bodies to dig up."

Bob: "I think that I would remember some bodies. I don't think you mentioned that. If you did I don't remember. Anyway, we can handle it. It's very late, Ernie; you don't want to do that now?"

Ernie: "No, tomorrow we will start fresh in the daylight and we will need a backhoe. Bob, my guys and I will take off and I'll call you in the morning."

Bob: "Not a problem; whatever we need, we'll get."

After assisting with the evidence, Ernie and the rest of the Quincy men left the area.

Friday, June 13, 1980

Ernie arrived at the office early and waited for the men to come in. While waiting he started the shooting reports. The reports for the drug buy and the report for the assist to Boston on the search of Leroy Watkins' home. Each man as he came in had to do a report on the shooting of the two men with Watkins and their individual parts in the search.

After Watkins was operated on, the detectives took the shell that hit Watkins as evidence. Detective Henry Griswold, the firearms expert, took the shell and did an analysis on it that showed that the weapon that fired the shell was an M-16. That specific M-16 was carried by one of Watkins men. None of the detectives carried that powerful a weapon.

This information proved to all of the men that Watkins was not shot by one of them or by one of their ricochets.

Ernie: "Guys, we have to file for a search warrant for the grounds of the Zoo, Franklyn Park."

Jack: "We don't need that, Ernie; they should let us do what we have to do."

Ernie: "You're wrong, what happens when the defense attorney asks for the search warrant that was issued by the court to search for the bodies?"

Jack: "Oh, yeah, you're right; they do have a tendency to be picky about those things. I forgot about that point."

Ernie: "I'll file for it. Call Boston and we'll be off."

Ernie typed up a brief affidavit requesting that the court issue an order to search for the bodies, based on information received from the two subjects. Sonia Levin, a/k/a, Chicken whose information described the temperament of the suspect Leroy Watkins and Petri Anderson whose information was received from the suspect Leroy Watkins.

Ernie took the completed affidavit and went to the Court, filed the paperwork and a search warrant was issued. He used a phone at the Court to contact Detective Hendrickson and tell him what he was doing and that he would meet him at the Zoo in an hour.

Ernie: "Bob, do you have any idea where we can get one of those machines that show what's underground?"

Bob: "Yes, I know that the museum has one, I'll call them and see if they can meet us at the zoo; we're looking for two bodies, correct?"

Ernie: "Yes, As far as I know two bodies."

Bob: "See you there."

Ernie went back to the office and told the men that he had obtained the search warrant and that he spoke with Detective Hendrickson. They were to meet Hendrickson at the Zoo in an hour.

An hour later, Ernie and the other Quincy detectives pulled up to the front of the Zoo. Parked in front of the Zoo was a truck from the Boston Museum of Art and Antiquities with a Mr. Hayes in the driver's seat. Behind him was, Detective Hendrickson in another car and a large trailer with a backhoe on it behind that.

Ernie: "Wow, you were fast, Bob."

Bob: "This is what you told me you needed."

They walked around the perimeter of the Zoo looking for locations that may be good spots to start checking for the bodies. They found two areas and Mr. Hayes from the museum and operator of the machine, found a third spot to check.

Across Blue Hill Avenue from the Zoo property stood city blocks of apartment houses. Many of these apartments over looked the Zoo area and the residents could easily see what the police were doing along the Zoo walls.

The men had checked two of the spots and were now checking the third when something hit the ground alongside one of the officers; no sound just a scraping and then nothing.

Standing there was Detective Lijoi, Hendrickson, two other detectives and a couple of uniformed men covering the area. They were all watching Mr. Hayes who was using his machine to check the ground for the bodies buried below the ground that they were standing on.

Ernie was talking with Det. Bob Hendrickson when one of the uniformed men standing behind them fell to the ground grabbing Det. Hendrickson on the way down in an effort to keep standing. They all gathered around the man and saw the he had a hole in his chest that went right through and left a larger hole in his back. He had been shot.

They pulled the man out of harm's way behind the backhoe. They tried to determine where the shot came from. Then there was another shot, ricocheting off the backhoe, another and yet another.

Ernie saw a curtain move and a person with what appeared to be a hand gun with a silencer on it standing to the side of the curtain. This person looked like it could be women and he thought she may have grey hair.

They called for assistance and an ambulance to help the man that had been shot, however it appeared that he was dead since the bullet went right through his heart.

They concentrated their efforts on getting to that apartment which was across the street directly opposite where the Police detectives and Officers were working.

Ernie worked his way from the backhoe to the bushes and trees along the Zoo wall. He went behind the bushes and along the wall to get a good distance away from the action. He crossed the street to the side that the houses were on. Ernie waved back to the men that he was OK and then Jack did the same thing.

Together they worked their way to the building where Ernie had observed the person in the window. There were no more shots fired and a total of nine shots had been fired. The entire neighborhood was quiet. The two detectives entered the building and went up to the fourth floor then figured out which apartment it was that Ernie saw the person in the window. The doors were very thin and could easily be pushed in. They decided on the apartment, Jack took a low stance while Ernie kicked in the door.

He raised his foot and kicked, the door lock gave and the door swung opened. Ernie was now standing in the doorway. Straight ahead of Ernie was an elderly woman, with grey hair, holding a hand gun she raised it and pulled the trigger, but the gun did not fire.

Ernie and Jack jumped behind furniture in the room, but did not return fire. The women pointed the gun again, pulled the trigger and the gun did not fire. The gun was empty.

Neither of the two men had it in their heart to fire back at an old lady who may not even know what she was doing. They both had the impression that she was in some kind of a daze and didn't really know what she was doing. When she pointed the gun, it was pointed too high each time. When the gun did not fire, she spoke.

Mrs. Watkins: "That stupid son of a bitch; he gives me a gun to watch his jobs and doesn't give me enough ammunition."

Ernie walked up to her, took the gun and sat her down.

Ernie: "Now tell us what you are talking about?"

Mrs. Watkins: "My son Leroy told me that if anyone went near that spot with digging tools to shoot them. He gave me this gun with just the few bullets that were in it."

Ernie: "Leroy? Are you Mrs. Watkins?"

Mrs. Watkins: "Yes, son, I think I am."

Ernie: "How old are you?"

Mrs. Watkins: "35."

Ernie: "How old did you say?"

Mrs. Watkins: "I am 82 years old."

Ernie: "Do you have children?"

Mrs. Watkins: "No, sorry."

Ernie: "Are you sure you don't have any children?"

Mrs. Watkins: "Of course I do – my baby Leroy."

Ernie: "Am I correct in saying that if you had more bullets you would have shot me as I came through that door?"

Mrs. Watkins: "Yes, I would do anything for my baby."

Ernie: "I can understand that, Mrs. Watkins, but it would have been murder. Do you understand that?"

Mrs. Watkins: "Yes, I understand, I'm 82 years old. What can they do to me, feed me the rest of my life?"

Jack: "Mrs. Watkins, you are under arrest for attempted murder. We'll let the District Attorney work this one out."

Jack: "Ernie, let's send her over to the hospital and have a doctor look she over. Obviously she has some dementia."

Ernie: "Yes, it is obvious. That was what I planned to do, Jack."

Detective Hendrickson walked into the apartment just as Ernie was cuffing the elderly women in the front and then he stopped and took the cuff off of her.

Ernie: "We don't need cuffs, do we, Bob? She has to go over to the hospital."

Bob: "No cuffs. I think we can handle her. One of the cruisers will take her over and stay with her."

The elderly women was taken down and placed in a cruiser and transported to the Boston police Station, District 3 for booking.

Bob: "Shall we get back to the search for the bodies?"

The men left the apartment, during the walk back to the site, Detective Hendrickson told them that this incident reminded him of a story about an incident that happened to one of his people several years ago.

1975 Boston

This is a story about Detective Jack Broland a black man, 5'8" tall, thin. 50 years of age, with a large mustache sporting the upper lip of his long face, a good man who always tried to do his job and never took advantage of anyone.

He worked as a narcotics detective in the City of Boston. He did search warrants on occasion and did a lot of surveillance; he seemed to like the surveillances. Often Jack would offer to do surveillances for the other men in the unit. He was the kind of the guy that would do the tedious, boring work, stay in the background and as I said on occasion he would get enough information on his own to do a search warrant of his own.

One night while doing surveillance on a house for another detective, Jack was approached by a man, named David, which he had arrested a few years earlier.

David: "Hi, Jack, how are you?"

Jack: "David, I'm fine thanks—and you?"

David: "Good, Jack, let me say thanks. Had you not caught me when you did I would be in serious trouble today."

Jack: "My pleasure, glad I could help you."

David: "Look, I'd like to help you out."

David proceeded to tell Jack about a house where some very serious dealing of cocaine was going on. Jack listened and wrote everything down that David told him. He thanked David for the information and then went back to the station to start a case report on the information. The next day Jack proudly turned in his report which indicated the entire story about how he received the information.

The Lieutenant liked the information and it fit with some other information that the unit had received in the past from a reliable informant. A reliable informant is someone who has given information in the past which had led to the arrest and conviction of a person for a criminal action.

Jack was given the case and he took off immediately, doing his surveillance—watching the building, checking the mailbox for names. There were two names in that building. On one side lived Mr. & Mrs. Furlough and on the other side was Mr. Robert Anderson. The target of the investigation was Mr. Anderson.

The surveillance went on for about two months and Jack observed numerous people coming and going from the duplex building. He would take the automobile plate numbers and run the numbers to find the owners then run the owners for criminal records and found that several of the people had been arrested for narcotics violations in the past.

Jack waited until he had plenty of information and until the man in the house had a good supply. He knew this by virtue of the traffic at the house and the days that the buyers showed up. He found that Thursday was the big day, the most traffic at the house, the most felons visited there.

On the following Thursday he waited for a known drug user to drive up enter the building and stay a short time. Jack followed the user after he left the building, called for a cruiser to stop him which was done. Jack pulled up and asked the man to exit the vehicle. Jack smelled the inside of the car and could smell that definite odor of marijuana which gave Jack probable cause to search the vehicle, but he found nothing more than an old joint and a crack pipe in the ashtray.

He walked over to the driver and searched the driver who had an $1/8^{th}$ of an ounce rock of crack in his pocket all wrapped up. Jack arrested the subject and transported him back to the station, he took the evidence and tagged and bagged it and turned it into the evidence locker along with a copy of his report on the arrest. The car was confiscated and towed to the police lot where Jack could do a better search at a later date.

This case was pulling together better than any case Jack had ever completed; the recent arrest along with all of the other information that Jack had gathered throughout his investigation put Jack into a position where he was now ready to do the search warrant affidavit.

Jack went over everything carefully piece by piece of the entire case and put it all in an easy to read and understand form for the courts. He took his affidavit down to the court house while the other men waited for him at the Police Station to assist him in his efforts to close this case.

While at the court Jack appeared before the Clerk of Court, the issuing authority, and answered some minor questions. The clerk wished him, good luck with the search and issued the Search Warrant.

Jack went to the station and told the men that the traffic usually started about 8 pm so the best time should be about an hour earlier, 7 pm.

Everyone was in agreement that since it was Jacks case, he and the backup men would be the first to enter the house with the front door crew. These are the men that use a special tool to knock the door off of its hinges, if necessary.

The other men would cover the windows and the back of the house in case anyone tried to get away, would only enter upon word that the people in the house or apartment were secure and the location was safe.

They were all ready and drove to the duplex residence.

Jack told everyone to make sure that once in the hallway, they are to enter the unit on the right. The unit on the left side is occupied by a man and his wife who are un-known to Jack.

The moment came, after several months of surveil-lance and investigation Jack was there, standing outside the door, ready to enter the unit. Jack knocked on the door and sang out, "Boston Police." No answer.

The men stepped up, hit the door with the large steel battering ram, on the second blow the door came down.

They heard screaming and saw an elderly women, about 80 years old, who was obviously coming to the door, slowly running around in a circle yelling and screaming, "He's back, he's back from the dead, he said he'd come back, he's back, he's back"

Jack walked over to her and grabbed her and finally calmed her down.

Jack: "Miss we are the Boston police and we have a search warrant."

She finally calmed down and Jack handed her a copy of the search warrant.

She looked at it and asked what it was for, she didn't know legal stuff, she always left that to her husband who passed away a couple of days ago. They just buried him that morning.

Jack: "Miss this search warrant is for narcotics."

Women: "You want all my husband's medications, there in our bed room I'll get them."

Jack: "No Miss, what is the address here?"

Women: "This is 456A Kennedy lane, young man."

Jack: "Guys, we hit the wrong place. The search war-rant reads 456A which means we are in the correct place, but the guy we want is in 456B Kennedy Lane."

Jack checked the mail boxes and found that the person he was after in apartment "B" had switched the names and numbers on the mail boxes to protect him against such an occurrence.

Jack apologized and left the home stating that everything would be repaired that day.

Back at the Zoo, the Grave Area

Ernie: "That's happened more than once, going into the wrong house. Did they eventually get the right one?"

Bob: "Yes, it took time, but they finally got it all straight."

All of the men joked about the incident and related it to the elderly women that they arrested a few minutes earlier. They arrived at the site of the third area to be checked when Mr. Hayes asked how many bodies they were looking for.

Ernie: "We were told that there should be two bodies here."

Hayes: "I can tell you for sure that there are more than two bodies here, I think there are four."

Bob: "Have you been able to pinpoint them?"

Hayes: "Yes, I believe that if you dig right from the wall out between those two bushes you should find them all; this area also happens to be opposite that apartment."

Jack: "What an idiot. He placed his mother in a position where she had to protect his private grave yard."

Ernie: "Bob, I'm sorry, but since this is Boston, this is all yours. Do you want to call the medical examiner and the morgue to pick up the bodies?"

Bob: "Sure, Ernie. Don't be sorry, what else would I do? At least this takes up the day."

Ernie: "Thanks, and please tell the medical examiner that we need any bullets that he finds in these bodies because I may have the weapon that was used."

Bob: "I will take care of it. Henry, will you pick them up when they are ready and test them?"

Henry: "I will be happy to take care of it, Bob."

The Quincy officers stayed until the four bodies were located and taken away; it was obvious that every one of them had been shot to death.

After the bodies were gone The Quincy Detectives left the area and went back to their office in Quincy.

It had been a long day and after making notes for their reports the detectives decided to call it a day and head to their homes, wives and girlfriends.

Chapter 18

The Hospital

Saturday, June 14, 1980

Ernie had breakfast with Teresa and saw the boys off to school. He had a cup of coffee with Teresa. She asked if he was going to stay in the narcotics field of police work or move on to another area less dangerous.

Ernie told Teresa that some day he would simply move into the office, take a permanent desk job and simply offer his opinions and ideas to the younger officers and detectives at that time, if they don't think that he is too old fashioned or old school by then.

Teresa did not push Ernie, but he could see that she was getting tired of the waiting and worrying about him and whether or not he would make it home at night. Ernie decided to try and let the subject die out on its own for the time being.

Teresa: "Ernie, this is not getting easier. You refuse to talk about the job. I read the news and watch the news on TV. I can see what is going on, especially when an officer gets shot by an old lady. I feel for the family of the man that got shot, but all I can think of, is that it could have easily been you that is being buried."

Ernie: "I know. I'll try to be more open with you in the future. But my silence has become a necessary habit for the job; silence is a protector; as a police officer we need it."

Teresa: "I understand. I just want to be kept in the loop, as you say."

Ernie: "OK, I'll do my best."

He finished his coffee and started out for the office, whistling to the mocking bird as he walked to the car and driving off with that smile that the mockingbird always gave him from their exchange of notes.

At the office he met with the other detectives who were all there to finish their own reports on the completion of the Leroy Watkins case. Ernie told them that his part of the case was not over, because he had to meet with Watkins, tell him about his mother and see what he has to say for himself about the bodies.

Jack spoke up and said that he had already called the hospital and the doctor asked if we should wait until Monday to speak with Watkins.

Ernie: "What did you tell him, Jack?"

Jack: "That as long as you agreed, I had no problem with waiting till Monday."

Ernie: "Monday it is. We'll go up there Monday morning about 9 am, baring interruptions. Will you be going with me, Jack?"

Jack: "You could not keep me away from that meeting."

The men completed their reports which took all morning. After lunch they gathered the reports together and Ernie took copies over to John Hageman, the District Attorney's office in Dedham.

At the district Attorney's office Ernie met with the DA who took the reports and read them over.

John: "You're telling me that this asshole had his own mother, who is ill with dementia, as a guard for his dead bodies?"

Ernie: "That's what she told us, I am not really sure she knows what was buried there."

John: "Do I detect a bit of compassion for her?"

Ernie: "She's 82 years old and those cell blocks are not that easy to sleep in."

John: "Get back to me after you speak with Leroy Watkins and I'll see what I can do for her. Remember, Ernie, she did kill a cop."

Ernie: "I think that she should be tested mentally because I am not so sure she knew what she was doing or saying."

John: "I tend to agree with that statement, Ernie. Get back to me after your meeting with her son, Watkins."

Ernie: "I will call you Monday."

On Sunday, Ernie and Teresa took the boys to the Boston Aquarium and once the sun started going down they treated the kids to some time at the St. Anthony Feast in the North end of Boston.

They had a great day and the Feast brought back to memory Ernie's life as a boy In Brooklyn and the feast they used to have.

Monday June 16, 1980

On Monday morning, at the office one of the men spoke of the religious feast in Boston which was held every year and is a tremendous party where everyone is invited to enjoy themselves in the streets of the North End of Boston. Ernie could not resist the opportunity to tell the men about the feast that he attended in his neighborhood in Brooklyn, New York, every year as he grew up.

Brooklyn 1940's, 1950's & 60's

Ernie was raised in an area that was predominantly Italian and Irish. In that area there were two Italian American clubs; one was the St. Andrew Club and the other was St. Sebastian Club, each of which had a separate feast each of the years that he lived there.

These clubs were frequented by what was then known as the Old Mustachios, the older Italian men of the neighborhood who were retired from various types of work. They would stay in the club all day long playing a common Italian card game called Setta Mezzi—Seven and a half—a game similar in some ways to the card game twenty one.

Each year they would put on a feast for all of the people that wished to come and take advantage of the speeches, music, singing, dancing, the Italian food that was sold on the streets and the games that were played. The streets were lit up at night with strings of hanging lights running across the entire street from one side to the other attached to poles high over the crowds of people that attended.

During the Feast period of one week they would have a special challenge for the young men of the neighborhood who would form teams.

In an empty lot where the boys played ball all summer, the men would erect a tall pole about 30 feet high, greased from the top down to the middle of the pole.

Nailed to the top of the pole was a cross of wood and hanging from the wood were long whole salami's , Prosciutto's, Capocolla, Provalone, Mortadella, Pancetta and more. Located in the middle at the very top of the pole was a ($50.00) fifty dollar bill to be split among the team that made it to the top.

At age 15 Ernie finally made it on to one of the teams along with both of his cousins, Lorenzo and Vincent. That year those boys used the usual strategy to get to the top.

A few boys, arms locked together, formed a circle around the bottom, then the next group on top of their shoulders doing the same and on and on until no one was left except the thinnest and smallest of them all, cousin Vincenzo.

Two years in a row Vincenzo made it to the top, cut all of the meats off and threw them down to the ground, took the money, put it in his pocket then slid down the pole to the ground where the entire team split the winnings and the meats and gave each of the other teams some of the meats. Those days for Ernie could never be replaced in his mind or his heart.

The detectives listened intently and asked questions about the pole climbing.

Henry: "Boy, you wouldn't see anything like that to-day, people would say you were trying to kill the kids."

Jack: "People have gotten too soft in my estimation, what do you think, Ernie."

Ernie: "Everything changes Jack, I don't even think about it anymore, I know one thing: when I was a kid we walked around with holes in our shoes that we filled with cardboard or folded paper, not anymore, the kids today wouldn't even know what that felt like."

Jack replied; "Yeah, I remember those days even here in the country."

Ernie: "Another thing, we use to walk to school, no snow days, there was no such thing. We would walk about five miles each way just to save a nickel for the bus. Then the bus ride went to a dime and we were really saving money. No such thing as a school bus in those days. I could go on and on."

Jack: "I believe it, Ernie, the kids today don't know how good they have it and they don't care."

Ernie: "Jack, do you want to go over to the Hospital and interview Leroy?"

Jack: "What about you, aren't you going?"

Ernie: "I don't think it's wise yet. Don't tell him that Petri is alive and don't mention me. I don't think he knows who I really am. Let's surprise him in court or talk to him separately and see what happens."

Jack: "OK. Henry, do you want to go with me?"

Henry: "Yes, I'll go, but you know the case so you do all the talking."

The two men drove to the hospital and were directed to the room of Mr. Leroy Watkins.

Jack: "Mr. Watkins, how are you feeling?"

Watkins: "I'm fine, which one of you pricks shot me?"

Jack: "We did not shoot you, sir."

Watkins: "Then who shot me?"

Jack: "Your men shot you by accident."

Watkins: "Where are those bastards? I'll break their skulls and use them as coffee mugs!"

Jack: "Both Herbert and Perry are dead and after analysis we discovered that the shell that was taken out of you fits the gun of the tall lanky guy."

Watkins: "Those two assholes belong dead after pulling something like that. Is Eddie dead also?"

Jack: "Who? That bystander that was there? We let him go."

Watkins: "You let him go?"

Jack: "Yes, why? Who is he?"

Watkins: "It's too late now, but he is the guy…" Watkins stopped talking.

Jack: "What's wrong? Did we miss something important?"

Watkins: "No, no, I guess you did the right thing. You got the drugs, right?"

Jack: "Yes, we got them. The drugs are not your biggest problem."

Watkins: "What do you mean?"

Jack: "Well, we have some bodies that you have to answer for. You get better and we'll talk after your preliminary hearing."

Watkins: "Bodies? What bodies?"

Jack: "Oh, yes, I almost forgot. Your mother is under arrest for shooting and killing a police officer."

Watkins: "You searched the wall?"

Jack: "Sir, before we go any further, you should know that you have the right to remain silent and not answer any questions. You have the right to an attorney. You have the right to have an attorney present at questioning or call an attorney before questioning and if you cannot afford an attorney one will be appointed to you by the court. Do you understand these rights?"

Watkins: "Yeah, Yeah, I understand, I've been there before."

Jack: "Do you wish to speak with us without an attorney? If you do, you may stop at anytime you wish."

Watkins: "Yeah, I'll speak with you."

Jack: "Sir, without an attorney, you will speak with us?"

Watkins: "Yes, without an attorney."

Jack: "To answer your question, yes, we found the wall at the zoo and the gun that you gave your mother to protect that area. She shot one of our men as you directed her to do."

Watkins: "How is she?"

Jack: "She's OK, in a retirement home under guard because we didn't want to place an 82 year old senile woman in a jail cell."

Watkins: "Thanks for that. What do you guys need?"

Jack: "Why did you kill those people that you buried at the Zoo wall?"

Watkins: "I didn't kill them."

Jack: "You didn't?"

Watkins: "No, some asshole I was working with named Peter killed them. That's all I know about the killing of those people."

Jack: "What do you know about this Peter? What does he look like?"

Watkins: "Nothing much, he's a white male, 5'8" tall, brown hair with brown eyes a lot of hair on his face and an afro, real curly."

Jack: "That sounds like that Eddie character we let go?"

Watkins: "Yeah that does sound like him, but get this straight, I didn't do it. You don't have a gun, no statements, no witnesses, nothing, just the drugs, so you guys are up a creek with no paddle."

Jack: "Mr. Watkins, we will look into this Peter person and let the District Attorney sort it all out at the trial."

Watkins: "See you then, guys, I can handle the drugs alone, no problem. I gave you the killer so that should help me and my mother."

Jack: "Don't you have concern for your mother?"

Watkins: "I will get her the best defense I can, she'll be OK. She's senile anyway. That info on the killer will help. My lawyer will see to that."

Jack: "Mr. Watkins, if that's all you have to say for yourself, we'll see you in court."

The two detectives left the hospital and drove back to the office where they completed a report on the interview with Leroy Watkins

Ernie read the report and began laughing at the fact that Watkins was trying to put the bodies on him as well as the drugs and did not realize that Eddie Pannoni, his buyer, was really Detective Ernie Lijoi Sr, the man he tried to scare by dropping the body of Sonia Levin, a/k/a Chicken in the park area of Quincy.

Ernie: "This guy has some real surprises coming."

Jack: "Ernie maybe you should visit him and see what happens."

Ernie: "I don't know, Jack, I guess I could go up and just stay a very short time. Who knows what he will say or do?"

Jack: "There are so many possibilities."

Ernie: "Yes, I'll wait until tomorrow and then go up for a few minutes."

Ernie finished up the day at the office and then went home.

Tuesday June 17, 1980

Ernie arrived at the office late because he stopped at the District Attorney's office to drop off the reports regarding the interview that Jack had with Leroy Watkins at the hospital.

Later that morning, Ernie changed his demeanor to
Eddie Pannoni and went to the hospital where he entered
Watkins room.

Watkins: "Eddie, they told me they let you go. How
the fuck did you work that out?"

Ernie: "My friend, I plan ahead."

Watkins: "Plan ahead?"

Ernie: "Yes, the buy money was not with me, I had ID
for another person with my face on it and I had a dog tied
up to a tree a short distance away. It all made sense to the
cops. I was just walking the dog and heard the shooting.
They let me go."

Watkins: "I think they may be looking for you now."

Ernie: "They'll never find me. I've got a more serious
problem though."

Watkins: "What's that?"

Ernie: "I have to go back to New York empty, I hate
doing that."

Watkins: "Fuck, no you don't."

Ernie: "What do you mean?"

Watkins: "I was in the service with a guy years ago.
We served in Vietnam together. He was and is connected,
very high on the totem pole."

Ernie: "Yes, I know people like that also, but how does
that help me?"

Watkins: "That's what I'm telling you, Eddie. You call
the number I give you and tell him I am here in the hospital."

Ernie: "Tell who, tell them what?"

Watkins: "Go down the hall to the phone booth and
call this number. Ask for Mr. Lucasie. Use my name Leroy
Watkins and the code name that he used to call me, 'the

bogyman'. Tell him that I'm here, to come visit me right away."

Ernie: "OK, but what if he won't talk to me?"

Watkins: "Just mention the bogeyman, he'll talk to you. It was a personal joke we had in Vietnam"

Ernie walked down the hall to the reception area and made the phone call.

Ernie: "Hello."

Unknown: "Who is this?"

Ernie: "My name is Eddie and the bogeyman Leroy Watkins said for me to talk to Mr. Lucasie."

Unknown: "Hold on."

Lucasie: "Hello, Leroy?"

Ernie: "No sir, I am his friend, Eddie. He's in the hospital in Quincy and said for you to come here, please."

Lucasie: "Did he say anything else?"

Ernie: "He just said to mention the private joke you had in Vietnam and the name bogeyman"

Lucasie: "Are you there now, Eddie?"

Ernie: "Yes sir."

Lucasie: "Stay there and meet me out front of the hospital in 20 minutes."

Ernie: "OK, sir. I'll be here."

After making that call Ernie called the office and made arrangements for the men to cover the arrival of Mr. Lucasie and get pictures. Then he went back to Leroy and told him his friend was on the way. The next thing was to go to the entrance and wait as instructed by Mr. Lucasie.

While waiting Ernie could see the men pulling in and getting into position to get pictures of the arrival of the big boss.

Ernie stayed in the front of the hospital for about 25 minutes when a long blue limousine pulled up and stopped in front of Ernie. A large white male got out from the front passenger side of the vehicle and opened the rear door and a white male dressed in a pin-stripped suit with a white shirt, open collar got out of the back seat of the car. He was about 5'6" tall, quite heavy set yet appeared to be muscular, slightly balding, clean shaven Italian male. This was Mr. Lucasie

Ernie: "Signore di buon pomeriggio" (Good afternoon, sir)

Lucasie: "Buono, buono, take me to him. You are Italian, Eddie?"

Ernie: "Yes sir, I am associated in New York, possibly with mutual friends."

Eddie's statement meant that they had mutual friends if Lucasie was a "made" man, in which case he would understand the expression, "mutual friends."

Lucasie: "I'm not that high yet, but it's going to happen shortly, I hear."

Ernie: "Congratulations in anticipo" (Congratulations in advance)

Lucasie: "Grazie, Grazie" (Thank you, thank you)

Ernie: "Here we are. This is his room." They walked into the room and Leroy called Eddie to the bed.

Watkins: "Eddie, do me a favor, leave us alone for a few moments."

Ernie: "No problem"

Eddie walked out of the room and waited outside along with the bodyguard of Mr. Fraido Lucasie. After a few minutes Mr. Lucasie asked Eddie to come back in and told his bodyguard to wait in the hall.

Watkins: "Eddie; Fraido will take care of your needs while I'm tied up with this situation."

Ernie: "That's fine, Leroy, how soon can we put something together?"

Lucasie: "The phone number that Leroy gave you to call me earlier is the number to reach me. We can get together tonight at the Horse Shoe Bar Lounge, which I own, just over the bridge from Quincy. Do you know it?"

Ernie; "As a matter of fact I do know the place. I was there last week. When I came into town a friend took me there."

Lucasie: "When I saw you I thought you looked familiar—that's where I have seen you."

Ernie: "Yes sir, so I'll see you there tonight."

Lucasie: "I'll be there."

Mr. Lucasie left to join his bodyguard. They left the area together.

Ernie then thanked Watkins for his help and left the area.

Chapter 19

The Mafia Takedown

Tuesday June 17, 1980 8PM

Ernie walked into the lounge called the Horse Shoe Lounge which was located just over the line in Boston, only one hundred yards from the Quincy town line.

This lounge took its name from the horseshoe bar in the center of the large room; to the left side was another large area for dancing with a juke box and a small stage for entertainment. On the right side were about 25 tables and along the back wall were several booths.

One of the booths was separated from the rest of them by a solid wall. This room had drapes hanging in front of it so that no one could see what was going on inside.

Ernie saw the bodyguard that drove the limousine, standing just outside of the draped room and walked over to him.

Ernie: "Hi, I was at the hospital this afternoon."

Guard: "Yeah, I know who you are, Eddie. Wait here."

The drapes opened and the guard told Eddie to go ahead in. Eddie entered a colorful room with red drapes hanging the entire perimeter of the room. Mr. Lucasie was sitting at a large table in the middle of the room.

Ernie: "Signore di buona sera" (good evening Sir)

Lucasie: "Buona, Buona (Typical Italian reply) Have a seat, Eddie."

Ernie: "Thank you sir"

Lucasie: "Call me Fraido, and I want you to know that I'm doing Leroy a favor here. I will fill your order for you. The payment will go to me, instead of him."

Ernie: "That's very kind of you, Fraido."

Lucasie: "In the future, you will deal with me, not Leroy, since he will be going away for a while. Leroy and I have discussed this. When he gets out you can make your choice and go back to him or stay with me."

Ernie: "Sir, both my New York family and I thank you for your kindness, generosity and understanding."

Lucasie: "No problem, no problem at all. Leroy and I go way back to Vietnam together. He is a great guy to have on your side in a firefight; of course we are starting to get a little older now and don't move so well, but we don't have to anymore."

Ernie: "Did Leroy tell you what I wanted?"

Lucasie: "Yes, I have your whole order and it's all ready for you, but I would like to know which of the five families' you are with? I have associated with all of them."

Ernie: "Fraido, I don't mean to be disrespectful, but that's not something I speak of at all. Not until I am very sure of the situation around me."

Lucasie: "I can respect that. We will speak of this again in the near future."

Ernie: "Thank you for your understanding."

Lucasie: "I like you, you're smart. That situation at the Quarries was unbelievable and you simply walked away clean because you think in advance. Once I am made, I will need people like you to handle things, my men could learn from you."

Ernie: "I must protect myself, my interest and my family."

Lucasie: "That's what I like, you're very sharp. I will have a position for someone like you, in time."

Ernie: "Fraido, where and when can we do this deal and close it out?"

Lucasie: "Here is what I want you to do; call Alberto in the morning, not too early around 10am is OK. You and he come to an agreement on where and when to do the deal and he will be there with the product for you."

Ernie: "That sounds like a plan, but who is Alberto?"

Lucasie laughed: "Alberto is my bodyguard, you have met him."

Ernie took the phone number of Alberto, said his goodbye's and left the lounge.

Ernie's day was finally over, he headed home and as soon as he hit the bed he was off to sleep.

Wednesday June 18, 1980

Ernie was awake early, the house was very still and quiet. He carefully got out of bed, took a quick shower, dressed and left the house so he did not disturb anyone.

As soon as he walked out the door the mockingbird started. Ernie was afraid he would wake the kids because their bedrooms were in the front of the house, so he drove off right away. Ernie was running over all the dangers and possibilities for the day in his mind and how busy this day was going to be as he drove to the office.

He arrived at the office and began doing his reports immediately about the meeting with Fraido Lucasie and his instructions to contact Alberto at 10 am on that morning. As he was finishing his report Jack Wade walked into the office with Henry Griswold and right behind them were

Jerry Gibson, Rick Bradshaw, Carl Robinson, the entire team was present.

Ernie: "I'm glad to see you guys, we have a big day. I hope you are all free because we have a major case to close."

They all put down their coffee and turned towards Ernie. They all started talking at once.

What happened at your meeting? What do we do next? How late will we be going on this? Ernie couldn't understand everything, with everyone talking and asking questions at the same time.

Ernie: "Guys, read this report, then we will talk. I will have a cup of coffee."

The men all read the report that Ernie just finished typing. They were amazed that Ernie had been accepted so easily and that this was even happening after the arrest of Watkins.

Jack: "This is amazing, Ernie."

Ernie: "I'll set up the buy for the evening so that we can have plenty of time to cover the meeting place. Second, we will do an affidavit so that we have a search warrant for Lucasie's Horse Shoe Bar Lounge. The second team will be ready to hit the lounge and arrest Lucasie and his body guard."

Henry: "Ernie, it shouldn't take a long time to do the drug buy and arrest."

Ernie: "You're right, Henry, after the drug buy we will join the other guys to search the lounge and clean that up/ How about some breakfast, guys? It's gonna be a long day."

All of the men got up and started out the door for breakfast. They would return to the office for the 10 am telephone call.

10 am that morning

All of the men were in the office waiting for Ernie to make the call to Alberto so that they could find out where the deal will happen. They could start setting up for the deal to protect Ernie who will be out in front as the buyer. They would do their best to make sure no one was injured.

Ernie dialed the number given to him by Lucasie and a heavy voice answered the phone.

Alberto: "Speak to me.

Ernie: "Alberto?"

Alberto: "Yes, who is this?

Ernie: "Alberto, this is Eddie Pannoni. Mr. Lucasie told me to call you this morning."

Alberto: "Si, Si (yes,yes), I am glad you called, I have everything ready for you. Is the money ready?"

Ernie: "No, I will have it all together late this afternoon. After what happened the last time I put all the money away. I have to withdraw it, all over again."

Alberto: "What time will you be ready?"

Ernie: "How is 5 pm tonight?"

Alberto: "That's fine. We will complete our business at the Horse Shoe Lounge."

Ernie: "No, I can't do that, I would like to stay on the south shore if we can, near that highway. I think you call it Route 128."

Alberto: "Why?"

Ernie: "I don't know the area that well. When I leave you, I go directly to New York and I can get right on the highway and avoid the traffic. I can take that road you call Route #3."

Alberto: "Where do you want to complete our business?"

Ernie: "How about the sports academy, I'll meet you in the parking lot. Once we are finished I can hop on 128 and head towards the Massachusetts Turn Pike."

Alberto: "Do you mean the one down by Canton Street?"

Ernie: "I believe so; that's what it says on the map."

Alberto: "That's OK. I can be there by 5 pm; bring a small van."

Ernie; "See you then, Alberto."

Alberto: "See you then"

Ernie hung up the phone; it was now 10:30 am. He advised the men as to the location and the time, a plan was made. Jack, who was in the other room talking on the phone with a relative that were visiting him walked into the room and saw Ernie placing his briefcase on the desk.

Jack: "The deal must be on, you're getting the brief case ready."

Ernie used the briefcase as a ploy so that the sellers of the drugs would believe that he had the buy money in it. In reality Ernie would close down the operation and make the arrest long before the briefcase was ever handled by anyone other than himself.

All of the men in the Special Services Unit knew the area where the buy would take place and had conducted other buys in that area in the past.

Ernie began writing the affidavit for the search warrant which would take some time because it had to take in all of the meetings with Leroy, the meeting at the hospital, the introduction to Fraido Lucasie and the meeting with Lucasie at his lounge and his conversation with Alberto.

The affidavit would also have to indicate the discussions with Lucasie in an effort to use this application as a search warrant and arrest warrant for Lucasie and his body guard.

After two hours of writing, looking at notes and piecing all of the information together, Ernie was ready to go to court and apply for the search and arrest warrants. An hour and a half later Ernie had all of the paperwork in his hands.

Ernie and Jack planned on meeting the men at 3pm to go over the strategy for buy bust that was scheduled for 5pm and to secure the finishing touches.

At 3pm everyone was in the office and the plan was rehashed.

Detectives Jerry Gibson, Rick Bradshaw and Carl Robinson would hit the club with a group of uniformed men and do the search warrant.

Detectives Ernie Lijoi, Jack Wade and Henry Griswold would do the buy bust then connect up with, Jerry, Rick and Carl after the bust went down.

Arrangements were made by Captain Richards to have four men and two cruisers held over from the first shift to accompany Detective Jerry Gibson and his team.

Jerry notified Boston since the Lounge was barely over the county line and into the Boston community. They asked what would be needed and Jerry requested two cars and two men for back up purposes.

This was more of a courtesy call than anything else. The Boston Police would do the same for any other department.

It was now 3:45 pm and everyone decided to go to the area and set up as best they could to be ready for the concluding moments.

Ernie stayed in the office, sat back on the small couch which was in another room to rest his eyes, but he could not fall asleep. It seemed like five minutes had passed, his eyes opened and the time read 4:15pm, he had to get to the meeting place. He got up and washed his face to wake up.

Ernie went over to the room with all the desks, opened his draw and grabbed his 9mm, Glock-22, with a 15 round clip and stuffed it under his belt in the small of his back and grabbed his briefcase, the two tools standard for the type of job that he was about to undertake. Ernie picked up an un-marked van from the vehicle pool and left the area. He arrived at the meeting place at 4:50 pm, parked his van, got out and looked around for his men.

The area was surrounded by trees and a small hill with the Sports Academy set in the middle of a large open area and the parking lot in front.

Ernie could not see anyone at first; then one of the men, Jack, made himself visible to Ernie. He was behind some trees. The second man, Henry, made himself visible; he was behind a parked tractor trailer across the street and signaled that they were ready. They did not have to wait long because the van pulled into the parking lot, Stopped at Ernie.

Alberto: "Eddie, how are you?"

Ernie: "OK, thanks, Alberto?'

Alberto: "Follow me."

Eddie got into his van and followed Alberto to the back of the 5 acre parking lot where he parked on the oppo-site side of the lot from Alberto with his van pointing at Alberto's van; this was a safety measure that Eddie had learned to take.

Alberto got out from behind the driver seat and went to the rear of the van where he opened one door and two men got out. They stepped away from the van and stood there looking around at the immediate area for trouble or the un-invited.

These two men has dark complexions, Italian men, well dressed in suits, each with what looked like Mac-10's, very small machine guns with a folding shoulder piece, very serious weapons, held along the side of their bodies.

Ernie: "Alberto, what the fuck is all this."

Alberto: "After what happened the last time, with Leroy, I was told to take extra precautions, just in case."

Ernie: "I guess that's understandable, but I thought that this was a friendly deal."

Alberto: "It's, just business; you know; let's get down to it, take a look at the product and make your decision."

Ernie: "Yes, I will."

Eddie walked to the back of the truck the two gunmen moved so that there was one on each side of the van, allow-ing him to pass easily, to the rear of the van. Eddie looked in, grabbed a key of cocaine took out his knife, made a small cut in one corner of the packaging and scooped out some powder which he spread between his fingers then took out a small chemical kit and placed some of the snow in the kit, shook it up and it turned a beautiful dark blue indicating a very high concentration of cocaine.

Ernie: "That's the blow, but which is the horse?" (Her-oin)

Alberto pointed out the two keys of heroin and Eddie went through the same process with a kit made especially for heroin testing and again a very high concentration of heroin.

Alberto: "I didn't expect you to have those test kits, Eddie."

Ernie: "Alberto, where I come from you better have them or you'll get fucked every time."

Alberto: "Yes, yes I understand; and my money?"

Ernie: "In the back of my van, I'll get it."

Eddie, adjusted his hat, (the signal), walked over to the back of his van where he would have some cover, opened the trunk and took out the briefcase. As he stood there with the van door opened and covering him, he reached for his Glock 9mm and yelled to Alberto.

Ernie: "Alberto"

Alberto stepped out from the back of the trunk to see what Eddie wanted.

Ernie: "Alberto, you and your men are under arrest."

They immediately started firing with the machine guns then ran behind the van for protection.

Henry had blocked the exit roadway by moving cruisers into the area of the only exit. Jack was on the opposite side. Alberto and his men were surrounded on three sides with open field behind them, it seemed like it was over.

Ernie: "Alberto, it's all over, there is no place to go."

Alberto: "Fuck you, we'll get out; we're three, you are only one."

Alberto and his two men did not know that Jack, Henry and others were covering.

The firing began, Jack had a perfect shot from his angle, he hit one of the men then Henry fired and hit the other, two men were down, but one could still fire.

Henry fired again and the man still firing was hit in the chest this time, now both machine guns were immobilized. Alberto yelled to Eddie that he will walk out quietly.

Ernie: "OK, Alberto put your hands on top of your head, walk out backwards."

Alberto: "I'm coming out."

Ernie stood up from behind his car and Alberto jumped out and fired one shot hitting Ernie in the leg. Henry and Jack both fired and killed Alberto.

By this time there were two cruisers close by and they pulled in and assisted in the clean up. Ernie and one of the assailants were transported to the hospital via ambulance. The other two bodies were taken to the morgue.

Ernie was treated for a minor wound, cleaned up, taped up and released. The second man that was hit died at the hospital.

Ernie got up and began to get dressed so that he could join the other men in the search.

Dr.: Where are you going? You.ve been shot in the leg, that's gonna start aching in a while."

Ernie: "I started this. I want to be in on the finish. I can rest later."

Ernie immediately went to the Horse Shoe Lounge with Jack and Henry, who wanted him to go home or back to the hospital. Ernie refused; he wanted to finish the case. They arrived at the Lounge. By that time all of the customers had been identified and released by the other detectives and officers.

Fraido Lucasie was sitting at a table with his body guard and Detective Jerry Gibson who was taking all of the information needed. The other men and the Boston police were doing the search of the location.

One Boston patrolman, John Bails walked into the room and asked whose case this was.

Henry looked at him and said; "Speak with Detective Lijoi."

Bails: "Who's that?"

Ernie: "I'm Detective Lijoi; what do you need?"

Bails: "I think you had better come down to the cellar."

Ernie followed the officer into the cellar and up to a walk-in refrigerator where the food was kept fresh and frozen for use by the cooks for the restaurant.

Bails: "Take a look in there."

Ernie opened the door, walked into the chest. At first glance he could not see what was supposed to be so interesting, than he looked under the bottom shelf.

Ernie: "What the fuck is this; it seems you got here at the right time, Bails."

Under the bottom shelf, on the floor were two bodies, it appeared that both had been shot with a large caliber shell, probably a 9mm, the one in front was dead. Ernie pulled the first body out to check the second body which was in the back and placed his fingers along the man's throat. He detected a faint pulse.

Ernie: "Call an ambulance right away, I want him here yesterday, this guys barely alive."

Bails called for an ambulance via his radio. They pulled the second man out and took him into the cellar where it was warmer and he could breathe easier.

Bails: "Does he need CPR?"

Ernie: "No, but he could use some oxygen."

Bails: "They just supplied our cruisers with oxygen, I'll get mine."

The officer ran out to his cruiser and returned with the oxygen which was placed on the dying man. This simple procedure and stopping the bleeding from his chest helped to keep the man alive long enough for the ambulance to get there and take over.

Ernie: "That was close, Bails, great catch. I am sure this guy will want to speak with you and you'll get the credit for saving his life in my report. I need you to write up a report on how you found the two bodies and what was done to save them."

Bails: "Yes Sir. Detective Lijoi. Why can't I sign your reports?"

Ernie: "No, because I want one directly from you. They may give you some sort of an award and I don't want to clutter it up for you. Who knows, maybe it's a detective spot for you?"

Bails: "Whatever you say."

Ernie went up to the first floor lounge area and spoke with Lucasie.

Ernie: "Henry, has he been given his rights?"

Henry: "Fully given and he signed the card."

The detectives and officers all had cards with the rights printed out and a place for the arrestee to sign for acceptance.

Ernie: "Mr. Lucasie, do you want to speak with us?"

Lucasie: "I speak to no one without my attorney."

Ernie: "OK, Henry, have you told him the charges?"

Henry: "No, thought you may like to do that."

Ernie: "Mr. Lucasie, you are under arrest for murder, attempted murder, distribution of illegal narcotics and the additional charges will be filed at your arraignment by the District Attorney."

Ernie: "Henry, were they packing guns?"

Henry: "Yes both of them were carrying 9mm Glocks."

Ernie: "Isn't that interesting? Mr. Lucasie, we found two bodies in the fridge in the cellar."

Mr. Lucasie simply shrugged his shoulders in an effort to indicate that he knows nothing about them.

Ernie: "Are you trying to say that you know nothing about them?"

No reply.

Ernie: "Well, here's something you should know, one of them is alive."

Lucasie looked at his bodyguard with disgust, but said nothing.

Ernie: "What's the bodyguard's name?"

Henry: "His name is Angelo Cresti. What charges should we place on him?"

Ernie: "Same charges, Henry."

Angelo: "Hey, you can't charge me, I didn't kill them."

The body guard had spoken.

Ernie: "Sorry, you seem to be the one caught in the middle here. We'll discuss it at the station. Take these guys in separate cars and keep them separated."

Aside from the guns and the bodies, there was no other evidence found on the premises. The men packed up locked the door and went back to the police station before going to the unit office.

Ernie arranged to have an officer stand by until the suspects could be interviewed. This was a precaution in case the detectives needed to return to the scene.

The first thing that Ernie did was take the bodyguard up to the interview room.

Ernie: "What's your name?"

Angelo: "Angelo Cresti."

Ernie: "How old are you, Angelo Cresti?"

Angelo: "I am 40 years old, you have all this information in front of you on my booking sheet, why ask again?"

Henry: "Confirmation of facts, Roberto. Would you like some coffee?"

Angelo: "No, thank you."

Ernie: "You're a little young to be going to jail for the rest of your life"

Angelo: "I ain't going to any jail for anybody."

Ernie: "Where did those two guys, the bodies that we found in the freezer, come from?"

Angelo: "I can't talk about that."

"One of those men is still alive and will talk when he comes around. You talk now or I will not be interested in what you have to say after he wakes up and starts telling me the entire story. I don't think we'll have a problem with him wanting to testify."

Angelo: "I did not shoot those guys."

Ernie: "Who did?"

Angelo: He just shook his head, "No."

Ernie; "Your choice; we'll take you back to your cell."

Alberto: "I hope you guys got them guns marked as to whose is whose, because I did not shoot them."

Henry: "We have them noted as to which is yours and which belongs to Lucasie."

Alberto: "Then you will find out."

Ernie: "You do not understand, Alberto; as long as you were there you are as guilty as he is, so maybe you're looking at 30 years instead of life. At forty years old is there a difference?"

Alberto looked at Ernie with surprise and shook his head.

Alberto: "What is it that you want to know, Detective?"

Ernie: "Why were those two guys shot?"

Alberto: "They were dealers that owed Mr. Lucasie money and showed no respect for Mr. Lucasie."

Ernie: "That's not the reason they were shot."

Alberto: "No, but that's part of it."

Ernie; "What's the rest?"

Alberto: "They came into the lounge and wanted to rob Mt. Lucasie. When they let their guard down they were shot."

Ernie; "That story means a lot, if it holds up."

Alberto: "It's the truth; their guns are in the cellar, under the stairwell."

Ernie: "Is there anything else that you want to tell me?"

Alberto: "No that's what happened. What can you do for me?"

Ernie: "I'll tell the District Attorney that you want to cooperate with him and we will see what he can do."

Alberto: "Then that's all I say until we can make a deal."

Ernie: "OK, let's see what the DA says. They will take you back to your cell now."

The officers standing outside of the interview room came in and took Alberto down to his cell. Ernie and Henry went into the Drug unit office. They told the men what was said and discussed. Ernie stated that he believed there was more to it, but they would have to go back and check for the guns under the stair well.

It was late and all the men agreed that they should call it a day and go home; Jack offered to search for the victims guns on his way home and hold them as evidence, if he finds them.

When Ernie walked into the house, Teresa could see that he was beat. He looked very tired to her then she noticed the torn pants and she could see the bandages through the torn area.

Teresa: "What happened, are you OK?"

Ernie: "I'm OK, I was grazed that's all, it stung like hell, but it's minor."

Teresa: "Ernie, you leave before anyone is up, you don't call and now you walk in and you have been shot."

Ernie: "Grazed, l wouldn't call it shot."

Teresa: "I don't care what you call it, I call it shot. I worry all the time."

Ernie: "I don't know what to tell you. I'm too tired to discuss it right now. I need a good night's sleep."

Teresa: "Go to bed. Do you want anything? Do you want something to eat or drink?"

Ernie: "No, nothing; just some rest."

Teresa: "OK, you go up and rest. Think about what I said, we need you around here. I don't want to visit a grave the rest of my life. I want you here with me."

Ernie: "I'll tell you this, maybe it's time for me to step down and help the younger guys. I don't know. I have to think about it."

Teresa: "Go rest, we'll talk tomorrow."

Ernie went up to their bedroom, laid down and fell off to sleep like a baby.

Chapter 20

The Trial

Thursday June 19, 1980

Ernie was up and ready early in the morning. Before going to breakfast he changed his bandage, the wound looked OK. He took the antibiotic while trying not to bother Teresa who was still sleeping. He went down to the kitchen and began making breakfast, just as he started; Teresa got up and took over the breakfast for him.

Ernie: "Teresa, about our discussion last night."

Teresa: "Ernie, I was just worried and tired, I'm happy that you are OK. Do you want me to change your bandage?"

Ernie: "I already changed it, thanks."

Teresa: "Did you take the antibiotic?"

Ernie: "Yes. I took it. About last night, I was tired; don't take anything I said to heart."

Teresa: "What do you mean?"

Ernie; "What I said about stopping this work and helping the younger guys. I help them anyway, but I'm too young to stop."

Teresa: "I don't know about that, you're getting up there in age for this kind of work. There are many other jobs on the department you could do if you wanted."

Ernie: "I've told you before, I like what I do. I feel as though I am helping society. Of course society doesn't know it, but that's OK with me and my team."

Teresa: "What do you mean?"

Ernie: "It would be nice for the whole truth to come out once in a while. That would give the team some credit. On the other hand if we get credit, then we lose our secretiveness and become ineffective."

Teresa: "That's nothing to worry about."

Ernie: "I don't worry, Teresa, just talking."

Teresa: "How does your leg feel?"

Ernie: "It's fine, no pain; just a scratch."

Teresa: "You changed the bandage, is there anything that I can do?"

Ernie; "I changed it after I showered this morning. We can change it again when I get home, I'll shower, and we'll change it."

Teresa: "OK, I will do it for you tonight."

Ernie; "Thanks, I'm off to the office."

Ernie finished his coffee and left the house for the office. As Ernie began to pull out of the driveway, Teresa came running out of the house and waving to Ernie. He stopped the car and went back into the driveway after Teresa told him that he had a phone call.

Ernie: "This early, who is it?"

Teresa: "He said he works with you."

Ernie parked the car, went into the house and picked up the phone.

Ernie: "Hello"

Jesus: "Ernie, this is Jesus."

Ernie; "Yes, Lord?"

Jesus: "As soon as you get to the office, call me."

Ernie; "I'm on my way there now; I'll call you in twenty minutes." Ernie hung up the phone.

The call made Teresa curious.

Teresa: "What's wrong, Ernie."

Ernie: "Teresa, just because I get a phone call doesn't mean something's wrong."

Teresa: "Isn't that the guy Jesus from Arizona?"

Ernie: "Yes."

Teresa: "Well that's three hours behind us so it's 4 am there. Why would he call you at 4 am?"

Ernie: "You don't miss much. Nothing to worry about, he had the all night phone duty and wanted to catch me before I went anywhere this morning, that's all."

Teresa: "Oh, but why? You're lying to me."

Ernie: "Don't worry; he wants to update me on the Ernesto case, that's all."

Teresa: "OK, see you tonight."

As Ernie drove to the office he wondered what it was that Jesus really wants to tell him that was so important that he had to call at 4 am his time and why not speak while Ernie was at his home. Very curious.

He walked into the quiet office, went to a desk and dialed Agent Jesus Martinez of the DEA in Arizona.

Ernie: "Jesus?"

Jesus: "Yes, Ernie, I have some bad news. You sitting down?"

Ernie: "What's wrong?"

Jesus: "We received information from an informant that's imprisoned with Ernesto Adelanto. This informant stated that he overheard a conversation between Ernesto and a Mafia lieutenant. During the conversation the name Eddie Pannoni was mentioned and the price of fifty thousand was asked for by the Mafia lieutenant."

Ernie: "What family is the Mafia guy associated with?"

Jesus: "I'm not sure, but I think it's one of the New York families or branches. Does the name Borgazino mean anything to you?"

Ernie: "No, not really."

Jesus: "They must be associated with the Black Hand or something. That price, if it's for you, is quite large."

Ernie: "Wow, my value is coming up; it used to be twenty thousand."

Jesus; "Ernie, this is no joke."

Ernie: "I know, but what can I do, sit and cry?"

Jesus: "I guess you're right. We will be working the case diligently. Keep your eyes open."

Ernie: "OK, let's keep it close to the breast until we confirm everything."

Jesus: "I knew you would say that. I already called Captain Richards before I called you. The people around you should know."

Ernie: "Jesus, what about my family, are they in any danger?"

Jesus: "I would say no. He's after you because of the case, that's all he wants. I doubt that he wants to swap dead families. He'll keep it between you and him—at least for now anyway."

Ernie: "Thank God for that!"

Jesus: "Yes, I'll keep you informed."

Ernie: "OK, don't call my house, my wife is too curious. I'll be here, at the office, every morning at this time."

Jesus: "OK, done."

Ernie: "Stay in touch, Jesus."

Ernie hung up the phone. The men began drifting into the office. At about 8 am Captain Richards walked in.

Captain: "Good morning, men, is everyone here?"

Henry: "Yes, we're all here."

Captain: "I received a call early this morning about Ernie and you all should know what is going on."

The men all gathered in the room, in an effort not to miss a word.

Captain: "Ernie, Jesus spoke with you this morning?"

Ernie: "Yes, he called me at home then I spoke to him from here."

Captain: "Then you are aware of the case?"

Ernie: "Yes Sir"

Captain: "Men, Ernie has another threat hanging over his head, a fifty thousand dollar contract from that Ernesto character—one of the main suppliers of cocaine and heroin to the United States, from Columbia and Mexico, that Ernie investigated with the federal agents."

Jack: "How firm is this contract, Captain?"

Captain: "Jack, good question. We don't know yet, but Ernie goes nowhere alone; at least one man will be with him at all times and if you guys are all tied up I will be with him."

Jack: "We have no problem with that, Captain, I have been working closely with Ernie and I will volunteer for the job." The rest of the men all stepped forward and offered any assistance that was needed.

Captain: "Everyone, please, one thing that we have to look out for besides everything else is a bomb in the car. Ernie will not drive his vehicle; he will take a different car every day from the yard. It will be checked out from stem to stern before he takes it. The belief is that his family is not threatened so that should not be a problem. We must protect him as he would protect any one of us. I would insist that he live here in the station instead of going home, but I also know that he would never agree to that."

This made Ernie feel both embarrassed and good at the same time, to be accepted in that way. After all they are putting themselves in danger just being around him.

Captain: "What do you have this morning, Ernie?"

Ernie: "Captain, I have the Leroy Watkins case and I have to go and get Petri Anderson and escort him to the court house."

Captain: "How long do they estimate this case will take?"

Ernie: "This should be an all day affair; maybe more than one day."

Captain: "OK, Jack, are you going with him?"

Jack: "Yes sir. That's partially my case, too, so I have to be there."

Ernie: "Good, you guys should be safe in the court house. Check with me at the end of the day."

Jack: "Will do, Captain."

Ernie and Jack left the office and went to the coffee shop.

Jack: "How serous do you see this, Ernie?"

Ernie: "I don't, the DEA has not confirmed any of this. It's an informant that gave them the information and the DEA is not totally convinced that it is true. Personally, I think that everyone is overdoing this a bit. We're somewhat premature on this whole thing."

Jack: "I see, so they are working on it? Will they be convinced once you're dead?"

Ernie: "Jack, all we can do is wait and see what happens. I don't like it, but there is nothing more to do. The Feds are good guys and will do everything they can to help. It could be just as easily one of them. One point though, I'm not gonna wait forever. Eventually I'll go after those

Preyers of society, whether the powers above us agree or not."

Jack: "I understand."

The two men entered the court room and took a seat. They waited for the court to be brought to order and for the Judge to take his seat.

The defense attorney had the floor first, which is standard in a case like this. His first move was to ask for a dismissal on the murder charges.

He stated that the government had no case for murder, no weapon, no witnesses. The trial was merely a sham to trick the defendant into saying something that may make it seem that he can be tied into those crimes because they don't want to go out and do the work necessary to find the real culprit.

The defense attorney went on to state that they were going to prove that the government had a double agent who was committing murders of behalf of drug dealers.

Ernie and Jack sat back and almost started laughing out loud after that statement because they knew that the defense attorney was speaking of Ernie and the Petri Anderson case.

This attorney was very good at his job; he had the case of Watkins' mother separated from Watkins case.

Because of this separation, his mother's case could not be mentioned in his case and visa-versa, but the defense had some surprises coming from the prosecutor.

No one wanted to see a senile 82 year old women go to jail because of her son. Not even the family of the four victims found at the Zoo wall or the officer's family. They all wanted the real assailant Leroy Watkins to pay for his crimes.

After the defense was finished presenting the outline of their case the motion to dismiss the Murder charges and all related charges to the murders was denied by the court.

A jury had been picked a few days earlier and the case was all ready to begin.

The first witness was Detective Jack Wade.

Jack went over the entire case through questioning by the prosecuting attorney. Jack was carefully avoiding the Petri Anderson matter with his answers.

The defense took over and to every one's surprise he questioned Detective Wade about Detective Ernie Lijoi, what Jack observed, where he was, when he observed it, why things happened the way they did.

Jack did his best not to bring up the Petri case, the gun or the shells taken from the bodies by stating that he was not involved in that part of the case which was true to fact.

At the end of the testimony the defense stood up and again asked for a mistrial and dismissal because there was no evidence to place a weapon in his client's hand, no witnesses and no weapon at this point.

After the judge denied the motions, Leroy Watkins stood up in the court room and was waving around a news paper clipping of Petri Anderson and yelling.

Watkins: "This man is dead because of a cop. A cop killed him, he called himself Eddie Pannoni."

The Judge yelled at Watkins:

Judge: "Mr. Watkins, if you make any more statements without your attorney, this Court will have your mouth taped and your hands cuffed."

Watkins sat back down. His attorney bent over and spoke to him very quietly so that no one could hear the statement. Watkins answered the attorney with, "Yes I will."

Because of all of the discussion about Petri Anderson's death, the prosecutor decided to place him on the stand next. The judge looked at his watch, called a lunch break and stated that the court would resume at 2pm.

Ernie, Jack and the District Attorney John Hageman, went to have lunch. While there they discussed the case in general and John indicated some of the strategy he would be using.

After lunch Ernie and Jack dropped DA Hageman off at the court house, and went over to the office to gather as much of the evidence as was needed for this trial.

They returned to the court house and the court room just as the court was being called to order and the Judge was entering the room.

The DA stood up and called Petri Anderson to the stand.

The defense attorney immediately started objecting and making all sorts of statements.

His first and biggest objection was that this witness was not on his list of witnesses.

The DA stood and stated that this man was supposed to have been killed at the request of the defendant and that he would prove that fact.

The judge listened to both sides and had a conference in his chambers after which he came out and made his decision.

The witness Petri Anderson will be allowed to testify.

Anderson walked into the room and Leroy Watkins went crazy and tried to throw his chair at him and then fought off the guards to get at Anderson. They held him down.

The court had Watkins cuffed and told his attorney that if necessary the court would tape his mouth or place him in another room where he cannot interfere with the trial.

"Yes, Your Honor," was the only thing that the defense attorney could say.

After Anderson testified about his conversation with the defendant, the fact that he was to get rid of the gun and his knowledge about the murders he was approached by the defense attorney. The attorney simply asked him what he was getting for testifying.

Anderson: "Nothing that I know of, sir."

Defense: "Then why testify in this case?"

Anderson: "I did not wish to be charged with those murders. I was in possession of the gun."

Defense: "Why did you go along with this falsehood of your death?"

Anderson: "Because Watkins threatened to kill me, and Detective Lijoi said that he would kill me."

Defense: "Your honor this is all hearsay testimony."

Judge: "Allowed, the court will strike the parts about what Mr. Anderson was told and the jury will not take those statements into consideration."

Anderson was finished testifying and he did a great job, he had been on the stand for over two hours. The judge decided to adjourn for the day. The case would continue in the morning at 10AM. This judge was not stupid he was actually giving the defense a last opportunity to make a deal with the DA, before Ernie testified.

In the morning Ernie would testify and that would put the icing on the cake. All of the testimony that was not allowed would be allowed coming from Ernie since it was first hand information.

Friday June 20, 1980

Ernie and Jack were at the court house waiting for the murder trial against Leroy Watkins to begin. Ernie would be called as the lead investigator and expert witness on the subject of narcotics.

At 10 am, the court was called to order and the Judge took his seat.

Judge: "Mr. Hageman, do you have any more witnesses to call?"

D.A. John Hageman: "Yes. Your honor, I would like the court to call Detective Ernie Lijoi Sr. of the Quincy police Department."

The announcement was made and Ernie arose from his seat in the back or the court room, walked up to the front, gave his oath and sat in the witness chair.

Hageman: "Detective Lijoi, how did you learn about the defendant, Mr. Leroy Watkins?"

Ernie: "Sir, I answered a call for assistance at the hospital where I met a black female named Sonia Levin."

Hageman: "Did Miss Levin have a nick name?"

Ernie: "Yes, Chicken"

Hageman: "Did Miss Levine have any tattoos?"

Ernie; "Yes a tattoo on her right wrist of a chain and heart wrapped around the wrist."

Hageman: "What did Miss. Levin tell you?"

Ernie: "Miss. Levin stated to me that her boyfriend, Leroy Watkins beat her up because she threatened to talk to the police about his activities and she wound up in the hospital."

Hageman: "Did you have other occasions to see Miss. Levin?"

Ernie: "Yes Sir I did, but I did not know it at first."

Hageman: "Would you explain that statement, please?"

Ernie: "Yes Sir. Detective Jack Wade and I answered a call for a dead body that was found in the park in Quincy. Upon arrival we observed a black female with her face so badly beat up that she could not be identified. I noticed a tattoo on her right wrist of a chain and heart wrapped around the wrist. That's when I knew that this girl was Miss Levine. This fact was later confirmed by her finger prints."

Hageman: "Did Miss Levine frequent Quincy?"

Ernie: "No Sir, her home base was Boston."

Hageman: "Was she killed in Quincy?"

Ernie: "No sir, it was later confirmed that she was murdered in Boston."

Hageman: "What could have brought her body to Quincy?"

Ernie: "Through investigation we discovered that she had another fight with Mr. Watkins, threatened to call me and was killed. Her body was placed at the park in Quincy in an effort to tell me to stay out of Boston and out of Leroy Watkins business."

The defense got up and started yelling, that this was supposition, assumptions are not evidence and on and on.

The court had to ask the defense to be quiet and agreed to a certain extent with him and told the jury to disregard that conversation where the detective assumed that she was killed by Mr. Watkins or that the killing and placing the body was a threat to the detectives.

The Prosecutor smiled knowing that the statement was made, the fact had been stated and the jury, as much as they may want to, could not disregard anything that they heard that morning.

It was now 11:30 am and the Judge called a lunch break until 1:30 pm. The court was recessed until that time.

Ernie and Jack went to lunch. Ernie—who was still under oath—was unable to discuss any aspect of the case until after the case was completed.

Their lunch conversation was about something that Ernie had been told by an informant regarding a Massachusetts Motorcycle gang called Heavens Devils, Rhode Island Mafia head, New York and some Politicians in Washington DC. Quite complicated, but interesting. An interesting, but complicated case which will require allot of work and time.

Ernie and Jack returned to the court house after lunch and waited for Ernie to be recalled as a witness.

The court was called to order the Judge took his seat, and the prosecutor recalled Detective Ernie Lijoi Sr. to the stand.

Hageman: "Detective Lijoi, did you have occasions to meet Mr. Watkins personally?"

Ernie: "Yes sir, I did"

Hageman: "Would you please tell the Court when that was and what happened."

Ernie: "On June 6th, 1980, I went to a party at the home of Petri Anderson where I was introduced to My Watkins by Mr. Anderson and I used the cover name of Eddie Pannoni. While there I had a discussion with Mr. Watkins. In an effort to make myself more acceptable to Watkins, I told him that I was not sure of Mr. Petri because he was recently arrested. Mr. Watkins indicated that he (Petri Anderson) would be taken care of. That he, Watkins, was going to kill Mr. Petri Anderson who had become a threat to his illegal narcotics business."

Hageman: "Then what happened?"

Ernie: "In an effort to save Mr. Petri Anderson's life I offered to do the job for him."

Hageman: "What happened then?"

Ernie; "The other detectives and I arranged what appeared to be the suicide of Mr. Anderson with pictures that were released to the newspapers. This would relieve Mr. Watkins of the threat of murdering Mr. Anderson, believing that he was already dead. This would, also, place me (Detective Lijoi) in a strong position to purchase drugs and acquire more information from Mr. Watkins about his illicit narcotics business."

From that point on, Ernie spent the entire day on the stand answering questions from the prosecuting attorney, identifying different narcotics and testifying to what they were, how they were cut and the street value of these narcotics after they were cut.

He also testified about the weapon that was taken in the Petri Anderson search warrant and the fact that the bullets taken from the dead bodies found at the Zoo matched the test firing of that weapon, the statement of Anderson and the investigation in its totality.

Ernie has been accepted as an expert witness by numerous court cases by the prosecutors and the defense attorneys of the past and now in this case.

The next Monday would be the defense turn to questioning Ernie and try to place holes in his story.

Ernie spent the weekend with his family and they went up to Maine for some fishing and relaxation.

That Friday night they arrived in Maine very late, put wood in the stove and went to bed as the house warmed up. That far north in Maine the house was still chilly over night from the cool night air.

The next morning Ernie and the boys went out fishing and caught some largemouth bass, white perch, a couple of small mouth bass and one decent brown trout.

They were heading back to the cabin to clean the trout and get it ready for lunch. As Ernie Sr., drove the boat, his son Joey and Ernie, had lines trolling behind them.

Joey's line began to go then Little Ernie's; they were both hooked up on fish. Little Ernie got his to the boat first; it was a three pound brown trout. Joey's line was much heavier and they could not figure out what it was until Joey got it to the boat. On the one lure were three fish. They were all trying to eat the same bait, at the same time and that's why they felt so heavy.

His son had a four-inch lure with three treble hooks, on each hook there was a fish. They were all small, about 1½ pounds each. This was the catch of the century.

Ernie still tells that story today to friends that are interested in fishing and he can see in their faces that most do not believe it since that is one of the rarest things that anyone has ever seen or heard.

Sunday morning they all got up early and went down to the kitchen for breakfast. After breakfast Ernie took the family to a small store which was about a mile from the house. The store owner had lobster tanks and sold the lobsters live or upon request, cooked them, for his customers. They looked at the lobsters, some were as large as ten pounds, but most were around one and a half pounds, perfect for one person. Before they left the store Ernie ordered four cooked lobsters to be picked up later that day around noon.

They went down to the Kennebec River Park in Augusta, Maine and spent some time there admiring the scenery, watching the fisherman fish for striped bass that came up river from the ocean to lay their eggs.

At 12 noon they picked up the lobsters, went home and had a feast. Teresa made some side dishes to go along with the lobsters. After lunch they closed up the house and started back for Dedham, Massachusetts, a three hour drive and arrived home at 6 pm.

Monday June, 23, 1980

Ernie met Jack at the court house; Ernie was due to testify on cross examination and was expecting a strong cross examination.

Ernie was called to the stand shortly after the court began and the defense attorney questioned Ernie on several subjects, but did not try to trick or confuse him.

Ernie was puzzled because the defense did not appear to be putting up the fight that he expected. Ernie sat there and answered all of the questions when the defense began to make it look as though Ernie placed the seed of the crime of murder in the mind of Mr. Watkins.

Defense Attorney: "Detective Lijoi, isn't it true that you brought up the point that Anderson should be murdered?"

Ernie: "No, Sir."

Defense: "Then Mr. Watkins just pulled that out of the air."

Ernie: "No Sir, he was afraid that Anderson would talk because Anderson had recently been arrested with a large quantity of Cocaine."

Defense: "No more questions."

Ernie was released from the stand and later spoke with the prosecuting attorney.

D.A. Hageman: "Ernie, this guy is going to look for something on appeal, that's why he didn't go after you very hard besides the fact that you have a fantastic reputation. If he went after you and could not break any part of your story he would have nothing to appeal on."

Ernie: "I figured that; I was only up there for about an hour, that's a short time in a case like this. I expected to be there all day. The defense didn't try very hard."

Ernie and Jack left the court house and would return when the jury came in, to hear the verdict. The wait was not long only an hour and the verdict was in. Leroy Watkins was found guilty and would be sentenced the following week.

Detective's Lijoi and Wade were pleased about the outcome of the case and also glad it was over. On their ride back to the office they discussed sports for change.

Brooklyn 1950's

Ernie was again reminded of being a child and playing baseball in an empty lot on Dean Street in Brooklyn, New York.

In those days there was no supervised play, no adults to tell the kids what to do and how to do it. The kids had their idols—the ball players in the news papers—which spoke of sports every day and all of the games.

One game in particular that Ernie could never forget was a baseball game where the boys, chose sides, picked the teams, in the usual way and began to play.

Ernie was not a pitcher, but for some unknown reason he was on the pitcher's mound and he did a great job of striking out almost every batter that came to the plate for the first four innings. He didn't know how he did that and never figured it out. It was strange.

Ernie and Jack arrived at the station and decided to finish up the reports on the Leroy Watkins case so that the case could be closed, the last report was merely a formality to indicate the trial and the findings of the court, the sentence could be filled in at anytime.

Chapter 21

The Attempted

Tuesday June 24, 1980

Ernie arrived at the office a little late and all of the men were there waiting for him. Jack wanted to work with Ernie on permanent bases which they discussed and both agreed to try it out.

The two men went for breakfast and coffee then returned to the station and began boxing up the evidence from the Leroy Watkins case to have it available for any appeal that may come up in a year or two. The phone rang.

Ernie: "Hello"

Unknown male: "Hi, is this that guy I helped pulled up from the Knox building when he fell through the skylight?"

Ernie: "Is this my cousin, Lorenzo?"

Unknown Male: "No."

Ernie: "Vinchenzo has passed on, so this can only be, Antonio?"

Antonio: "You got it, how are you, Ernie?"

Ernie: "I am fine, Tony, how long has it been?"

Antonio: "I bet it has been 20 years, it's nice to be speaking with you after all this time."

Ernie: "It had to be you, there were only three people on that roof and you caught me by my hood just before I fell through the skylight and down those six stories, then you guys all pulled me back up to the roof."

Ernie: "Antonio, how are your mom & dad?"

Antonio: "They have passed on; my sister is doing OK, how about your family?"

Ernie: "My parents passed on a few years ago; everyone else is OK, thanks."

Antonio: "Sorry to hear that."

Ernie: "Tony, how did you get this number?"

Antonio: "China was out on Long Island visiting Bob, the guy that lived next door to us."

Ernie: "Yes, Yes I remember Bob and China both."

Antonio: "Anyway he ran into your sister and they had a long talk and he asked how to contact you, she gave him this number and said you are always working. I hope it's OK to call you here."

Ernie: "Yes, it's Ok, but why did you call instead of China."

Antonio: "We were talking and I said that I wanted to call you first because of the Knox Factory incident, Ernie, what's wrong, you seem to be a little cautious."

Ernie: "No, I am just cleaning up some cases and I am both surprised and happy to hear from you."

Antonio: "Ernie, I cannot believe that you are a cop, after all the shit with the gangs. The running of the bags for the men and all the things that went on as kids; I couldn't believe it when China said you were a cop. I always figured you would become one of the guys, you know what I mean?"

Ernie: "Yes, Tony, I do and that's why I left New York as a kid. I saw that coming and wanted to get away from it before it became a reality."

Antonio: "Look, take my number, (789-555-4050) and when you get straightened out give me a call."

Ernie: "I promise I will call you in a week or two, right now I have something going on that I can't explain yet."

Antonio: "I'll expect to hear from you soon, stay healthy."

Ernie: "You too."

Ten minutes later Ernie received a call from agent Jesus Martinez of the DEA.

Jesus: "Ernie how's things?"

Ernie: "I'm doing fine and you?"

Jesus: "Good thanks, some info for you; you know that lieutenant that I told you about?"

Ernie: "Yes, the Mafia lieutenant that spoke with Ernesto in the prison yard?"

Jesus: "Yes, before his arrest he was tied into Vegas and New York, as a member of the Borgazino Family who are associated with the Black Hand."

Ernie: "Black Hand, that's the real bad guys, they don't fuck around."

Jesus: "That's right. The mob goes to them for most hits that are important to them."

Ernie: "OK, but Ernesto is not mafia, why would they put a hit on me for him?"

Jesus: "I don't understand it either; they usually will not do anything like that for an outsider."

Ernie: "All I can do is wait for now, but I will not wait forever."

Jesus: "Don't do anything rash. This can still be up in the air. I'll let you know more, soon."

Ernie hung up the phone and turned to Jack Wade telling him that he was going to take the day and get some needed rest. Jack understood and told Ernie that he would drive him home.

Jack: "Ernie, you have had a few tough weeks you deserve a rest."

Ernie: "Thanks Jack I hope the other guys see it that way."

Jack: "Believe me no one is going to complain that you take a half day off."

Ernie: "OK, then, I'm out of here."

Ernie left the office and drove directly home, went in the house and lay down on the couch. Teresa was not home, probably out shopping, he thought.

The next thing he knew Teresa was waking him for dinner, he did not hear the kids come home, he did not hear Teresa come in and he did not hear the television as the boys watched it. He had been out like a light.

That night Ernie and Teresa took the boys to the ice cream shop in Westwood called the Bubbling Brook. The boys liked going there because they received plenty of ice cream and were never rushed to decide what flavor they liked.

After they finished the ice cream, they returned to Dedham and parked the car in the square. They walked around the square for a while looking in the real estate windows at the real estate deals of the week, the shoe store at the new designs, the wedding store at the new wedding dresses and gowns in the window and then returned home.

Ernie still felt tired so he went up to bed, after a few minutes Teresa walked into the bed room.

Teresa: "Ernie, are you OK?"

Ernie: "Yes, I'm just a bit tired; I finished up a case that took a lot out of me in a lot of ways."

Teresa: "As long as you are sure you are OK. Your arms, your jaw or your neck don't hurt do they?"

Ernie: "No, Teresa, I'm not having a heart attack, I'm just tired. I'll be fine in the morning."

Teresa: "There is such a thing as denial, you know."

Ernie: "Yes, I know, I'm not in denial. I just need some rest without worrying about a case that I am on."

Teresa: "OK, rest. I'll sleep in the other room so that I won't bother you."

Ernie: "You don't have to, but whatever you think is OK."

Ernie fell off to sleep and slept all night as though the night never happened.

The next morning Ernie got up and felt great, back to his normal self, had a cup of coffee with Teresa and told her that he received a call from an old friend, a boy he grew up with, Antonio.

Teresa was happy for him since she knew that he had tried connecting with some of his old friends over the years from time to time. In many cases they were dead or had become very heavy users of illicit drugs which in Ernie's mind were the same as being dead.

He never had any contact with any of them until the call he had that day from Antonio who seemed to be OK.

He finished his coffee and left the house for the office and as he closed the door behind him he heard the mockingbird sing to him. Ernie replied with the same jingle he always uses and the bird picked right up on it. They went back and forth with the jingle for a few minutes then Ernie got into the car and drove off.

On his way into work he decided to take the Blue Hills Road which is a road that is peaceful and quiet with plenty of trees and a nice scenic overlook at the top of the largest hill in the Blue Hills.

As he pulled in at the top of the hill he heard what sounded like a shot and the passenger seat window blew into the car. Ernie had glass all over him and a few minor cuts.

He jumped out of the car ran to a tree and as he ran the few feet to the tree he pulled him 9MM weapon. He looked around the entire area on the passenger side of the vehicle and saw nothing. The hill was quiet, the birds were singing and the squirrels were running up and down the trees playing their little games.

He could barely make out the fire tower at the very top of the hill which was on the driver's side of the car and figured if someone was anywhere they were probably in the tower.

Ernie called into the police headquarters, on his two way radio for assistance, stating his location and that he had been fired upon. Cruisers were on the way.

He slowly worked his way up the hill by going from tree to tree and constantly keeping a visual in all areas as he went.

A few minutes later he heard the cruisers pull up and his radio started squawking.

Henry: "Ernie, where are you?"

Ernie: "I'm Ok, on my way up to the fire tower. Be careful."

Ernie reached the base of the tower which was built of cobblestones in a circular fashion, with a lower entrance and stairs inside to reach the covered platform at the top.

He waited for one of the men to catch up to him so that he was covered as he went up the stairs. Henry Griswold caught up with Ernie, He asked Henry to cover as he went up the stairs.

Ernie carefully took the stairs and reached the top, no one was there, Henry came up and they searched the top for anything. In one corner Ernie found a spent piece of brass from a MAS-49, a French-designed semi-automatic infantry weapon. Ernie looked down at the road.

Ernie: "You know Henry, something isn't right here, because the angle of trajectory is all off. The bullet could only penetrate the window and my passenger seat. The shooter never had a shot at me. He couldn't see me from this angle I was on the other side of the car, driving."

Henry: "You're right, this guy may not have been trying to kill you."

Ernie: "No, just trying to scare me. Very curious. What if someone accidently fired his weapon towards me. All we can do is hold the shell and take the bullet out of the car and keep it on file."

Henry: "Unless we get lucky and find a print on the shell casing. It could happen."

Ernie: "That's a long shot, Henry, but we will try."

Henry: "What do you think of these threats against you?"

Ernie: "My honest opinion, until now, is that this whole thing is all to keep me on edge and worried about everything and everyone. I will not fall for that game."

Henry: "Ernie, I have a question for you?"

Ernie: "What is it?"

Henry: "Over the years, this unit has taken down a lot of people and each time someone takes over the street business of the person we arrest."

Ernie: "Yes, that's true."

"Who do you think may take the place of Ernesto in Mexico, Leroy Watkins in Boston and Fraido Lucasie who is connected to Vietnam, New York and Rhode Island?"

"I don't know, but I do know one thing. This threat may be serious. Anything can happen. That guy Ernesto is a real nut and his associates, the Borgazinos, in New York are a strong group. I will have to be careful.

~*~The End~*~

Look for future books in the Ernie Lijoi Sr,/Eddie Pannoni series at Argus Better Book Publishing:
http://www.a-argusbooks.com

And Ernie's sites www.erniersr.com and www.thepreyers.com

Ernie Lijoi Sr.

Other Books in the
Eddie Pannoni Thriller Series

by
Ernie Lijoi, Sr.
from A-Argus Better Book Publishers

*****

Destructive Obsession

*****

Meth or Myth

*****

The Butcher of Boston

*****

The Cash Mule

*****

The Tunnel